Love is
a time of enchantment:
in it all days are fair and all fields
green. Youth is blest by it,
old age made benign:
the eyes of love see
roses blooming in December,
and sunshine through rain. Verily
is the time of true-love
a time of enchantment — and
Oh! how eager is woman
to be bewitched!

LYONHURST

Belinda Lemaître was born out of wedlock — and abandoned by her mother's rich, snobbish family. She was brought up in France and never told of her heritage. Curiosity drives Belinda to visit England and Lyonhurst, the great country mansion where her mother still lives as an invalid. Here, she discovers her past and secretly comes into the employment of her mother. Suddenly, as she is readying to reveal her true identity, Belinda is entrapped in a terrifying web. A handsome gentleman courts her love, and a killer waits — until they are alone . . .

RONA RANDALL

LYONHURST

Complete and Unabridged

ULVERSCROFT
Leicester

First published in Great Britain in 1962
under the title of
'Walk Into My Parlour'

First Large Print Edition
published 1997

British Library CIP Data

Randall, Rona
    Lyonhurst.—Large print ed.—
    Ulverscroft large print series: romance
    1. Love stories
    2. Large type books
    I. Title
    823.9'14 [F]

    ISBN 0–7089–3831–0

Published by
F. A. Thorpe (Publishing) Ltd.
Anstey, Leicestershire
Set by Words & Graphics Ltd.
Anstey, Leicestershire
Printed and bound in Great Britain by
T. J. International Ltd., Padstow, Cornwall

This book is printed on acid-free paper

For Biddy Parker,
in appreciation of all her hard work

The Birth

"TAKE the child," the man ordered. "Give it to the Sisters of Mercy."

There was a cry from the bed. He turned his back upon it.

Shocked, the Mother Superior protested, "But, m'sieur, it is your own grandchild!"

"A bastard spawned by a whoring daughter and a French peasant! I'll not acknowledge it as any kindred of mine."

His shoulder was seized, spinning him around so violently that he rocked on his heels.

"I am no peasant, m'sieur. I am Pierre Lemaître, son of Jacques Lemaître, Advocat of Clermont-Ferrand."

The man shrugged aside the young man's grasp, straightened his jacket, glanced contemptuously at the youth's bespattered military uniform, and said, "Son of a provincial lawyer? Is that supposed to impress me? We have them in England; two a penny. And look at

3

your rank — a mere corporal! I repeat, a peasant, with the behavior of a peasant, the look of a peasant as well."

Pierre Lemaître, twenty-two, dark-eyed, Gallic in appearance and temperament, clenched his hands in an endeavor to control his anger, and failed.

"M'sieur Tredgold — "

"Sir Humphrey," the man spat. "Address me properly, if you dare address me at all."

"*Sir* Humphrey — my apologies! I was under the impression that I was not addressing a gentleman. If I look as unkempt as a peasant at this moment, it is because I have trudged through rain and mud for hours to reach your daughter. Now that I am here I shall look after her. That was my reason for coming."

"A deserter into the bargain, eh?"

"My battalion is breaking up. It is a case of every man for himself, but call me a deserter if you wish. I can think of worse names for a father who turns his back on his own daughter. I shall not turn my back on mine, believe me. Our child, mine and Kathy's, shall neither be given away nor rejected. She will bear my name and so will Kathy. We will legally marry. That is why I am here."

"You'll be court-martialed for desertion before you even get a chance to! As for hoping to marry my daughter, she is barely sixteen, underage even in this country let alone her own. I'm getting her out of France before the Maginot Line is completely demolished. The Germans have already broken through, so perhaps you're not a deserter after all, merely a coward on the run with the rest. What do you think is going to happen to you when Hitler's troops are your masters? Do you think a daughter of mine is going to be allowed to face *that*?"

"I notice you say 'a daughter of mine,' not 'my daughter.' There is a difference, sir. One is merely a possession, a thing belonging to you, not a child to be loved and understood. It's a pity Kathy's mother died before her father did."

The Englishman turned on the Mother Superior, standing nearby with the infant in her arms.

"Get him out of here! Why he was

admitted in the first place, I fail to understand."

"He was admitted because he is the child's father, m'sieur, and therefore had every right."

"And you call this a convent for young ladies — you, the Mother Superior? There's nothing the slightest bit maternal or superior about a woman who pretends to be their guardian, but who turns a blind eye on the seduction of her pupils, so don't expect me to address you by that hypocritical title. If there were time, I'd fight your complicated French laws to drag the name of this school in the dust, but as it is, I'll waste neither the effort nor the money. Get my daughter ready to travel at once. France is falling and the sooner we get back to England, the better."

The cry from the bed was repeated, tinged now with desperation.

"Sedate her, can't you? Silence her somehow. Then dress her."

"M'sieur, I protest! It is only a short time since she gave birth."

"She is young and healthy, and since she has behaved like a gypsy in the hedgerows, she can emulate the breed and be up and on her way. Besides, I've brought her old nurse to look after her. Harriet! Are you there, Harriet?"

The door, slightly ajar, was pushed open and a stout, motherly woman stood on the threshold.

"Yes, Sir Humphrey, I'm here."

"Well, don't just stand there! Attend to Katherine. Get her up and ready to travel."

"But, sir, she isn't fit — "

"She has to be fit. Good God, woman, don't you realize how serious the situation is? *France is falling.* If the country capitulates, and capitulate she will, we'll be trapped. Interned. Do you know what that means? Interned for the duration, and God knows how long that will be. And God knows what sort of camps we would find ourselves prisoners in!"

The old nurse moved reluctantly to the bed, holding out her arms and gathering its occupant close to her ample bosom.

"Harriet! Don't let him take me! *Pierre!*"

"I am here, *chérie.*"

His arms replaced the woman's, cradling

the girl's fragile figure. Smoothing the hair back from her damp brow, he murmured words of reassurance and love.

"Get away from my daughter."

Humphrey Tredgold was a heavily built man, and all his weight was behind him as he pulled the Frenchman away.

"Listen to me, Katherine. I am your father. I have come to take you home. You are underage and no one — *no one*, understand? — can prevent me."

"I want my baby! I want to stay with Pierre! Please, Father, don't force me!"

"You are making it necessary. Forget the child. You'll soon get over the loss of it."

"*Never!*"

"I say you will. You will come home, and no one will know anything of this episode. In no time at all it will be in the past and you'll pick up the threads of your old life in England."

"I shall never forget my child, nor Pierre. I shall get back to them somehow."

"Not so long as I am alive. Lemaître, get out of the way. And you, Harriet — if you don't get my daughter dressed,

I swear I'll drag her out of that bed and do it myself. I've a car outside to take us to the airport, and the aircraft I chartered to bring me here is waiting on the tarmac."

Pierre flung himself between the bed and Harriet's reluctant figure.

"Kathy stays. We vowed never to part. We knelt in the little church of Mont-Dore and took our vows together."

Humphrey Tredgold laughed.

"Unblessed by priest or bishop? How sentimental, how touching — and how binding! Those whom God hath not joined together can always be put asunder. No priest would have conducted a marriage service for a girl underage, nor for one who was a pupil at a nearby convent. He would have contacted the Mother Superior beforehand, and even you, madam — " He turned back to the nun. "I believe even you would have had to forbid any marriage, doubtful as I now am of your integrity. When I sent my daughter to this convent I understood it to be a place where the pupils would be protected and cared for. I was mistaken. Is no vigilance exercised here?"

"As much as possible, m'sieur. Indeed, I believed the maximum, until this happened. But at least give me credit for notifying you at once, and if Katherine managed to keep secret assignations outside school hours, I take full responsibility."

"How *did* she manage to? That's what I would like to know. Hurry, Harriet, *hurry!*"

"Sir, she is weak — "

"Too weak to be moved!" Pierre blazed. "Reverend Mother, keep her here, I beg."

"Alas, my son, I cannot. She is, as her father says, underage. He is her rightful guardian; I am not. Moreover, she is an alien and only the law can intervene, and for that, there has to be just cause. Removing a girl to her rightful home because she has had an illegitimate child would be considered the best possible cause for taking her there, believe me. Her father has the law on his side. He cannot be stopped."

"He can be stopped from giving my child away! The Sisters of Mercy shan't have her. I shall."

"And how will you care for her, my son? How will you bring her up? It is true that France is falling. Any minute now, we will be under German occupation. What will you do then?"

"Join the Resistance. Plans for the Maquis are already under way. Here in the Auvergne the force will be active, from the heights of the Puy du Sancy down into the valley of the Dordogne. The forests beneath the Capucin to the Puy-de-Dôme will be alive with members of the Maquis."

"And while you are working with them, under cover day and night, who will look after your daughter?"

"I shall," said a feminine voice.

All heads turned. Standing within the door was a slim young woman, slightly older than Pierre. At the sight of her, he cried, "Françoise! Thank God, you've come. Kathy is being taken home. It is criminal — "

"But, as the Reverend Mother says, it cannot be prevented."

The girl on the bed, now half dressed, cried weakly, "Françoise — oh, Françoise, they are taking my baby away

11

from me and separating me from Pierre! But I shall come back. After this horrible war is over, I shall come back . . . "

"I shall come to England for you, chérie. We will be together again, for always."

"Of course you will," Françoise said calmly. "Meanwhile, have no fear. Your child will be loved and cared for."

"She must be baptized," Kathy urged. "Please call her Belinda. It was my mother's name."

"She will have yours also." Pierre's voice broke, and the lines of fatigue on his face were deepened by grief. "And she will have my family name — Lemaître. My father will arrange it by what you call deed poll in your country. This I promise."

Kathy's father declared, "That will satisfy me well. I want no bastard bearing my family's name. And who, may I ask, is this young woman?"

"Françoise Lemaître, Pierre's sister," said the Mother Superior. "She teaches needlework to the pupils."

Something in the woman's voice, and in the way she doubtfully looked at

12

Françoise, caused the man to ask, "Is that all she does?"

"No, m'sieur. Sometimes she takes the girls for walks. They are not allowed to go into Mont-Dore except under supervision, and since Mademoiselle Lemaître lives there and comes daily to the school — "

"She is in a position to arrange assignations for them, I suppose?"

"I meant no such thing! Merely that since she is a native of the place she knows the best walks on which to take them, and the best shops at which they can spend their pocket money — "

"And the best way to arrange meetings with the opposite sex?"

Françoise Lemaître had a very determined chin. It tilted defiantly now as she interrupted, "I introduced your daughter to my brother, yes, but the meeting was accidental, and that is the truth. We were waiting outside a shop in the Rue Menadier while some of the girls were inside. It was only natural for Pierre to stop, and only natural for introductions to be made."

"And after that, future meetings were

also 'accidental,' I suppose? Do you live alone, mademoiselle? A flat of your own, perhaps?"

"I have a small modiste's shop in the Rue Rigny, with rooms above. I teach needlework to the convent pupils to supplement my income."

"And how else do you supplement it? By allowing your premises to be used as a brothel?"

The crack of Pierre's hand across Sir Humphrey's arrogant face jerked the man's head violently.

"That is only a sample of what I would like to do to you, but one day I will pay you back for your words *and* your actions — *sir*. When I come to England to claim Kathy, I swear before God you will never see her again."

"And *I* swear before God you will never have access to her."

"This war will last longer than anyone expects. By that time she will be of age, free to make her own choice." The Frenchman turned to Kathy, now dressed and sitting weakly on the bed. "Promise to wait for me, my precious love . . . "

She clung to him, weeping bitterly. "I

14

promise, Pierre! I promise!"

Her father wrenched them apart, picked up his daughter, and carried her from the room. She was as light as a doll in his arms.

"God save her," Pierre choked. "Dear God in heaven, take care of her . . . "

Belinda's Story

1

THERE was nothing to warn me, as I stood at the entrance to Lyonhurst, that I had reached a threshold in my life and that beyond those imposing wrought-iron gates lay a world in which I was to become involved irrevocably and alarmingly, as in a cul-de-sac from which there was only one exit, and that exit barred. How did one escape from a trap of one's own making when others — strangers, enemies — stood guard, ready to pounce?

But on this particular morning the sun shone, the air was clear, my life was free. Had I been wise I would have walked away and never returned to stare through that ornate barrier. But wisdom had never been part of my makeup nor ever would be, according to Françoise.

"You are your father all over again, Belinda, reckless and impulsive. You will never learn to think before you act but, bless you, I would not have you change, any more than your mother would have wished your father to."

As always, I refused to discuss my mother. When Françoise dared to plead on her behalf, as even now she sometimes did, I turned a deaf ear. I had managed well enough without her all my life, and would continue to.

So it was illogical to be standing at the gates of my mother's home, knowing full well that I should never pass through them, but possessed by a quixotic desire to do so. I had convinced myself that curiosity and nothing more had urged me to visit Oakwell during college recess, and that I should be more than willing to shake the village dust from my feet and return to London at the earliest opportunity. Yet here I was, three days after my arrival, still lodging with Mrs. Tracey at the village store, still pretending to be an art student on a sketching holiday, and still wasting my time.

How could I ever gain admittance to Lyonhurst, and why should I want to? The place meant nothing to me, and my mother meant nothing to me — despite all the pathos Françoise had put into her story. Try as she might to convince me that my mother had wanted to keep me, Francoise had never succeeded in alleviating the doubt in my mind. I had been rejected by my mother and remained unacknowledged by the Tredgold family, and for that I hated them. I was the child whom Françoise, my father's elder sister, had adopted as her own, saved from war-ravaged France, and struggled to rear against unbelievable odds. For that I loved her.

How she had managed to support me in those early impoverished days I cannot imagine, for her little modiste shop in Mont-Dore, which was used as local headquarters for the Maquis, had been forced to close down when escape had been essential.

"What did I do?" she had once echoed with a laugh when I asked that question. "I grabbed a few clothes in one hand and you in the other, and fled with the rest."

"Why didn't you leave me behind? A baby must have been an encumbrance. Someone would have looked after me."

"Leave behind the child of two people I cared for deeply? Never. People like your mother and father are rare. They loved each other completely, and both wanted you. Never forget that."

Yet I found it hard to believe that my mother had wanted me, since she had never returned to claim me when the war ended. Only my father had proved his love for me, and Françoise her loyalty. It was to her that I owed allegiance. She had taken the place of my mother and, as far as I was concerned, she would occupy that place forever.

I turned away from the gates of my mother's home and, as I did so, heard a rush of sound nearby: a swift thudding upon earth. I whirled around. On the opposite side of the lane was a sloping meadow, hedge rimmed, and it was from this meadow that the noise came, that tingling of excitement, that breathless apprehension which the sudden sound of galloping hooves brings, spelling danger. I stood rooted and expectant while the thudding grew, swelled, ceased abruptly, and burst into a violent surge of air and flying mane as horse and rider soared over the hedge and came straight toward me at a gallop.

I leaped aside. I felt slithering earth and stones as I catapulted backward into a ditch. For a moment I lay winded and shocked, scarcely aware of a man's shout and the flurry of hooves hastily reined. And then he was scrambling after me and I was struggling to rise, aware that I was shaken and bruised and, ridiculously, wanting to cry. As he swung me onto the verge again, I sobbed furiously, "You clumsy *fool*, careening about the countryside like that! Do you think pedestrians have no right in these lanes?"

His hands were on my shoulders, steadying me. Perhaps my dislike of his touch was due solely to anger and shock. Whatever the reason, I pulled away from him and made ineffectual attempts to brush myself down. My hands were shaking and badly scratched. Fortunately, I was wearing slacks so my legs were protected, but there was an ugly tear in one knee. That quickened my anger, for the slacks were new, well cut, and with Françoise's elegant stamp on them.

"Look what you've done!" I hurled at him.

A smile touched his mouth. Even in my present state I was aware of its sensuality.

"I suppose it's useless for me to apologize? People rarely use this lane, so I took it for granted that it would be clear."

I felt he was the type of man who took much for granted, whether he had the right to or not, but my quick anger had subsided, leaving me feeling ashamed and rather foolish. After all, no harm had been done. I was alive, with no broken bones and merely a few scratches and a pair of torn slacks as souvenirs. I felt that I had made an enormous fuss about nothing.

"Are you badly hurt?"

"Not in the least," I replied shortly.

"Then I presume shock made you turn on me like that?"

"I suppose so. I'm sorry, though I think you deserved it. Leaping that hedge was crazy as well as arrogant."

"Arrogant!"

"Yes. Arrogant. You have an arrogant face and an arrogant voice."

He burst out laughing, not in the

least displeased. He seemed to find my description complimentary and I sensed that he was the type of man who didn't care what opinion a woman held of him so long as it was not one of indifference. I also realized something else — now that he was assured no harm had been done, a little pleasant dalliance wouldn't come amiss. Since he was good-looking and presentable, why did I want to avoid it? I enjoyed the company of men, so my reaction was illogical.

I turned away, searching for my portfolio of sketches. It lay on the grass, its contents spilled, my pad of drawings lying open. The man picked it up, studied it, and said, "An amateur artist, I see."

Patronizing as well, I decided.

I took the sketchbook from him, scarcely noticing the page at which it had fallen open. I thrust it back into the portfolio and straightened a few loose pictures. I saw the man look at them with interest and, because of his use of the word 'amateur,' I hastily covered them. When I looked up, the sensual mouth was no longer smiling and he seemed to be studying me with an intensity which I found embarrassing.

I turned, anxious to be gone. A few feet away his horse stood waiting, not daring to crop the grass, out of fear I felt. I liked the horse better than his master, and touched his mane as I passed. He whinnied with pleasure.

"You have a way with you. Rufus has a fiery temper and a habit of displaying it with strangers."

I was annoyed because the man walked by my side, so I smiled briefly in dismissal and continued down the lane.

Behind me, there was the sound of hooves as he remounted and followed. Within a minute he had reached my side again, and reined.

"Are you sure you're all right? I would like to make amends somehow."

"You have nothing to make amends for," I answered, wishing he would accept dismissal and stop pestering me, but his horse barred my path and I was forced to tolerate his deepening scrutiny.

"Bruises, shock, cut hands, and torn slacks? Do you regard all that as nothing?"

26

"The bruises can only be minor, the shock has already passed, the cuts are nothing but scratches, and the torn slacks I can mend. Good afternoon."

"But I am not ready to say good afternoon." He added abruptly, "Who are you? Where are you staying?"

I opened my mouth to say, "I'm a hiker on holiday," just as I had told Mrs. Tracey. Instead, I walked on without answering and was thankful when he let me go without further hindrance. I heard the horse's hooves as he turned and galloped away. Something made me pause and watch his departure. He sat easily in the saddle, his body responding effortlessly to the horse's movements. Then they were away, light and shade playing upon the flying mane and glossy coat and the man's strong back. The dust in their wake fanned and swirled and began to settle.

I went on my way, glad that I should never meet the man again.

By the time I reached the village I had recovered both my poise and my temper, and now wanted to forget the incident. I decided that should Mrs. Tracey notice my scratched hands and torn slacks, I would make the excuse that, finding the main gate locked, I had tried to get into the grounds of Lyonhurst some other way in the hope of sketching it, but unfortunately failed.

It was true, up to a point. I was an art student, although actually studying dress design. My sketching block, for this trip, was merely part of my props, my luggage consisting of the suit I had traveled in, a rucksack, and an artist's portfolio. I had walked from Ockenbury to Oakwell, painting as I went — the ancient abbey, village cottages, anything architectural so that my desire to make sketches of Lyonhurst would appear more convincing when the time came. I could think of no other excuse to get within the gates.

Had I had any common sense, I would have abandoned the whole idea, in which case all that followed — the bewilderment, the fear, the danger, and the terror — would never have come my way. But I had inherited my father's stubbornness, that tenacity of purpose which had made him fight on with the

Maquis until he was finally caught and shot. Perhaps the tragedy of his wasted life had turned me against my mother and her family even more. Perhaps I harbored some obscure desire to seek revenge for his sake, although in what way I had no idea. I had not grown up with such a desire consciously.

The bell which heralded customers in Mrs. Tracey's shop pealed loudly as I entered. She beamed at me from behind the wire cage which separated the post office from the general store.

"Well, dear, had a good morning? Let me see your sketches." When I produced them, she studied them admiringly. "My, but you're clever!"

As usual, I was touched. I wasn't a talented artist, just good enough to get by and with sufficient ability to put my designs on paper, but Mrs. Tracey didn't know that. To her, my sketches were wonderful and she was proud of her present lodger. Never before had an artist rented her spare bedroom. "Hikers mostly, dear, or cyclists. Nice, of course, but not like yourself. Wish I could have one of these as a souvenir, that I do.

Then I could hang it up and remember you by it."

"Take your pick!"

Delighted, she did so, begging me to sign it for her, so I scribbled my initials in the corner. I sometimes signed my sketches, or not, according to my mood. If I was pleased with a sketch I signed my full name; it was no more than a whim, a small conceit, an indication that I wasn't ashamed of a particular piece of work.

As I put away the remaining drawings, one of Lyonhurst fell to the floor. Mrs. Tracey picked it up, studied it, and said, "Now whatever made you draw those old gates? I shouldn't have thought there was anything interesting about them. They've been closed for many a year and must be rusted on their hinges!"

"Even so, they're beautiful. I wish I could get beyond them to sketch the house."

"Oh, you'll never do that, dear. Lots of people have tried, journalists and photographers and people like that, because it is one of the most famous country houses in England, but no one ever succeeds. Nor ever will, I reckon, even though Sir Humphrey has passed on. His word was law when he lived and I can't see it changing even though he's dead. His daughter would never go against his wishes."

At the mention of my mother I turned away, wanting to hear more and yet half afraid to, afraid also that Mrs. Tracey might detect my curiosity, but she was busy closing the shop for lunch and not looking in my direction.

"You don't mind a cold meal, do you dear? Millie didn't turn up today so I've had to keep my eye on the postal as well as the general, and on top of everything I had to deliver a registered parcel to Doctor Harvey."

I'd heard a lot about David Harvey, the village doctor. His name was mentioned with awe and respect because he had been the medical officer on an expedition to the Himalayas, and on another occasion, climbing alone, had been marooned on a ledge on Scafell for three days in a blizzard. Such episodes, I gathered, he dismissed. Reserved, Mrs. Tracey called him. Tough, I thought.

"Couldn't it have been delivered by

the morning mail, Mrs. Tracey?"

"It could've, I suppose, but it was marked urgent so I guessed it must be medicines and thought I'd better get them to him. Then I remembered he'd be out on his rounds. Luckily, his part-time secretary was there."

"Is that all the help he has?"

"It's all he can afford, I imagine. He's a village doctor, remember. None of your smart London surgeries for Doc Harvey. Country born and country bred, he is." She gave a dry laugh. "I can just imagine him telling those fancy London ladies to go home and do a good day's housework!"

"All London women aren't idle, Mrs. Tracey. Most of them work very hard, and have to."

"No offense, love. I meant the rich ones. Those neurotic creatures spending their husbands' fortunes in expensive Harley Street consulting rooms."

"Rich women anywhere can be idle and neurotic, Mrs. Tracey."

"True enough," she agreed. "Like Sir Humphrey Tredgold's sister. Now there was a spoiled creature for you! Took what she wanted from life without caring if other people were hurt. Of course, she was hurt herself in the end. You can't go around stealing other women's husbands and not pay the price."

I was startled. This was the first I had heard of any other relative. I didn't even know that my mother had an aunt.

"Sir Humphrey Tredgold?" I echoed casually. "And who is he?"

"He isn't anymore. He's dead, like I told you."

"Oh, you mean the owner of Lyonhurst?"

"That's right. It's been in the Tredgold family for generations, but what'll happen to it now he's gone, nobody knows and everybody wonders."

"Didn't he leave a widow? And what about his sister?"

"He lost his wife when his daughter was a child. Some say that's why he clung to Miss Kathy so much. I still think of her as Miss Kathy in spite of her title. As for his sister, she died young, too. Overdose of sleeping pills. Accidental death, they called it. Aye, they're a tragic family one way and another, and just about the biggest tragedy is Lady

Katherine herself."

"Why?" I asked, keeping my face immobile and my eyes expressionless. To hear someone actually talking about my mother was shaking.

"Because she's never married and never had the chance to, that's why. Her father saw to that. Shut her up at Lyonhurst as if she were a prisoner, all her life."

"Oh, come, Mrs. Tracey! People don't behave like that in this day and age! If she had wanted to escape, she could have, surely?"

"Not that man's daughter, believe me. I don't expect a girl like you to understand because you come from a different world and a different generation. Poor Miss Kathy didn't have the freedom young people enjoy today. She was dominated by her father. So was everyone belonging to him or working for him. He was a king in his own domain and, my goodness, he was a tyrant!"

"If I had been his daughter, I would have run away."

"If you had been his daughter, you wouldn't have had the means or the opportunity to. The only time that poor

34

girl left Lyonhurst was to go to a finishing school in France, and goodness knows what happened there. Came back sort of changed, she did, but not in the way we'd all expected. I mean, she wasn't all polished and sophisticated, like a girl just out of finishing school. She was so quiet and pale everyone thought she must have been ill and that she'd be her own bright self again in time, but somehow she never was. And from the day her father brought her back, he never let her out of his sight."

"I repeat, she should have run away."

"It's easy to talk, my girl, but what could someone like Miss Kathy do? How could she have earned her living, brought up the way she was? Her father took good care she wasn't trained for a career or anything. And with all their money she didn't need to be."

"You seem to know a lot about the family, Mrs. Tracey."

"I know all about everyone, dear, and can you wonder, keeping a village post office? And old Harriet, Miss Kathy's nurse, used to chat to me a lot once upon a time. Don't see her in the village much these days, she's pretty housebound now, but she used to drop in for a regular chat. It wasn't surprising because life must've been lonely at Lyonhurst and became even more so as time went on. The old man kept as few servants as possible. Didn't trust 'em, he said. Didn't trust anyone, if you ask me. Not even his own daughter. When she came back from France he acted like her jailer. No wonder the poor thing never married. No man was good enough for her, in her father's eyes, and I must say Miss Kathy herself never seemed interested in anyone. The only person in her life was her father. There now, I hope you like homemade pork pie?"

I said truthfully that I loved it, and sat down, my mind running on my mother's family and the home which should, Françoise insisted, be mine by rights. She was wrong about that, of course. Quite apart from the fact that an illegitimate child had no legitimate claim, Françoise had been as ignorant as I about the existence of my mother's aunt.

"Did she leave any family?" I asked.

"Who, love?"

"Sir Humphrey's sister."

"None that anyone has ever heard of. She never married. Not that marriage vows, especially other people's, meant anything to Prudence Tredgold. Prudence! Anyone who had less would've been difficult to find. She was a good-for-nothing trollop. You don't have to belong to the lower classes to be one of those."

I ate on, saying nothing, my mind too occupied with the surprising revelation that my mother's autocratic family had harbored anything so scandalous as a nymphomaniac. I felt a certain wry amusement, but anger as well, for of all things in life I hated injustice the most. That was why the Tredgold rejection of myself and my father had festered in my heart all these years. And now to find that they had worse things of which to be ashamed than a daughter who fell in love with a penniless foreigner! Prudence had not been so unwise as to give birth to an illegitimate child, but her lovers had been plural and taken for physical satisfaction alone. I, if all Françoise said was true, had at least been conceived in love. But sometimes I wondered if she painted a kinder picture of things, for my benefit.

"I suppose they had no pity for her, either."

"Either?" Mrs. Tracey echoed.

I said quickly, "I meant for either Prudence or the woman whose husband she fell in love with."

Mrs. Tracey sniffed.

"She fell in love with too many husbands, that was her trouble — if you could call it love. Man after man she had to have. One man alone could never satisfy her."

"Poor thing," I said gently.

"You needn't waste your pity on the likes of her!"

"I don't think pity of any kind is ever wasted."

I changed the subject by complimenting her on her pork pie. My morning's exercise had whetted my appetite. Since arriving in Oakwell I had walked to Lyonhurst and back every day, and each time got no nearer than those impenetrable gates. Undoubtedly they held a challenge, and this surprised me, for my decision to visit Oakwell had been entirely spontaneous. Nothing had been further from my mind when I read of my unlamented grandfather's death as Françoise and I sat at breakfast one morning in our flat on Brook Street.

Sir Humphrey Tredgold, Bart., at his Kentish home, Lyonhurst . . . one of the oldest families and finest estates in England . . . well-known figure in hunting circles . . . Sir Humphrey leaves a daughter, the Lady Katherine Tredgold . . . Will Lady Katherine retain the family seat, or will she, as some think, hand it over to the National Trust? Speculation is idle until Sir Humphrey's will is made public . . .

There was more. Something about the entire village of Oakwell being in mourning and the passing of a grand old English gentleman. I had hurled the newspaper across the table and said, "So he has gone, Françoise."

Françoise, elegant in a housecoat which could only have been designed by her, sipped black coffee and replied absently, "Who is gone, *chérie*, and where?"

"My grandfather. As to where, I could give a good guess, and I hope he gets a hot welcome."

Slowly, Françoise laid down the letter she was reading and picked up the newspaper. "So," she commented in her heavily accented voice. "So." That was all, but it spoke volumes.

Handing the paper back, she had continued, "The world will be a better place without him. He had no heart. But if the doors of Lyonhurst should be opened to anyone, it is you."

"They can remain closed as far as I am concerned. I am happy as I am, thanks to you."

Françoise had given me one of her long, assessing glances, then said, "I can see you mean it. You're as stubborn and proud as your father, bless you."

And that was the way I intended to remain.

"You are right," I told her. "The world will be a better place without him. As for my mother, she can live in comfort at Lyonhurst for the rest of her days. She has lived well enough without me, and I without her."

"Have compassion, Belinda. She loved your father, and wanted you whole-heartedly."

"*He* wanted me more than she did. It was he, and you, who cared for me.

"Because life contrived it so! Kathy was younger than you are now! She was scarcely sixteen, underage, and overruled by parental authority. Although she was the child of a wealthy family, she was penniless herself. Her father kept her so, and with good reason. He was determined that she would never again escape his control, although she resolved to get back to Pierre somehow. Then France fell — and you know the rest."

I did indeed.

"I shall never believe that she forgot you," Françoise insisted.

"Well, I don't suppose any woman could forget giving birth, but that doesn't mean that she wanted an illegitimate child — or at any rate, not for long. Otherwise she would have tried to find me when the war ended."

"There must have been reasons. Good

reasons, impossible to overcome. This I shall always believe and this I want you to believe."

"I'll try, Françoise, for your sake. You lost your job as sewing mistress at the school because of what happened."

Françoise shrugged expressive shoulders. "You call that suffering? I hated teaching, and the job merely supplemented my earnings. Losing it meant that I had to work harder at my dressmaking, and look where it led me! Could anything have been more fortuitous from my point of view?"

"You were generous, you and my father. A child born as I is rarely so fortunate."

"Don't talk like that. And don't take a wrong view of your birth. Kathy and Pierre regarded themselves as man and wife and took what steps they could to sanctify their union, in their idealistic way. They exchanged vows in the house of God, which were as binding to them as any form of marriage contract and worth more than a mere piece of paper legalizing their union in the eyes of the world. Neither of them would have gone through a form of marriage with anyone else after that."

From a side street in a mountain village of the Massif Central to the heart of Mayfair — this was the route Françoise had embarked on when she escaped to England with me, with nothing to pave her way but outstanding talent and dauntless determination. Now she was one of London's leading dress designers, charging fabulous sums for her magnificent gowns, listing among her clientele the wealthy and famous; but success had not changed her. She was still a hardworking dressmaker as well as guide, mentor, and friend to me. She was all I had in the world. I needed no one else, so this sudden urge to see my mother's home was totally inexplicable.

I had always assumed that my mother still lived, but had no idea of what had happened to her. In order not to dwell on the pain I felt because she had never claimed me, I deliberately avoided looking for her name in the social columns. I had inevitably pictured her as another man's wife, mother of another man's children, for this seemed inevitable. The reference to her in Sir Humphrey's obituary notice, however, confirmed that she still bore the Tredgold name.

Was it this which sparked in me a desire at least to see the house where she lived? College was in recess and for three weeks Françoise would be away at the Continental dress shows, and I was at loose ends, so why shouldn't I visit Oakwell and see my mother's birthplace? I had nothing to lose . . .

Once conceived, the idea grew. Had I suppressed it, I would never have tumbled head over heels into trouble, or have been stalked by bewilderment and fear and a final, terrible danger. I would have stayed safely in our hardworking *couture* world, in which I hoped to follow as successfully as Françoise, instead of packing a rucksack and sketching materials the day after she departed and calling to her secretary Hilda on my way out: "I'm off on a hiking trip, Hilda — where to, I don't know, but the idea of being alone in the flat upstairs for three weeks or possibly more doesn't appeal to me. I expect I'll be back long before Françoise returns. Once she gets caught up with those Continental fashion folk she can hardly tear herself away."

Hilda had smiled and agreed. "She's obsessed with it, isn't she? Fashion, I mean. It's her life. I suppose that's why she never married. A pity, really. She's such an attractive woman."

I paused to give the remark only fleeting consideration. Why Françoise had never married wasn't a question I had ever dwelt upon. She was a single-minded woman, full of drive and determination, but beneath her veneer and dedication to work she had a big, warm heart. I, of all people, knew that.

"There isn't a man in the world good enough for her," I told Hilda as I waved good-by.

★ ★ ★

I became aware that Mrs. Tracey had been talking for some time. "Why don't you visit Ockenbury and sketch the abbey there? You'll never get nearer Lyonhurst than those old gates, believe me."

45

"I sketched the abbey on my way here. Besides, I hear that Lyonhurst is beautiful. I don't see why the owners should be averse to visitors, especially artists who want to immortalize their home!"

"Once upon a time, they wouldn't have minded, but that was long ago, before Sir Humphrey closed the gates on the world. The few people who go there now have to settle for the side entrance."

"That sounds highly unsociable. But I thought you said the old man was dead. What about his daughter? Wouldn't she be more approachable?"

"I doubt it, love. She's as reserved as her father was, though I never dreamed she'd get that way. As a girl she was so friendly. A mischief, too, her nurse used to say. Now the pair of them live alone in that great place, hardly ever going out. I expect old Harriet'll go wherever her mistress goes now."

"Why should she go anywhere? Why shouldn't she stay right where she is?"

"In that great barn, all by herself with only Harriet to keep her company? Just about the worst thing she could do, I'd say. No, you mark my words, she'll get rid of it. They do say she'll hand it over to the National Trust and maybe it wouldn't be such a bad idea, then the likes of us can enjoy it. The grounds are beautiful. Oakwell village fête used to be held there every year, when I was young. It was the tradition. Then suddenly the old man put a stop to all that; shut himself up like a recluse, and his daughter with him. What a life for the poor girl!"

I said nothing. I had to be careful, think before I spoke — a maxim Françoise had always tried to instill in me and which I never found easy to follow. "Think before you act, and count ten before you speak." By this ruling she had climbed in her career. Caution and tact, she declared, were lessons she had learned the hard way. Sometimes I wondered if I would ever learn them. At that moment I had no desire to, nor had I when standing before those immense gates earlier. The impulse to turn the great iron lock and march up to the house had been strong. Not a sign of it could be glimpsed from the road. Beyond the gates a winding drive, flanked by massed rhododendrons, curved away out of sight. I had even skirted the high walls of the estate, searching for a viewpoint and finding none. A rear gate, presumably for tradesmen, had yielded nothing either, and a side entrance, probably the one to which Mrs. Tracey referred, seemed to open merely onto endless shrubberies.

So unless I could think up some plan, or be presented with some miraculous opportunity, I should return to London without even glimpsing the house in which my mother lived.

Little did I dream how near that opportunity was, or anticipate the unexpected hand which fate was to hold out and which, without thought, I was to grasp, allowing it to propel me into a position from which there could be no escape, and for which I could have no one but myself to blame.

2

ELPING Mrs. Tracey to clear the table, I listened with some amusement to her insistence that it seemed all wrong for a young girl like me to go around sketching moldy old ruins. "Should've thought you'd prefer the promenade at Margate. Plenty going on, plenty to see. Why don't you move on there, love, and have a good time? Not that I want you to go. I've enjoyed your company."

I promised idly to think about it.

It was time to open the shop again. The communicating door stood ajar and I could see the Canterbury bus stopping outside, its passengers alighting. Among them was the wife of the village school's headmaster. She was small and spry and bustling, full of self-importance. She hopped from the bus straight toward the shop and rattled the latch impatiently.

"Shall I open up, Mrs. Tracey? You have a customer. Mrs. Butler."

"Oh, her. Impatient as usual, I expect."

"I'll see what she wants."

Mrs. Butler didn't want to buy anything. She had been shopping in Canterbury and was laden, advertising the fact that she didn't think Oakwell's shops worth patronizing. She didn't thank me for opening the door, nor for holding it while she entered, nor for shutting it behind her.

"How *awful* it is to be without the car! Public transport is something I'm just not *used* to!" She broke off and surveyed me with a patronizing little smile. "I don't think I know you, do I? You're a new assistant, I take it?"

"No."

"A relative of Mrs. Tracey's then?"

"No, again. I'm her lodger, Belinda Masters." I gave an English interpretation of my surname, as I had done to Mrs. Tracey, because it was easier than having to spell it out. "What can I do for you?"

"I've a letter — now where *is* it?" She rummaged in a cluttered handbag and produced it triumphantly. "I thought Mrs. Tracey might send it along for me — "

"If that's another letter for free delivery, Mrs. Butler, I'd remind you that I sell stamps."

Mrs. Butler's head jerked around indignantly.

"It isn't a letter of *mine*. My niece from Canterbury entrusted it to me — the one who was going to stay at Lyonhurst."

Curiosity got the better of Mrs. Tracey. "Your niece, going to stay at Lyonhurst! Why, they haven't had a visitor for years!"

"Well, she wasn't going as a guest, exactly . . . "

"Oh, I see. You mean she was going to work there. I didn't know she was in domestic service."

"She most certainly is not! She's a nurse — well, a sort of nurse. No drudgery, nothing messy, you understand. A superior companion; always lives as one of the family, of course. Now she's off to Majorca suddenly — "

"To take a job?" There was nothing Mrs. Tracey liked more than a good gossip. And this was certainly news. Mrs. Butler's niece had been bound for Lyonhurst to fill the job of a companion.

"She'd be going to look after Lady Katherine, I take it," Mrs. Tracey continued.

"Yes. I imagine she misses her dear father who has passed on."

I failed to see how Mrs. Butler's niece could take the place of an elderly gentleman, but Mrs. Tracey seemed to find the idea acceptable.

"Yes, indeed. No doubt she's lonely. And now your niece is letting her down, you say?"

"I said no such thing! She is sending word at once. Dear Gillian is so conscientious that as soon as she heard that her present employer wanted her to travel to Majorca with her she couldn't *dream* of abandoning her — "

"Not for a holiday in Majorca, I'm sure."

Mrs. Butler ignored that. "She wouldn't even leave it to the employment bureau to send word, because she was due to arrive today and a letter wouldn't arrive until tomorrow — "

"So she asked you to deliver it for her, and it's such a long walk, all of three miles — and you with no car!"

"It's gone in for servicing," Mrs. Butler said stiffly.

"So you'd like me to take the letter for you?"

"Well, you do run the post office, and you do deliver mail when necessary. I saw you taking a parcel to Doctor Harvey only this morning . . . "

"That was urgent."

"So is this."

"But it isn't mail. Doctor Harvey's was. Besides, I can't leave the shop — "

"But I can," I volunteered. "In fact, I'll be passing Lyonhurst on my way to Margate."

My voice, and the hand I extended, were both absolutely steady, which surprised me, for my heart was beating a wild tattoo. Here it was, the opportunity for which I'd been waiting. The open sesame. Without any planning or scheming, it was presented to me by fate.

Mrs. Butler thrust the letter into my hand. "Thank you *so* much, Miss Masters. Good-bye, good-bye!"

The door closed. Mrs. Tracey sniffed eloquently. "That niece of hers must be as mean as herself. Too mean to send a telegram, it seems."

"I'm glad she didn't. This give me the opportunity to see Lyonhurst before I leave."

"So you're taking my advice, love. Well, I can't say I blame you, sorry as I am to see you go. There's nothing in this quiet village for a young girl like you."

I pretended to agree, saying as I headed for the stairs, "If I find the old house worth sketching, I'll do one or two and then be on my way . . . "

The letter was almost burning my hand and the impulse to open it was strong, but I resisted until I had parted from Oakwell with Mrs. Tracey's eager insistence that I should "have a good time in Margate, dear!" ringing in my ears. Not until the village was well behind did I pause on an isolated stretch of road, slit the envelope, and extract the letter. It didn't tell me much — no more than Mrs. Butler had already divulged.

It was a wild gamble, but I knew I was going to take it. I tore the letter into fragments and scattered them in a nearby ditch, where a muddied stream swallowed them forever.

3

THE house stood majestically amidst sweeping acres. Against my will, I was awed. That troubled me, for I had no wish to be impressed by the place or to experience anything but idle curiosity.

Beneath my reaction was an awareness that from this earth my roots had partially sprung, but I was more conscious of excitement. This was a daredevil scheme which I wouldn't have missed for the world, a reckless step which I was quite unable to resist. In any case, it was too late to turn back. The double doors of Lyonhurst were opening, revealing an old woman in a plain black dress, a gray woolen shawl about her shoulders. Her alert mind shone from her eyes, which were bright and sharp. There was also a certain annoyance in her gaze.

Harriet, of course. She had the stamp of an aging nanny and the air of a family retainer, the sort of dignity a woman achieves after serving a household for most of her lifetime.

Before I even had time to speak, she acknowledged me with a grudging, "So you've arrived, Miss Conrad, and about time, too."

"I'm sorry. I was delayed a little." I spoke apologetically, carefully feeling my way.

"A little! Expected you first thing this morning, we did. All day long her poor ladyship has been asking for you. Is that all the luggage you have — a rucksack?"

She eyed it with surprise and disapproval. I could understand the surprise, for a rucksack seemed rather unconventional luggage for a nurse-companion. Then she saw my portfolio and studied it curiously.

"I sketch a little," I explained. "It's just a hobby."

"Well, you can leave your stuff here. Buxton will take it to your room."

The next moment I was stepping across the threshold and following her bent figure along a vast marble-floored hall with a vaulted roof. On either side, sweeping marble stairs curved out of sight. The place was magnificent, but chilling. I suppressed a shiver. This wasn't a home. It was a mansion without a heart. I wondered how it had ever produced a girl so gay and passionate as my mother was supposed to have been. Gaiety didn't belong here, not in this cold baronial hall with its somber pillars, dark portraits, and echoing floors.

Harriet's step, despite her years, was as brisk as her voice. She proved to be surprisingly garrulous, which suggested that having someone to talk to was a rarity for her. This chattering made it unnecessary for me to contribute to the conversation and I was glad to let her prattle on. I wanted to learn all I could to help my impersonation, for I had given no consideration to the unknown Gillian Conrad — her qualifications, her experience, or even who had engaged her — but now ragged edges of alarm brushed against my mind. How could I hope to impersonate successfully someone about whom I knew not the slightest detail? The most trivial mistake could be my undoing.

I wanted to turn and run. I could hear the staccato echo of my heels as they marched in Harriet's wake across the stone floor, and wished I could speed them in the opposite direction. But my feet moved onward as if of their own volition. There could be no turning back now.

"A pity you were delayed, Miss Conrad, but I suppose it couldn't be helped. It's just like everything nowadays. As I told her ladyship myself, it's wait, wait, wait. That's all we ever do, whether it's for a plumber or a parcel. Everyone's hoity-toity nowadays, no matter who. It's all this welfare state that does it! Everyone's equal now, or so they say." She sniffed. "I belong to the old school, so I'm out of date, I suppose, but I know my place and am not ashamed of it. As I was saying to Mr. Deacon only yesterday, I was born into service and I've stayed in service and there's no stigma attached to being a servant in *my* mind. I could see he approved, but then he's a gentleman, so of course he would. Doctor Harvey, now, he's different. Doesn't even think the same way. 'Stop being so self-righteous,

Harriet,' he said. 'Self-righteousness is a form of conceit.'

"Did you ever hear the like of it? I gave him a good straight look and he knew what I was thinking all right, but even so he had the audacity to laugh. 'The trouble with you, Doctor,' I said, 'is that you're not religious.' At that he laughed even more. 'And what has religion to do with it, Hattie?' he says, knowing full well I dislike being called Hattie. So I told him straight. 'If you were religious,' I said, 'you'd have respect.' That's what I told him."

"And what did he say to that?" I asked. The more I could get her to talk, the more I would learn, and it was necessary to learn all I could about the doctor with whom I was going to be in touch.

"What did he say?" The black shoulders shrugged. "Something about the only thing he respected was human life and human courage. Of course, he isn't the gentleman Mr. Deacon is. *His* manners leave nothing to be desired, but the doctor's very often do. You haven't met him yet, so wait until you do."

I felt relieved, because her words

meant that Gillian Conrad had not been interviewed by the doctor. There was no reason, of course, why she should be; a companion didn't have to be a qualified nurse.

Even so, my spirits rose. Hurdle number one, meeting Dr. Harvey, could be faced without fear.

The old woman's footsteps halted beside a heavy door. "This way, if you please." She held it open for me, and as I passed through I was conscious of a change of atmosphere. The marble floors, the vaulted ceilings, the carpeted corridor leading to some distant part of the house, the cold, disused feeling all vanished as the warmth of an efficient central heating system met me.

My reaction must have been self-evident, for Harriet smiled wryly. "Different, isn't it? And all thanks to Mr. Deacon."

"And who is Mr. Deacon?"

"Her ladyship's solicitor — Matthew Deacon, son of the late Sir Basil Deacon, who became a leading judge shortly before his death, but his son has no such ambitions. 'I'm quite content to be a country lawyer, Harriet,' he said to me once. 'I've no desire for fame or glory.' Yes, a real gentleman is Mr. Deacon."

The relevancy seemed a little illogical, but I let it pass.

"Her ladyship only uses one wing of the house now," Harriet continued as she led the way. "The rest is shut up, and a good thing, too. The manor is too big and sprawling to manage in these days, and so I told Mr. Deacon myself. He agreed. If it hadn't been for his, persuading Lady Katherine to withdraw into this part of the house and be warm and comfortable in it, we'd still be shivering."

"Didn't she want to live in just one wing?"

"Oh, dear me, no! She would never do anything of which her father would disapprove and Sir Humphrey always insisted on occupying the whole of the place, as his ancestors did in the days when servants were two a penny. By the time he passed on, there was only myself left to run the house with whatever help I could get from the village — and Buxton, of course. He's gardener and handyman, but not much good about the house."

I wondered why the proud Sir Humphrey had allowed the staff to deplete so drastically, and said so.

Harriet's bent shoulders shrugged again.

"It was his wish. He had an aversion to replacing the old servants. Wouldn't have strangers in the place, he said, and that was that."

A tyrant, Mrs. Tracey had called him and Mrs. Tracey, it seemed, was right.

"But surely, now that he is dead, Lady Katherine can run the house as she pleases?"

"Lady Katherine is content," Harriet answered evasively, and changed the subject abruptly. "You'll handle her gently, won't you? She isn't like other women, you understand."

"What do you mean — not like other women?"

The old lady looked at me sharply.

"Surely you were told?"

"I was told nothing, except that I had to look after her."

She clucked her tongue impatiently.

"Then you should have been! Ah, well, never mind, you'll have Doctor Harvey to turn to, and though I say it myself, you couldn't have a better doctor. Knows his job, all right. I'll give him his due there."

Why did I feel that, despite her condemnation of him, she really liked the man?

Harriet's neat black figure came to a halt beside another door. She tapped on the paneling, then turned the knob and held the door open for me to enter. As she did so, something in her manner and her voice changed. The brusqueness, the touch of impatience, the dryness were gone, replaced by a gentleness and a note of indulgence as she said, "Well, here she is, my dear. Here's the nice young lady, come to keep you company."

I braced myself. I was about to meet my mother, the woman who had rejected me, the woman for whom I could feel nothing.

Imperceptibly I lifted my chin as I walked into the room. It was long, with tall windows overlooking the gardens. Placed between the windows was a high-winged chair and seated on it a small figure almost doll-like in its fragility.

My mother had been barely sixteen when I was born and now she was approaching forty. She looked much more than that. There was a shrunken look about her which was aging, plus something I could not define, something which suggested that she had withdrawn into herself, away from life.

When she turned and looked at me, I felt nothing, no apprehension, no fear, no need to brace myself any more. Only curiosity filled me as I went to meet her, and as I did so my footsteps echoed like a rhythmic beat upon a drum. The floor, I noted subconsciously, was bare and highly polished, with just a few scattered rugs.

The small woman in the wing chair watched my coming, and it wasn't until I was within a few feet of her that I stood still abruptly. I had been aware that she held something on her lap, but I hadn't glanced at it until now. A lapdog, I had assumed. Or a cat. A pet of some sort. But I was wrong.

It was a doll.

A doll with flaxen hair and a blue-eyed waxen gaze, a doll dressed absurdly in a frock several sizes too large. The doll's diminutive head emerged rather grotesquely from this garment, lolling in the crook of her arm, cradled like a baby.

My mother lifted her finger and laid it against her lips. "Hush," she said softly, "Belinda is asleep."

4

A CHILL ran through me as I realized what Harriet meant when she said that my mother was not like other women.

But I hadn't expected this. Beneath my shock I was strangely moved. I was looking at a woman who had retreated from reality into a world of her own, a world in which she nursed the child she had lost. A child called Belinda.

I heard myself saying, "I won't waken her, I promise."

I saw Harriet's look of relief and approving smile. She crossed the room and adjusted the cushion at my mother's back. "There, there, my dear, now you won't be alone anymore. This is Miss Conrad, who has come to look after you."

"*And* to look after Belinda," my mother corrected.

"Of course, my love, of course."

The old lady's voice was full of

maternal affection and above Katherine's head she gave me an imperceptible nod of approval.

I had won her over. I had adopted the right approach, and Harriet was to be my ally from that moment on. As for myself, I felt curiously weak. This was a moment for which I had been totally unprepared.

I had arrived at Lyonhurst with a sense of adventure and repressed excitement. Now all that had gone, leaving me vaguely ashamed. But what could I do to make amends? Announce my true identity and plunge this unfortunate woman into even more drastic shock? What useful purpose would that serve? I had come here as Gillian Conrad, a nurse-companion, and the best thing to do was to keep up the pretense for a few hours at least and make my getaway as soon as I could conveniently offer an excuse. In that way no harm would be done and no one need ever know my true identity. I would go back to London and tell no one where I had been — not even Françoise, when she returned. I would leave Katherine Tredgold to her secret dreams and forever afterward pity her. That much good, at least, would come out of this visit.

My mother held out her hand to me. It felt fragile and brittle in my own. I had not been aware of how young and strong my own was until this thin little bundle of bones was grasped within it. The skin was almost transparent and there was a pathetic helplessness about her hand.

She looked at me with eyes which seemed to reflect all the weariness of the world, and said, "Welcome to Lyonhurst, my dear. It is nice of you to visit me."

It was almost as if she were saying a party piece instilled into her when young: How to Greet a Guest, Lesson One — from a Victorian book on etiquette. Then I saw the tired eyes looking at me shrewdly and I realized that, although part of my mother's mind had retreated from the world, the rest of it was very much alive and quite surprisingly acute.

I withstood her scrutiny quite calmly, despite a sudden apprehension, although in appearance I was distinctly different from my mother. My hair was dark, almost black, while my skin, Françoise had repeatedly told me, was as olive as my father's. My nose was what the French call *retroussé* and the English, less elegantly, snub. My eyes were the deep gray of Pierre's and my eyebrows, I had once observed from a photograph of him, matched his own, winging upward, which imparted a look of somewhat surprised amusement.

"You resemble your father far more than your mother," Françoise had frequently told me, but right at this moment I prayed that the resemblance was not noticeable, and that time might have dimmed my mother's recollection of him.

"It was good of you to come," she repeated. "I hope you will be happy at Lyonhurst."

"Thank you, Lady Katherine."

"Of course, I don't need nursing, merely someone to keep me company," she continued with a touch of childish defiance. "It was the doctor's idea and so Matthew engaged you at once. Matthew is so kind to me. More thoughtful than a brother."

At that precise moment footsteps

echoed on the terrace outside. A moment later they paused on the threshold of the French windows. With his back against the sunlight stood the solid figure of a man. I couldn't distinguish his features, but although the expression on his face was concealed, I could tell from his stance that he was angry.

Harriet was still standing beside my mother's chair, and as she looked toward the windows her face showed relief. There was reassurance in her touch as her hand rested briefly on Katherine's shoulder.

"Here is the doctor to see you," she said comfortingly. "Now you will have nothing more to worry about. You'll be well looked after between the pair of them."

So this was David Harvey — climber, explorer, adventurer, and village doctor. I studied the man with interest — strong, muscular, possibly a boxer in his student days. He was not handsome by any means. On the whole, his appearance was quite ordinary, but I knew that he possessed distinguishing qualities, for he had accomplished much in the world of endurance and physical endeavor.

Besides being the Medical Officer on that Himalayan trip, he had accompanied an expedition to the Brazilian jungle, from which he had returned with a wound in his back caused by a native spear thrust. A fellow member of the expedition had become separated from the rest of the group in a part of the jungle from which no white man had ever been known to return. Searching for him, David Harvey's naked back had been the target for a concealed spear, the bush hiding the attacker. He fell, crashing through the undergrowth, spread-eagled upon the dead body of his missing companion. But for that spear thrust, the man would never have been found, and despite it, the village doctor from Kent dragged his dead colleague back to base for a decent burial.

"He said the only thing he respected was human life and human courage . . . " Harriet's words echoed in my ears and I thought that at least he respected the right things and if that wasn't religion in the conventional sense, perhaps it was better. If psalm-singing and cant didn't enter into Dr. Harvey's scheme of things, at least he was not a hypocrite.

My mother's voice recalled me with a jerk. She was holding the doll toward me and saying, "Take Belinda, will you, dear?"

Automatically, I reached out and took the doll. The garment in which it was dressed was even bigger than I had realized, and I guessed that it was a dress which my mother herself had worn as a child. Now she had passed it on to this waxen image into which she imbued imaginary life. With this inanimate doll she consoled herself, playing with it as she had played with it in childhood.

A strange sensation ran through me, a mixture of curiosity and sadness. I found myself regarding Katherine Tredgold with different eyes. Could she have been so indifferent since she cherished this doll in my place, calling it by my name, believing it to be the baby she had lost?

She rose from her chair and went to meet the doctor, both hands extended. A change had come over her. In laying aside her doll she had returned to reality.

This switching from past to present took me by surprise, but was one to which I was to grow accustomed.

"David," she said, "what a pity you couldn't have come earlier! Had I known, you could have picked Miss Conrad up at the station and brought her here."

"Miss Conrad?" the doctor echoed sharply, and looked across at me.

He had stepped into the room and now the light shone fully on his face. I could see he was astonished. His heavy brows met in a frown.

"Miss Conrad?" he repeated. "But that is impossible!"

There was only one thing to do. I met his glance squarely and said, "How do you do, Doctor Harvey?" and held out my hand.

I felt rather ridiculous, standing there with a doll crooked within the curve of my left arm and holding out my right toward a man who was regarding me in doubt and disbelief. He had a direct and disconcerting glance, but I met it steadily. I saw a pair of dark eyes, piercing and intelligent, a stubborn chin, a firm mouth, and knew that I could be

73

afraid of this man if I allowed myself to be.

He ignored my outstretched hand.

"But this is ridiculous!" he said. "This girl cannot be Gillian Conrad."

5

"MY dear David," said my mother, "what do you mean? That she isn't what you expected? She isn't what I expected either. So young. So attractive. Not pretty, no, but a piquant little face, don't you think? All the companions I have ever known were middle-aged and drab, but this one isn't and I am glad. Belinda will love her."

She held out her arms for the flaxen-haired doll and I laid it within them. Pity was stirring again, a dangerous emotion, I reminded myself. I hadn't come here to be won over by my mother. Curiosity and nothing more had brought me; once satisfied, I would go. Nothing would make me change my mind about that.

David Harvey glanced at Katherine and his face softened. I felt he had been about to say something, but now changed his mind.

Harriet said, "I'll bring tea at once."

"None for me, thank you, Harriet. I haven't time. I just looked in on my rounds," the doctor said.

Harriet departed even so, and I was alone with my mother, who didn't suspect me, and with the doctor who did.

He said to me briskly, "Well, I'm glad you've arrived, Miss Conrad," but there was sarcasm in his voice and still that hidden note of anger.

All right, I thought, if you want to be angry, do so. I can be angry, too. It's as good a defense as any other and certainly better than fear.

"You're right, Lady Katherine," he continued. still with his eyes on me, "she isn't a bit what I expected."

I took a plunge and said boldly, "Surely the employment bureau told you what I was like?"

"Not that you were so young."

"I don't recall telling them my age."

Well, that was true at least, I reflected wryly, and hoped the answer would pass. Apparently it did, for David Harvey made no comment, but I felt he wanted to say something and would have done so had we been alone. I was determined

76

that we should not be and that he would have no chance to cross-examine me.

My mother was cradling her doll, caressing the flaxen hair with a tender hand. It was a heartrending gesture and I turned my eyes away. Had she touched her own child's head in such a manner, the day it was born?

"Did you have a good journey, Miss Conrad?" Dr. Harvey's voice was abrupt and clipped.

"Very good, thank you."

"And what train did you catch?"

The question was a blow, but before I had time to rally, the door opened and mercifully Harriet entered with tea.

"I brought three cups just in case the doctor feels like changing his mind. Will you pour, my dear? I usually do it for her ladyship, but since you are here . . . "

Thankfully, I went to the tea tray, glad for an excuse to avoid Dr. Harvey's disconcerting glance. I took one cup and saucer from the tray and laid it aside deliberately. Promptly he sat down and said, "Two lumps for me, please."

I poured a cup for my mother and carried it across to her, taking the doll from her arms and laying it comfortable upon a nearby chair.

"Has Harriet made some of her queencakes today?" she asked.

Harriet had. I picked up the plate from the tea trolley and handed it to her. Then I poured my own tea and lastly the doctor's, dropping two lumps in with defiant little plops. He accepted the cup with frank amusement. The man annoyed me, and since my mother was obviously not a sick woman physically, I hoped his visits would not be too frequent.

With an indulgent sigh my mother said, "How I needed this tea! Belinda has been so naughty today — full of mischief, quite tiring me out!" She turned a loving glance upon the stiffly smiling doll and I saw that the waxen lids, edged with sable eyelashes, were closed.

"She is sleeping very peacefully now," I put in.

Across the room the doctor studied me reflectively. What lay behind his glance I couldn't be sure, but I felt a certain measure of approval because I was humoring his patient. But what else could I do in the circumstances, since I had come here ostensibly to companion her?

I finished my tea, laid my cup aside, and said, "I believe my luggage has been sent up to my room. I wonder could I — ?"

"But, of course, my dear. How very thoughtless of me to detain you!"

My mother turned to me. "You must forgive me," she said quite normally. "Living alone, one becomes self-centered."

She was back in the present again, a childless woman accepting her lot. Someone ought to take that doll away from her and make her face up to reality, I thought, then realized that the thought was a harsh one and that if the pretense gave her some measure of comfort, what harm could it do?

I was disturbed by the realization that she was seeking affection by clinging to an inanimate toy. I had known this woman for no more than half an hour, yet already pity had given way to sympathy and sympathy to understanding, despite the fact that I had spent my lifetime condemning her.

I had no wish to become enmeshed in any personal relationship or feel any sentimentality, so I made my escape thankfully. I hoped that by the time I returned, David Harvey would have gone.

* * *

It didn't take long to unpack my rucksack. It held little enough. Too little, I realized, for in my haste to impersonate Gillian Conrad, I had given no thought to the question of clothes. A girl taking up residence in a household such as this would have brought a more adequate wardrobe than for a walking tour. I would have to think up some excuse — that the rest of my luggage was being sent on, perhaps. I reflected that since I had been lying very glibly for the past hour I should be able to continue easily enough. On my first free afternoon I would go into Canterbury and buy a few things. But that meant that I was no longer planning to make my getaway at the earliest opportunity.

I shrugged the thought aside. I would

face each moment as it came and let fate take control, as it had done competently up to this moment. Meanwhile, I studied my room with interest. It was charming, but, like the rest of the house, rather shabby. Upholstery and curtains needed renewing. Carpets were worn. All these signs of decay had been evident downstairs, suggesting that the Tredgold fortune was sadly depleted.

My room, with Queen Anne sash windows, overlooked the park. Every view from the house must be magnificent, I reflected, for the grounds spread away on all sides, green and undulating and wooded. I could imagine my mother as a girl riding through the park, young and carefree, her hair flying in the wind, little dreaming what life was to do to her.

I turned away, wishing devoutly that I had not come. I had been stupidly impulsive and now regretted it. How could I possibly hope to get away with this impersonation? Sooner or later I would be found out. It would be better by far to slip away quietly and never return than to plunge this poor woman into deeper turmoil and shock.

A door leading from my room revealed an old-fashioned bathroom. Bath salts had been thoughtfully provided, and I lay for a long time in the scented water, feeling oddly content. Even the doctor's unexpected denouncement failed to disturb me unduly, for logic told me that if he had any proof of my impersonation he would have produced it. Instead, he had let the matter ride. So what had I to worry about?

When dressed, there was nothing for me to do but go downstairs again. I had to take up my duties and count myself lucky that they demanded nothing more highly qualified than the home nursing course which I had taken at school.

At the foot of the stairs I met my mother, accompanied by the doctor. She smiled and said, "Ah, there you are, my dear. How quick you have been! When I was your age I spent hours dressing. In fact, I still do. I suppose I'm vain, aren't I, David?" She gave him her hand, saying, "Miss Conrad will look after me now. I always have a rest after tea and then take my time over dressing for dinner. Good-bye, David. You must come to dine very soon — unless you plan to go adventuring again?"

"Not for a long time, Lady Katherine, if ever. My practice must come first, from now on."

Until the next challenge comes your way, I thought. You're the sort of man who could never resist a new adventure.

"Over to you, Miss Conrad," he said. There seemed to be a hint of mockery in his voice.

I turned my back on him and led my mother upstairs.

"Hush," she said softly, glancing down. "Belinda is still asleep. We mustn't waken her."

Falling in with her mood, I walked quietly beside her. I heard the doctor's footsteps retreating across the hall below and was glad to hear him go.

★ ★ ★

It took some time to settle my mother, for first Belinda had to be attended to. It might have appeared farcical for a middle-aged woman and her companion to administer meticulously to a doll's

83

needs — undressing it, bathing it, putting it to bed for the night — but the whole ceremony was conducted with great solemnity. My heart was wrung with sadness, but I tried to adopt a professional attitude, reminding myself that this was no more than humoring my patient and that it need not represent something deeply personal.

The whole business was disturbing and I was much too involved personally to feel any amusement. I failed to delude myself.

"There!" she said tenderly, when at last the doll had been placed in its cot and carefully covered up. "She's asleep again already." She stooped and kissed the painted cheek. "Good night, my darling," she whispered.

It was ridiculous to want to cry. I turned away swiftly, hiding my reaction. For how long had she behaved this way? Surely the tyrannical Sir Humphrey would not have tolerated it in his lifetime?

"There now," I heard her saying, "if you will unhook my dress and pass me that robe — yes, that one, the blue — I'll lie down for a while and take my nap. Dear Harriet always insists that I rest before dinner. Not that I need to, of course. I only do it to please her."

She lay upon the bed and I drew the counterpane over her, tucking it in lightly, aware of an odd sense of protection which I had never experienced before.

"I'll come back in an hour," I whispered and quietly left.

★ ★ ★

The great house was silent. In the distant regions of the kitchen Harriet was no doubt preparing dinner. I was free to roam at will through the house or through the grounds.

Automatically, I turned toward the drawing room. This, I was to learn later, was my mother's favorite room in which she spent most of her day. I was thankful the doctor had gone. I was free to relax at last, to be myself, to be Belinda Lemaître for a brief time before assuming once again the identity of Gillian Conrad.

I sank down upon the window seat with a sigh, content to gaze out upon the sweeping gardens. Everything was quiet and at peace, and so was I.

I was startled when a man's voice spoke behind me.

"I'd like a word with you, my girl."

I turned with a start. David Harvey had risen from a deep chair beside the fireplace and now stood before me — solid, aggressive, and challenging.

There was accusation in his voice as he demanded, "Well, what's your game? What are you up to?"

6

HIS words echoed in the silent room, deadly as pistol shots.

"I — I don't know what you mean."

"Oh, yes, you do. You telephoned my office this morning and left a message with my secretary, saying you couldn't keep your engagement here, that you were off to Majorca with your current employer. I must confess I thought it odd, since your employment should have terminated at the end of last week, but my secretary assured me that was what you said. It was lucky she was there to take the message; she only comes part-time. I tried to give you credit for at least taking the trouble to send word. People walk in and out of jobs nowadays without any consideration for employers. My secretary added that you had written directly to Lady Katherine, so I hurried straight over, only to find you had arrived after all. What the devil are you playing at?"

I sat quite still, aware of sickening confusion. The only way to parry his disconcerting approach was an equal frankness, but in the circumstances it wasn't easy.

I took a steadying breath. I had been foolish. Just how foolish I dared not contemplate, but I had to stick to my guns. I glanced at his face and a little current of apprehension shivered through me. No lie was foolproof and faced with this man's obvious skepticism, I began to realize just how flimsy my pretense was. There was only one thing for me to do, brave the situation somehow, and since the best method of defense was attack I weighed right in.

"You seem very doubtful of me, Doctor. I might even say suspicious. Why?"

I hoped my voice sounded more confident than I felt.

He answered heatedly, "I would doubt anyone so unpredictable! The employment bureau recommended you highly, but now I wonder why."

"I'm surprised that you should engage

anyone solely on the recommendation of an employment bureau," I retorted.

"Unfortunately, I had no choice. Anything Matthew Deacon says goes with Katherine Tredgold and he went ahead and engaged you. Since my patient's main need is peace of mind, I approved. Deacon can do no wrong in her eyes and, in any case, it is better to humor her."

"I shall be glad to do the same."

"It is your duty to do so," he retorted. "And since, apart from the brief medical facts I gave you in my letter, I've had no chance to prime you about her condition, I will admit that you played up to her very well."

I asked carefully, "Is there anything more I should know about her? I think the information contained in your letter needs enlarging upon."

"Physically she is pretty sound. She sleeps badly, of course, and her mind continually vacillates between the past and the present. There is little we can do about her disturbed mental condition, except to exercise the utmost patience. Ever since the reading of Sir Humphrey's will she has been in a considerable state of nervous tension." He finished abruptly, "You still haven't answered my question."

"What question, Doctor?"

"Don't evade. I want to know why you backed out of the engagement, and then turned up without warning."

"My patient recovered sufficiently to travel alone, so I was able to come after all."

"Within an hour of telephoning? Do you really expect me to believe that?"

"You may be skeptical about it if you wish. She had a slight relapse, but it turned out to be not so serious after all. I was able to leave her in the hands of relatives until she was to go to Majorca, and then I departed immediately for Lyonhurst."

He gave me one long, penetrating glance. It discomfited me, but I met it squarely.

He shrugged and turned aside.

"Well, I hope you will prove reliable now that you are here, and I'm thankful you didn't send the same message to Lady Katherine. The slightest shock can

90

throw her completely off balance."

"She is already unbalanced, isn't she? Her obsession with that doll is abnormal."

"Abnormal, yes, but understandable and harmless. There is a reason for it, of course, but that I cannot confide in you. I can tell you little about her personal life, except that it has been desperately unhappy."

"If I am to help her, Doctor, it would be as well to put me in the picture more fully. The nature of her unhappiness, for instance — "

"A doctor can't betray a patient's confidence," he answered abruptly. "All you have to do is to keep her company, have patience and understanding, nurse her when necessary, and leave the rest to me."

He turned to the door. His movements, like himself, were quick and impatient. He was an impatient man altogether, I felt, and yet, as far as Katherine was concerned, I sensed his compassion and was touched by his concern for her.

"May I ask one thing, Doctor?"

"What is it?"

"How long has Lady Katherine been like this?"

I didn't really want him to say "ever since she was a girl," although that would have explained her rejection of me. If separation from Pierre and her child had tipped the balance of her mind, if she had retreated into imaginary motherhood as a form of immediate consolation which, as the years passed, became the real thing for her, I could understand and forgive everything.

"Only since her father's death," he said. My reaction must have been self-evident, for he went on, "You might understand better if I explained that Sir Humphrey disciplined his daughter into almost abject obedience. His word was her law. She was dutiful, obedient, and completely repressed — until the will was read. The will was a surprise to everyone, for miraculously it gave his daughter freedom, which no one who knew the man would ever have expected, and straightaway she did something which she must have been longing to do for many, many years. She opened a room which had been locked by her father long ago. It was the room she had occupied as a girl. He had barred his daughter from there when she was not yet out of her teens, insisting that she should occupy a room opposite his own. He was like a jailer."

"The man was a sadist!" I cried.

"Unhappily, yes, but against parental tyranny which stops short of physical abuse the law in this country provides little or no safeguard, and mental cruelty is always hard to prove. Sir Humphrey's particular brand was the product of an iron will which only an equally strong person could have fought. His daughter couldn't match it. She became docile, subdued, in time completely cowed, although occasionally she revealed flashes of rebellion which were always speedily crushed. That was why, at his death, she was bewildered by freedom. Instead of reaching forward, her mind slipped back — back to her old room, in which her girlhood belongings were hidden. The first thing she seized was that doll. I was with her at the time. Harriet had asked me to come over because she was anxious about her. Katherine seemed to have completely rejected the present and reverted to the past. There was only one thing she wanted to do and she had to do it at once — unlock that room, perhaps hoping to find herself again. Harriet and I entered it with her. The doll was perched on a window seat. Katherine stood looking at it, then suddenly gathered it up, cradling it and crying over it and calling it her baby. 'It is Belinda,' she said. 'I have found Belinda!' That was the name she gave to the doll as a child."

I tried to speak, but could find no words.

"She has cherished the doll from that moment," he continued. "In other ways, she is perfectly normal, although unhappiness and loneliness have taken heavy toll of her physically. Fortunately, there is nothing harmful about this obsession with the doll. It is a manifestation of frustrated motherhood and in time, I hope, will be assuaged. Meanwhile, I want you to try to understand."

"I have no need to try."

Something in my voice made him look

at me, then he put his hand on my shoulder and said in a tone of surprise, "My dear girl, had I thought the story would distress you so much I wouldn't have told you."

"Distress me?" I echoed.

"You are crying, Miss Conrad."

And so I was. I put the back of my hand to my cheek, and it was wet.

I managed to say, "I will take good care of her, I promise."

He gave my shoulder a kind little shake. "You'll have me to reckon with if you don't. Heaven knows, the poor soul is in sufficient turmoil over this other business without the additional upset of nursing difficulties. If you don't satisfy me, you'll be out. Understand?"

"I understand. But I shall probably fulfill my duties better if I don't have to put up with antagonism from you, and if I could know more about any other causes of Lady Katherine's nervous tension. What, for instance, do you mean by 'this other business'?"

"The matter is strictly between herself and her lawyer, although as her friend

95

as well as her doctor, she did confide it to me. That, however, doesn't concern you. As for antagonism, there'll be none from me so long as you do what you have been brought here to do. That's all I shall require of you."

At the door he turned. "Was that your luggage I saw Buxton carrying upstairs?"

"The rucksack?" I asked coolly. "Yes, Doctor. Why?"

"It struck me as being both odd and inadequate."

"It is perfectly adequate for me."

I felt that, this time, I had put him in his place, and watched his retreating back with satisfaction.

And yet, the interview left me dissatisfied and curious. I was intrigued by the situation at Lyonhurst and wanted to know more about it, more about the will, more about this other business which concerned only my mother and her lawyer, but which was, apparently, so important that it placed a strain upon her. I assumed it was something to do with financial affairs.

I began to debate whether to reveal my identity to my mother, then again decided against it. I felt that I would instinctively know when the moment was ripe. Meanwhile, I resolved to carry off the situation for as long as I could get away with it.

7

LIFE at Lyonhurst ran to a pattern, admirably supervised by Harriet. She was devoted to her mistress, and I soon realized that if I wished to remain here I would have to maintain Harriet's approval, for anyone she disliked would be out in no time. All the same, I wasn't prepared to curry favor with her. I had never been able to pander to people just to get on the right side of them.

Fortunately, I liked Harriet and felt it was reciprocated. Like the doctor, all she asked of me was that I should look after Katherine kindly and tolerantly.

"I've never cared for companion-helps much," she confided one day, "and as for nurses about the place, they drive me mad. We had one here when my late master was taken ill and, my goodness, did the household know she was around! She even tried to interfere in the kitchen, but I soon put a stop to that. 'Nursing's your job and running this house is mine,'

I said, 'and I take orders from no one but Lady Katherine herself.' When the master died and the shock of everything affected my mistress, and Doctor Harvey decided that she needed someone besides myself to keep her company — and he was right, mark you, I can't be with her all the time — I said to him, 'All I ask, Doctor, is that you don't get that nurse back."

"He didn't engage me, anyway. Mr. Deacon did."

I broke off abruptly. For the first time, one obvious and terrifying contingency presented itself — that my mother's lawyer, in taking the initiative as he had done, might have interviewed the Conrad girl. Why hadn't I thought of this before? I searched frantically in my memory for Dr. Harvey's words. *"Anything Matthew Deacon says goes with Katherine Tredgold, and he went ahead and engaged you . . . "*

Personally, or solely on the recommendation of the bureau? The question flickered alarmingly in my mind. If he had actually met Gillian Conrad, I was sunk, but if he had made all arrangements directly with the bureau, I was safe.

What was the legal penalty for impersonation? I wondered apprehensively. Matthew Deacon would certainly know.

I became aware that Harriet was speaking.

"Well, thank goodness he did. Trust Mr. Deacon to pick the right type! That was what I said at the time, and I was right, although I must say you are younger than we expected."

"I look much younger than I actually am," I lied, wondering, for the first time, how old Gillian Conrad actually was.

"It must be those perky features and that short hairdo — what the French call *gamine*, isn't it?"

"I don't know what the French call it," I lied.

"Well, it's very pretty, anyway."

My mother had said the same thing only this morning. "I'm glad you are young and attractive, Gillian. I wouldn't have been nearly so happy with someone middle-aged and starched. Doctor Harvey chose you very well."

"It wasn't Doctor Harvey who chose me, Lady Katherine," I had reminded her, "it was Matthew Deacon."

"Of course! I remember now. Matthew is so good to me. Just like a brother."

As usual, at the mention of Matthew Deacon, a light of approval came into my mother's eyes, but also a touch of anxiety.

"I wish he had news for me," she had sighed. "The waiting is becoming unbearable."

"Waiting for what?" I'd asked gently.

"For everything to be settled, of course."

Money, I thought. In what sort of a state had Sir Humphrey left his affairs?

My mother picked up her doll and held it close, pressing her cheek against its waxen one and slipping away into her own private world again. Much as I longed to ask further questions, instinct warned me not to.

I was becoming very concerned about Katherine's welfare. I couldn't fail to, for her charm was endearing and she displayed a concern for myself which touched me deeply.

"I don't want you to be lonely or bored here," she said more than once.

"This huge old house is really no place for a young girl, but life will come back to it. I am determined that life will come back!"

"Do you ride, my dear?" she asked one day.

"No, Lady Katherine. I've never had the opportunity."

"What a pity! There are horses in the stables. Cooper could pick a gentle mount for you and teach you to ride. We must have a word with him about it."

"Who is Cooper?" I asked Harriet, later.

"Cooper?" she echoed in surprise. "We had a groom called Cooper, twenty years ago."

* * *

Scarcely a day passed without Dr. Harvey calling to see his patient, but I was very rarely alone with him. From the professional point of view this was pleasing, for the fact that he sought no private discussions with me implied that, as far as fulfilling my duties went, he was satisfied. He uttered no criticism — on the other hand, he offered no praise.

Illogically, I found his attitude disappointing. He made me feel unimportant and I resented that. I was accustomed to my fair share of attention from male students at school and perhaps this had spoiled me a little.

"You are a *coquette, chérie,*" Françoise had once accused. "You like to flirt."

"And why not?"

"Flirt if you like, Belinda, but not too much and not for too long, for, if you do, you will be unable to recognize the real thing when it comes."

Where the heart was concerned, as in other things, Françoise had a Frenchwoman's wisdom.

In the excitement of coming to Lyonhurst, I had temporarily forgotten Françoise. Now a sense of guilt stirred. Had she known that I had arrived at my mother's home under false pretenses, she would certainly not have approved. Nor would she have understood. "It would have been far wiser to contact the Tredgold lawyers and reveal your identity. You have made a mistake, little one. You are asking for trouble." I could hear her saying it, but thrust the warning aside. I knew what I wanted to do and, wisely or foolishly, I was doing it.

"Stubborn, that's what you are," she would say. But even if she disapproved of what I had done, she would say it with indulgence and not a little admiration, for Françoise admired courage and audacity, qualities which her brother had possessed in good measure.

"Life challenged him," she once said, "and he challenged it back."

Which was precisely what I was doing now.

But for three weeks, at least, I need not worry about Françoise, and for three weeks she would certainly not be worrying about me. She would be lost in a world of her own, the world of fashion in Rome and Florence and Paris, so even if I wrote and even if my letters reached her — which I doubted because she took infinite precautions against receiving correspondence when away — she would be too busy to read them. She would push them aside with characteristic impatience, for as far as her work was concerned Françoise had a one-track mind and nothing was ever allowed to interfere with it.

For the time being, then, I was on my own, completely cut off from my normal life and from the one person most closely bound up with it. I could be Gillian Conrad for as long as I wished — providing I was not found out.

★ ★ ★

My step was light as I returned from a walk in the park one day, and as the house came into view I felt a bond of familiarity with it. Buxton, the handyman, was prodding ineffectually with a hoe and he nodded to me with a kindly smile. He was really too old to be handyman, let alone gardener. It made me feel sad to see the grounds so neglected. Lyonhurst was rapidly deteriorating. Casual labor from the village was employed spasmodically, but it needed more than incidental labor and Buxton's inadequate efforts to maintain what had once been a flourishing estate.

As obvious as the deterioration of the grounds was the depletion of the

Tredgold family fortune. The many signs of encroaching decay were positive proof that if there had once been money, there wasn't much of it left now.

Sometimes I ventured into Harriet's kitchen, where she would warn me not to get in her way, but she allowed me to lend a hand now and again. My diligent French upbringing had equipped me well on the domestic side and Harriet was surprised by my culinary knowledge.

"I've always been interested in cooking," I explained, "especially in more unusual dishes than roast beef or steak and kidney pudding."

"Then my late master would have approved of you! Fussy about his food, he was. 'You can keep your plain home cooking,' he'd say. 'Give me a dinner that's fit for a king!'" Harriet finished with a sigh. "That's what he considered himself to be!"

"It sounds as if you didn't like Sir Humphrey very much."

She shrugged. "He was all right in his way. A fair employer."

"But not a human being?"

"I didn't say that," she retorted sharply.

"Anyway, he's dead now."

And one shouldn't speak ill of the dead — that was what she was implying. But I refused to be put in my place.

"From what I have heard he seems to have been rather inhuman, Harriet."

"And what have you heard, may I ask?"

She stood in the middle of the kitchen, looking at me. She had blunt, forthright features. An honest woman and not one of whom to make an enemy. All the same, I liked her and wasn't afraid of her.

"The doctor told me a little about him. It was natural that he should, since I came here to look after Sir Humphrey's daughter. If his personality had an influence on her, I shouldn't be kept in the dark about that."

"No," Harriet admitted grudgingly, "I suppose not. All right, then, he was a harsh man. I admit it. He was my master, my employer, and for all his faults he treated me well. When the will was read he had remembered me — a pension, and a permanent home here. I'm grateful for that. It would have been hard for a woman of my age to go out into the world looking for other employment. For more than forty years I've been at Lyonhurst, coming here first as a nursery maid and then, when Miss Kathy was two, becoming her nurse. When she grew up, I stayed on for her sake. She needed a mother, poor lamb. All the same, I'll speak no ill of Sir Humphrey now that he is dead."

"Why should you? And I'm glad he remembered you in his will. Was it an interesting will?" I finished casually.

"Very interesting, and certainly a surprise. A surprise to everyone."

"Is that what Matthew Deacon is working on now?"

"And what do you know about that, pray?"

"Again, only what the doctor told me. He is anxious about his patient's nervous tension. So, naturally, when Lady Katherine said she wished Mr. Deacon had news for her, I wondered if the two things were linked."

"I see. Well, I admit that I wish he could produce some news for the poor dear."

"Why is it so important, Harriet?"

"If Lady Katherine hasn't told you, it isn't for me to do so, nor for you to ask. And now get along with you. I've dinner to prepare. We've a guest tonight."

"I'll give you a hand," I said. As I broke eggs into a bowl and began to whip them I asked casually, "And who is the guest?" Since my arrival the only visitor to Lyonhurst had been the doctor. Apart from him, my mother seemed to have no contact with the outside world.

Harriet tasted the soup, smacked her lips approvingly, and said, "It's Mr. Deacon. Didn't her ladyship tell you? Well, maybe she forgot, with that poor wandering mind of hers."

Matthew Deacon, the man who had engaged me, the lawyer with whom, I had hoped, my mother only communicated by post. So long as he remained safely in some stuffy legal office I was safe, but the moment he stepped across the threshold of Lyonhurst, what would happen?

This was the first real glimmer of danger, the first flickering red light. What should I do? Plead a headache and remain in my room? Even as the thought presented itself, I pushed it aside. Foolish and impulsive I might be, but I hoped I was no coward.

When I had finished helping Harriet, I went back to my room thoughtfully. I was afraid, yet beneath my fear the challenge of the situation quickened a sense of excitement. The doctor had accepted me — on sufferance, perhaps, but at least he believed me to be the real Gillian Conrad and would continue to believe it so long as Matthew Deacon didn't cut the ground from beneath my feet.

Dinner would not be ready for well over an hour. I had time to bathe, change, and relax before going along to my mother's room to attend to her. This was her hour for a predinner rest and I could picture her on the old-fashioned bed, with her doll either cradled in her arms or lying within the cot beside her. The cot in which she herself had slept in as a child, the doll she had played with, a baby frock she had worn — these were the things from which Katherine derived comfort now. They meant more to her than the great neglected house, the deteriorating grounds, the empty stables, the bygone glories. These were but shadows from an unhappy past, from which she escaped only when nursing the child she had lost.

I gave myself a mental shake. Was I, too, beginning to regard that waxen image as human?

I moved swiftly to the wardrobe. Within hung the few clothes I had brought with me, slacks and sweater, an uncrushable sheath dress which packed into the minimum of space, and a raincoat. I had traveled in the slacks and sweater, carrying or wearing the raincoat, so that my rucksack contained only the dress, a change of underwear, nightwear, and an extra pair of shoes. This left room, in an inner pocket, for the small morocco-bound Bible without which I never traveled, for it had belonged to my father.

I opened the Bible. It was a French translation and there were passages he had marked and to which I turned whenever I felt in need of some mental communication with him, or desired some spiritual guidance or strength.

"*The Lord is my shepherd; I shall not want. He maketh me to lie down in green pastures . . .* " The reassurance of the words brought comfort to my heart, and I read on. "*Yea, though I walk through the valley of the shadow of death, I will fear no evil . . .* "

He had walked through that valley. He had lain down in green pastures. He wanted for nothing now.

I put it away, no longer afraid, for whatever I had to face could be as nothing compared with all he had gone through. If exposure lay ahead — well, I had asked for it. No one but I could be blamed if I had laid a trap for myself and walked right into it.

★ ★ ★

I wore the sheath: sleeveless, straight, cut by Françoise herself and made with the exactitude which was her yardstick. I looked good in it and felt confident.

Outside, a threatening storm darkened the sky, overshadowing my room. I felt my privacy invaded, so I drew the curtains in swift defense. I was alone again, safe and secure with the shabby furniture that was made up of a hotchpotch of Victoriana and genuine antiques. Some of the pieces were lovely — a small Pembroke table, a Sheraton mirror, a walnut teapoy which loving hands had once polished with pride — but now the pieces looked ill at ease amidst cruder items, of which the gaunt wardrobe was one. Huge, overornate, depressing, it dominated the room like a large wooden sarcophagus.

Somehow the atmosphere of this room was characteristic of Lyonhurst — apathetic, tired, neglected, a place in which no one took any interest anymore. The house had grown old prematurely, as my mother had done; it was forgotten, as she was. It had ceased to live as part of her had. Loneliness pervaded the place like an unhappy spirit.

There was also a curious atmosphere of waiting, a sort of suspended animation which was even stretching its tentacles toward myself, so that I felt frustrated and charged with increasing curiosity.

I glanced into my mother's room and saw that she was still resting. She slept like a child, her cheek crushed against the doll's artificial one. There was something a little bizarre and certainly unnatural about the contrast between the smooth waxen face and the human one, and yet, of the two, my mother's seemed the more childlike at that moment. It betrayed a vulnerability which the doll's mask — expressionless, unnatural — could never reveal.

I closed the door softly. There was time enough to waken her. She could rest awhile and I could relax and prepare for the meeting with her lawyer. I found that I was even anticipating it with a touch of apprehension, for the old familiar sense of challenge sparked in me. If I could get through the occasion without disaster, it would be a gratifying triumph.

I paused at the foot of the stairs, surveying myself briefly in an immense mirror in which was reflected the entire sweep of stairway. I ran a critical eye over my makeup, dress, and shoes. In turning away, I saw a man standing within the entrance to the drawing room, watching me.

I was caught unawares, my guard

down. It was impossible to conceal my astonishment, for he was no stranger to me. I had met him once before. He had almost ridden me down in the lane outside.

We remained quite still. His face was inscrutable, and yet I sensed that his surprise was as great as my own, even bordering upon astonishment underlaid with a reaction which I was quite unable to identify.

I descended the last two steps slowly. He remained where he was, watching my approach. When I was halfway between the staircase and the double doors of the drawing room, I stood still again, faintly angered by his manner. He seemed to have the air of a master watching the advance of a servant. It disconcerted and annoyed me. I wanted to defy him and, if possible, snub him. Unhappily, I was in no position to do either, for I guessed his identity. Who else could he be but Matthew Deacon, my mother's lawyer, who had the power to expose me as a fraud?

8

I STOOD there, waiting for him to speak. I knew instinctively that he was a clever man and certainly more experienced than I, with the added advantage of an astute legal mind. I was merely a girl who had deliberately placed herself in an embarrassing and vulnerable position. He held every weapon. All I could do was defend myself somehow, so I waited for his attack.

He smiled. The change was so unexpected that it momentarily floored me. He came to meet me with hand extended, but I still felt that he was sizing me up, doing swift calculations in his mind and finding all the answers.

"So we meet again," he said pleasantly. "You have no idea how much I wanted this, although I had little hope of ever bumping into you again unless fate took a hand. I'm grateful to it for doing so."

My fingers were in his and his touch was as smooth as his smile.

He didn't release my hand immediately. He stood looking down at me and somehow, despite the pleasant smile and the flattery of his words, I sensed that his every nerve was alert and watchful and suspicious.

This is it, I thought. The game is up, and it serves you right. Did you really expect to get away with it indefinitely?

I was unable to speak. I was making a desperate clutch at composure and hoped that my face didn't betray it. Apparently it did, for he said, "You are as surprised as I, but not so pleasurably, I see."

Pleasurably? What did he mean by that? I didn't delude myself that this man had been pining for a sight of me. He was not the type to eat his heart out over women, although he was certainly attracted to them, undoubtedly replacing one with another without conscience or a backward glance. I sensed the merciless, self-seeking quality of his attention and was not flattered. If it had been David Harvey who complimented me, I should have responded in a truly feminine way. The realization surprised me, for the doctor and I were not exactly friends.

Our relationship was strictly professional. The doctor was not interested in me as a woman. It was strange that only at this moment should I wish it otherwise and realize that I had wanted it from the beginning.

Matthew Deacon was waiting for a reply, watching me with friendly scrutiny.

I pulled myself together, and admitted that I was indeed surprised.

"But not pleased? I am sorry about that. I suppose, frightening you the way I did the other day, I could hardly expect you to greet me with any enthusiasm, but I did want to atone, remember?"

We had turned toward the drawing room and now he stood aside for me to precede him, inviting me to enter with a gesture of his hand. Quite involuntarily, words flickered through my mind.

'Will you walk into my parlor? said the spider to the fly . . . '

Ridiculous words, and quite inapt.

I went ahead without looking at him. A fire burned in the immense dog-grate, sending leaping shadows about the room. Harriet had not yet lit the lamps, despite the sudden darkness of the storm. This surprised me, for she was meticulous in her attention to duty. I seized upon her error in order to change the subject, crossing swiftly to a standard lamp and switching it on.

"Harriet appears to have left you in darkness. I must apologize for that. I expect she was anxious to get back to the kitchen — she does practically everything in this household. I often wonder how she manages."

"So do I. No, don't switch on another lamp, please! You look charming in this light."

"Thank you," I answered pleasantly, but switched on the additional lamp just the same.

He said gallantly, "You look just as charming in any light, apparently. Daylight, lamplight, both are kind to the young."

I studied him. He was standing beneath the light and the electric bulb spotlit his face, revealing lines of self-indulgence. I realized that he was older than I thought. Riding against the wind, his color high, his hair windblown, he had given a different impression — one of youthful vigor and health.

"Well," he said pleasantly, "don't you think we ought to introduce ourselves?"

There was a sound from the door. It was Harriet.

"I beg your pardon, sir — and yours, Miss Conrad. I was coming to turn on the lamps. I didn't realize Mr. Deacon had arrived . . . "

She bustled across to the fireplace, threw on another log, straightened up, and said, "Thank you for answering the door, my dear. I didn't hear the bell."

"Nor did I. Where is Buxton, Harriet?"

"Buxton, miss? In the butler's pantry, pretending to be busy in case I need his help. He has been there this past hour, polishing and repolishing glasses — a job like that he can do sitting down, and if there's anything Buxton hates it's exercise! Fetching and carrying for me comes under the heading of exercise, in his lazy mind." She shrugged and added, "Was there something you wanted him for?"

"No, thank you, Harriet. I merely thought he could have stoked the fire instead of you."

She sniffed her contempt.

"Buxton isn't so considerate as you are." Moving toward the door, she remembered that drinks had been set out, and indicated them.

"Thank you, Harriet."

The woman nodded briefly, smiled at Matthew Deacon, and departed.

The man was looking at me intensely. I had the feeling that he had been staring at me in such a way ever since Harriet addressed me as Miss Conrad. No wonder he was puzzled. A swift glance told me that stupefied might be a more apt description.

He recovered quickly and said with a slightly mocking smile, "*You* are wondering how I gained admittance, and *I* am wondering why I didn't recognize you as Gillian Conrad."

The words were casual, the tone light, but his eyes were accusing. I felt a chasm yawn at my feet. He had moved away from the light, but even in shadow I was aware of his watchfulness.

I took the plunge and answered, "But of course I am Gillian Conrad. Who else could I be?"

"Who else, indeed? My surprise is due to the fact that the employment bureau told me your age was thirty. You are not even approaching that. Why did they lie? Or did you?"

"I did," I confessed humbly, adding with what I hoped was a helpless and touching appeal, "Please understand, I wanted the job very badly."

"But companion-helps are greatly in demand in these days of diminished domestic staffs and expensive private nurses."

"That is true, but not in country houses such as this. In lesser private houses, yes, but jobs in England's stately homes are few and far between."

He threw back his head and laughed aloud. I didn't blame him. The words sounded ridiculous and my excuses thin.

"That isn't surprising, since there are few stately homes left!"

"Precisely," I agreed.

"I do believe you are a snob, my dear. Does background really matter so much to you? Why? So that you can boast to your friends later, quote titles, say casually, 'When I lived with Lady-This or the Duchess-of-That . . . ' and make them all feel small?"

"Certainly not!"

His laughter remained.

"Now I have angered you and you are even more attractive when angry."

I moved toward the door. "I must see to Lady Katherine."

"Wait!"

I despised myself for obeying, but was afraid. I turned and said as distantly as possible, "Yes, Mr. Deacon?"

The laughter had gone. His voice was gentle as he said, "My dear girl, I don't blame you for lying about your age, although, had I interviewed you myself, I certainly wouldn't have engaged anyone so young. The only thing which puzzles me is how you managed to convince that very exacting and highly reputable bureau."

"They didn't interview me, either," I answered with truth. I was scarcely aware of what I said, for I was conscious only of relief. He had never met Gillian Conrad, never spoken to her . . .

His next words checked my elation.

"Is this true? Do you mean to tell

123

me that an employment bureau like the Marlborough, with a reputation second to none, would actually recommend someone without even interviewing her first? I understood that applicants on their books had been thoroughly investigated."

"That is true!" I declared wildly.

"Then why did you say, 'They didn't interview me, either'?"

"I meant for this particular job. They interviewed me when I first registered with them, so they knew my qualifications."

Lies, lies, and more lies. One led to another like a tangled skein of wool.

He was silent. The log Harriet had thrown on the fire began to spark, erupting in sharp little explosions. A coal crashed into the hearth. A lantern clock upon the mantelpiece ticked with sudden loudness, matching the hammering of my heart. The silence lengthened, and he continued to watch me until I felt like a butterfly on the end of a pin which, in a little while, he would slowly begin to dissect.

I made a weak clutch at self-defense.

"I'm sorry you don't believe me, Mr. Deacon. Fortunately for me, Doctor

Harvey does. Since he is satisfied with my credentials, I doubt if anything you say could persuade him to dismiss me."

"How can he? Only Lady Katherine can do that."

"He could influence her."

"So could I."

"I'm aware of that."

"Indeed? And how?"

"A solicitor always has a certain influence over his clients."

A slight dilation of the nostrils and a tightening of the lips indicated his annoyance at hearing Lady Katherine referred to merely as a client.

He said, "I can, of course, take the matter up with the employment bureau."

Panic hit me. This was a contingency I had completely overlooked, rushing headlong with impetuosity into this situation. It was even likely that an establishment with such a reputation for integrity would send him an apology and offer a replacement.

I took a grip on myself. Long ago, Françoise had told me how members of the Maquis were trained to remain impassive in the face of danger, to conceal emotions and fear and quench the impulse for flight. As a child I used to relive her stories, pretending that I was my father and emulating his courage. I did so now.

"Do so if you wish, Mr. Deacon."

He gave a quiet laugh and shook his head.

"My dear, why should I make trouble for you?"

"If you doubt me — "

"Why should I doubt you? If David Harvey is satisfied with you, far be it from me to criticize." He held out both hands. "Come, let us be friends!"

I didn't want to respond. I didn't want his friendship, but couldn't afford to be without it.

He drew me quite close, so close that I was aware of his animal magnetism.

"I knew it," he said quietly.

"Knew what?"

"That you were warm and passionate."

I wanted to ignore the insinuation in his voice, but it had a compelling quality as strong as the man himself.

"I knew it when you turned on me so furiously the other day," he continued, "like a little wild animal. It delighted me. And I knew it earlier, of course."

"Earlier?"

"When we spoke on the telephone. Remember?"

I didn't remember. I searched frantically in my memory for any telephone conversations I had had since coming to Lyonhurst.

"Surely you do remember?" he insisted. "You were at the Marlborough Bureau when I telephoned them. You had worked for a client of mine before her death — Mrs. Hubert Clayton, wife of the financier — and because her husband spoke highly of you, I naturally remembered you the moment David suggested that dear Katherine should have someone besides Harriet to look after her. I knew you had gone to the Claytons through the Marlborough, so I contacted them at once — with Doctor Harvey's agreement, of course. I telephoned immediately, to save him the trouble."

Why the elaborate explanation? I wondered fleetingly.

"As luck would have it, Miss Conrad,

127

you had called to see them that very day, at that very hour, because your current engagement was coming to an end. Miss Wade, the proprietress, promptly put you on the line and we discussed the job and settled all the details. It is hardly necessary for me to recall all that, since you know it already. But I do recall that I liked your voice. Strange," he finished softly, "that you don't remember our conversation."

His voice was like silk. His hands still imprisoned my own. His magnetism was still powerful, almost mesmeric. I could not draw away.

"Now that you speak of it, Mr. Deacon, I do remember." The answer branded me as rather stupid, but at least my voice was steady.

He released me abruptly. It was like a reprieve, a chance to escape. I wanted to run from this cat-and-mouse game.

"You could do with a drink," he said practically, and moved across the room.

"No, thank you. I must go to Lady Katherine. She will be needing me."

"I said you needed a drink." He poured one and handed it to me. Touching my glass with his own he continued, "Here's to our better acquaintance. And I'm sorry I frightened you."

"You didn't frighten me in the least. Why should you?"

"Because you thought I might undermine your position here, and I can't blame you for fearing that, any more than you can blame me for being suspicious."

"Why should you be suspicious?"

"Puzzled, if you prefer the word. That lie about your age was naturally something which needed explaining, not only by you, but by the employment bureau. I told you they gave your age as thirty." He strolled over to the fireplace and now stood leaning upon the mantelpiece, regarding me with a bland and disconcerting gaze. "Perhaps I should interrogate them about that."

I lifted my glass and drank, but there was no taste in my mouth, no relief from dryness and the arid flavor of fear.

"And then, of course, there was your voice . . . "

"My voice?"

"It was so different. Much more

mature. Certainly the voice of a woman of thirty . . . "

"Telephones can play tricks."

"Sometimes, yes," he acknowledged, and his tone held a note of final dismissal. "Let's forget the whole thing, shall we? And you will forgive me?"

"For what?" I parried lightly.

"For putting you through an uncomfortable inquisition. I must say you faced up to it pretty well."

"Thank you." I put down my glass and turned to go, but suddenly he was beside me again. He had the ability to move swiftly and relentlessly, reminding me of the moment when I had watched him ride away into the woods, turning his horse's head with a swift unerring movement and driving the creature with merciless determination.

"One moment, Gillian. The name is Gillian, isn't it? You haven't said you forgive me. You didn't say it the other day, either. I have much for which to make amends. Please let me know you better. Let me see you again."

This time I moved resolutely toward the door.

"Of course you will see me again. You will see me whenever you visit here, Mr. Deacon."

"Matthew."

"And you have nothing for which to make amends."

"All right, if you say so. But I still want to know you better. I feel we have much in common."

"I cannot imagine what." I had reached the door. My hand was on the knob.

"Can't you?" he said quietly and with a world of significance.

I looked back at him, searching for an answer and finding none and wondering why I thought it even necessary. Somehow this man compelled an answer.

As I hesitated he smiled, and this time his smile had an intimate quality.

"We were very much aware of each other just now. Don't deny it, Gillian."

"Not in the way you believe . . . " I said swiftly and without thought.

"Then in what way?" he taunted.

I refused to answer because I didn't want to acknowledge the strange, compelling bond I had felt between this man and myself.

At that moment my mind produced a question which had leaped at me earlier and had then been submerged by his cross-examination. I put it to him abruptly.

"Who let you in? Harriet didn't. I didn't. Buxton didn't."

"Lady Katherine, herself, perhaps . . . "

"She couldn't. For one thing, she never answers the door and, for another, she was asleep upstairs. That was why I left her for another half hour."

"Then you must hurry to her now. We have been talking for much longer than that. As for who let me in, I did so." He put his hand in his pocket, then dangled a key before me. "I am one of the few people — in fact, I do believe the only person — who has a key to Lyonhurst. It was Lady Katherine's idea, to enable me to visit her whenever I wish. Since her father's death we have had a lot to discuss, and perhaps," he finished modestly, "she trusts me more than anyone else, because I am closer to her."

When I made no answer, he continued, "You must indulge her little whims, my dear, whether you like them or not."

"I do indulge them, Mr. Deacon. That is one of my duties."

"Then you must not begrudge her the comfort of a close family friend. Henrietta, my mother, grew up with Katherine's mother and the family friendship has always been strong."

I smiled an acknowledgment and left the room, shutting the door carefully behind me, but even after it was closed it seemed as if Matthew Deacon's penetrating glance followed me.

9

THE threatening storm had broken and my mother was crying like a child. She was alone with the thunder and the darkness, and terrified. I could hear her wild sobbing as I approached her room, and I ran swiftly down the passage.

When I flung open the door and switched on the light, she screamed. When I gathered her up in my arms she beat upon me helplessly. She didn't know me, didn't want me. I was a stranger of whom she was afraid.

The doll had fallen to the floor. I picked it up and placed it in her arms for comfort. She seized it desperately, but my further attempts at pacification only increased her terror, so that she resisted with the instinctive self-defense of an animal. She bit me.

The attack was sharp and vicious, prompted by fear. My reaction was equally sharp, for I was taken by surprise, recoiling from her to suck my injured hand. I tasted blood and somehow that made the whole thing more frightening. Normally she was frail, with no more strength than a blade of grass, but suddenly she was tempered with hatred and strong as steel.

"Harriet! Harriet!" she screamed, but Harriet was far out of hearing in the kitchen wing of the house. I was both glad and sorry about that. I could have done with her help, but wanted to manage without it. I sat down on the bedside and attempted to reassure the terrified woman, but she shrank farther into the pillows, still trying to beat me off. I was dismayed by her mistrust, but even more by the realization that she didn't know me. I was an enemy, an unknown face emerging from the dark, a creature of terror conjured up by the storm.

"Go away! Go away!"

The high, frenzied note in her voice struck a chill into me, for it was the voice of the temporarily insane. I couldn't deal with this alone. Someone had to help me, but not Harriet, nor Matthew Deacon. This was an emergency which only the doctor could handle.

The telephone stood upon an Adam table just outside the drawing room downstairs. Even with the doors closed, Matthew Deacon might overhear and I wouldn't put it past him to eavesdrop. The man filled me with great unease and he was the last person with whom I wished to share such a situation. He would blame me for it, and he would have justice on his side, for it was I who had left Katherine to awaken to the darkness and the storm, so I said to her desperately, "It's me, Gillian. There is nothing to be afraid of. Listen to me, trust me, please!"

She turned her face into the pillow and screamed for me to go.

I went swiftly downstairs. The double doors leading to the drawing room were closed. Nevertheless, I picked up the receiver gently, trying to subdue the betraying sound, but the ping of the bell and the whir of the dial seemed to vibrate loudly in the wide hall. I held my breath, listening to the distant ring at the end of the line, fearful in case the doctor was out. When I heard his voice, the relief was indescribable.

I cupped my hand around the mouthpiece and begged him to come. He didn't waste time with elaborate questions — a few brief queries and then, "I'm on my way," and the line cleared.

I sped back upstairs, my feet soundless on the shabby carpet, but I was only halfway up when Matthew Deacon's voice arrested me and I turned and saw him standing within the drawing-room entrance, watching me.

"Is anything wrong?" he asked.

"Nothing," I said, and went on my way, giving him no chance for further comment or question, but when he came striding up the stairs after me I wasn't surprised, merely annoyed. I turned on him and asked where he was going.

"To see Lady Katherine, of course. Something is wrong."

"Nothing is wrong, and I cannot allow you to bother her now. She is changing for dinner."

We had reached the landing and were standing at the entrance to the passage leading to my mother's room. The sound of her weeping could be heard quite plainly. Matthew Deacon nodded toward her door and said, "Do you consider there is nothing wrong with *that*? She is crying. She is hysterical. I can hear her."

"She is upset because when she awakened I was not there, thanks to you. It was you who delayed me." I turned toward the bedroom, but when he persisted in accompanying me, I stood still again and said bluntly, "You are wasting your time, and mine. Please go back to the drawing room. Lady Katherine will be herself again very soon."

He laughed.

"Herself? My dear Gillian, she hasn't been herself for a long time, and never will be. The creature is crazy. Why pretend you don't know?"

I hated him. I hated the callousness of his words and his utter indifference to suffering and fear. Even if what he said were true, pity, not contempt, should come from a man who professed to be so close a friend.

I went into my mother's room and

shut the door in his face. Not until later did I reflect that this was guaranteed to antagonize him. Matthew Deacon wasn't the kind of man to enjoy a woman's defiance.

He took the hint. He didn't tap on the door or demand admission. There was silence from the long corridor.

My mother's frenzy had now become uncontrollable sobbing, her terror undiminished despite the reassurance of the light. She still didn't know me. I went into the adjoining bathroom and returned with a cold sponge, gently wiping the tear-mottled face. She shrank away, but I persisted, holding her chin firmly with one hand and murmuring endearments as I administered to her. They came quite naturally, but she failed to hear them, lost as she was in her world of doubt and fear and mistrust. When I accidentally touched the doll in her arms, she hit out at me blindly.

"*Leave her alone!* You shan't have her. You *shan't*! She's mine! My baby! You shan't take her away from me!"

"I wouldn't dream of taking her from you," I said gently.

"Oh, yes, you would! That's why you're here! That's what you've come for, to steal my baby, to hide her, to send her away! But someone else is coming. Ah, you didn't know that, did you? You thought you could creep into my room like this and snatch her from me, but I'm cleverer than you, much cleverer! And so is dear Matthew. *He* will stop you."

I stood beside her, helpless and bewildered, unable to do a thing. She was rambling and incoherent. She was delirious. She was insane. Or so said dear Matthew contemptuously. But she trusted Matthew, not me.

Right now I had no time to dwell on such things. I was baffled by the situation and prayed for David to come. Words, endearments, verbal reassurances, all were inadequate and I dared not administer a sedative without his medical approval.

She lay there, staring at me with a blank look which, nonetheless, held a terrified awareness. She screamed at me to go, but I remained, afraid to leave her and hopeful that in a little while the familiarity of my face might spark recognition in her mind. Her fragile hands clawed at the bed covers, alternately fingering her baby's dress or fondling her hair. And there was I, regarding that lifeless doll as a child because her belief in it, her intensity of love for it, and her utter dependence upon it were so real that contact with them became infectious.

I moved away from the bed. At all costs I had to remain calm and emotionally detached, but it wasn't easy. Finding her in such a state had been a shock and I was aware, as I glanced out of the window, that my own hands were trembling. My interview with Matthew Deacon had disturbed me more than I cared to admit, and now this situation threatened to break my self-control. At any moment the doctor would arrive and he mustn't find me like this.

Praying for him to come, I stared down into the drive as if the very urgency of my need could conjure his appearance. Behind me, Katherine rambled incomprehensibly. Here and there words stood out from the muttered tangle. "Gone . . . gone . . . He has sent her away . . . He has hidden her . . . No, Father, no!"

The clock ticked. My mother wept. The shadows of the room shrank back, seeming to listen and wait. The storm had ceased, but rain still fell with monotonous regularity. I turned from the window and crossed to her bed, but her eyes were closed and she didn't see me. The artificial yellow hair of the doll was wet with her tears.

I felt a compassion so great that I wanted to cradle her in my arms and never let her go. Life had beaten her down, wounded her so deeply that no one could guess the intensity of her suffering. I had not fully comprehended it myself until now. This was a woman who had given birth in joy which had been turned into shame. She was not made of the stuff which could stand up to adversity. She had not been brought up to it, nor had she been encouraged in independence in her youth. A girl of her background had been taught complete subjection to parental authority.

Helpless, pitiable, and defenseless was how I saw my mother now.

The sound of wheels on gravel brought me swiftly to the window again, relief pounding in my heart. Headlights swept up the drive. There was no concession to a speed limit in the way David drove his car that night, and beneath my agitation I was aware that his driving was characteristic of him — forceful, direct, but absolutely under control. I had never been so glad to see him. I cast one swift glance toward the bed and then hurried downstairs, determined that neither Harriet nor Buxton should answer the door, and certainly not Matthew Deacon.

I should have known that he would be there before me. The sound of David's car brought him promptly into the hall, and as I reached the top of the stairs and the ancient bell jangled on its iron chain, he was already opening the front door.

David brushed past him without a word and came striding toward the stairs. I met him at the foot. Something about my face made him pause and to my surprise his hand touched my own. His mouth tilted in a brief smile. That was all, but reassurance overcame my alarm.

He went upstairs; I followed. Behind us Matthew Deacon's voice rapped out, "What's going on? What has happened?" When David took no notice the man added peremptorily, "I demand to know, Harvey. I have the right."

David paused and looked back at him.

"Right?" he echoed. "What right?"

"The right as Katherine's lawyer . . . "

"Being her lawyer doesn't give you the authority to question me about her as a patient, any more than being her doctor gives me the right to question you about her as a client."

He turned away and hurried to my mother's room.

She didn't recognize him. He gave her a swift professional glance, then took hold of her wrist and felt her pulse. She tried to pull away, but although his touch appeared to be gentle, his hold was firm. His examination was quick and thorough, his experienced eye sizing up a lot, then he opened his bag, took out a hypodermic case, and handed it to me.

I knew what he wanted me to do and I almost panicked. Never in my life had I sterilized a hypodermic, but at least I had seen it done and I now delved frantically into my memory for instructions. I dealt with the instrument in the bathroom, and returned with it in a shallow bowl covered with a clean towel. I held the bowl toward the doctor and he picked up the hypodermic, saying as he did so, "I understood you had sufficient nursing training to know how to give injections."

10

THE sudden cessation of her weeping brought silence to the room. Her breathing seemed to be the only sound. The doctor stood beside the bed, looking down at his patient, and without glancing at me asked, "Don't you know how to give an injection?"

"Yes, but I was disturbed. Finding her in such a state unnerved me."

"Surely you have dealt with hysterical or frightened people before?"

There was nothing I could say. I had faced so many questions and answers tonight that I was at a loss for ingenuity. I was afraid to speak.

"I want to talk to you," he said, "but not here." He pulled the coverlet gently up to my mother's chin. "I'll wait for you downstairs."

"Not in the drawing room," I said swiftly. "Mr. Deacon is there."

He raised one eyebrow quizzically,

saying nothing. I hurried on: "I know you wouldn't wish to discuss your patient in front of him."

"I never discuss my patients in front of anyone not directly concerned."

Although his tone was not one of reproof, I felt faintly reprimanded nevertheless. My earlier fracas with Matthew Deacon, followed by the scene with Katherine, seemed to have left me very much on the defensive, and I knew that a hint of this was revealed in my voice when I answered, "He is concerned as her lawyer."

"But not as a relative," David pointed out, and turned to the door. "I'll wait for you in the morning room."

I cleansed the hypodermic and gave a final glance at my sleeping mother, patted my somewhat disheveled hair into place, picked up the medical bag, and left it in the hall downstairs. I didn't even glance at the drawing-room door as I went on to the morning room, for suddenly I didn't care whether Matthew Deacon emerged again or not. I was tired and emotionally spent; all I wanted was to be alone. I had no appetite left for dinner and wondered whether Harriet would be annoyed if I asked merely for a glass of milk and some biscuits in my room.

David was standing with his back to the fireplace, facing the door.

"What happened?" he asked abruptly. "What brought on the attack?"

"Fear. Alarm. She wakened to the storm. It was my fault. I should have returned to her earlier. When I went to help her dress for dinner, she was sleeping so peacefully that I hadn't the heart to waken her, so I came downstairs for half an hour. There was plenty of time, I thought. Then I was delayed."

"By Matthew Deacon, I suppose."

I had to admit it.

"Asking all sorts of questions?"

"Merely renewing our acquaintance. Previously he only interviewed me by phone."

"I know. I was present at the time." When I looked surprised, David continued: "Lady Katherine was in a disturbed emotional state following the reading of the will, and Harriet had sent for me. It was obvious, as it must now be

148

obvious to you, that the poor soul needed someone with her constantly. Deacon took the initiative and telephoned the bureau."

"Was that why you resented my coming — because you didn't choose me yourself?"

"Partially, perhaps."

"Then you did resent me. I thought so."

I tried to keep a wry note out of my voice, but failed.

"Matthew knew you already, of course, since you had looked after Henrietta Deacon. I agreed that in the circumstances a renewal engagement would suffice, so naturally I reacted to your unpredictable behavior."

I echoed without thought, "Henrietta Deacon?"

"His mother."

"But I didn't look after her. I looked after the wife of a former client of his, Hubert Clayton, the financier." I clearly remembered Matthew Deacon mentioning this.

"He said it was his mother. That was how he knew you, and why he was able to recommend you, and why I raised no objection to your coming."

"You must be mistaken. And surely, since you are the only doctor in Oakwell, Henrietta Deacon was your patient, in which case you must have met any nurse or companion she employed."

"I was away on an expedition at the time. Another doctor took my place."

"The Himalayas, or Brazil?" I asked.

"Brazil." He glanced at me and humor touched his mouth. "So you remember that yarn, do you?"

"Was it a yarn? The reports seemed to be authentic. Then, of course, there were television interviews with all members of the expedition. You refused to be interviewed yourself, I remember."

"Naturally." His tone was curt, and I realized how embarrassed a man such as he would be by applause and publicity.

He switched back to the subject we had been discussing. Little as I wanted to, I had no choice but to face it again.

"Are you quite sure you didn't work for Henrietta Deacon?"

"Quite sure."

Hubert Clayton's wife, Matthew had

said, and Hubert Clayton's wife I had to stick to. Besides, the solicitor had been quite emphatic that it was solely on Clayton's recommendation that he remembered me. If the unknown Gillian Conrad had actually looked after his mother, he would have known at once that I was an impostor.

I said, "Lady Katherine thinks very highly of her lawyer, doesn't she?"

"Yes, indeed."

"She regards him almost as a brother."

"And who told you that?"

"Both Mr. Deacon himself and Lady Katherine. She has even let him have a key to the house, so that he may come and go as he wishes."

"Why not? If it reassures her . . . "

"Why should she need reassurance?"

"You know very well that she is highly strung and nervous. With only Harriet and old Buxton in the house it is good for her to have a man to rely on."

"She has her doctor."

"And now you, her companion." He smiled unexpectedly.

"Then I take it you have accepted me?"

"Have I any other choice?"

"Companion-helps are replaceable."

"If unsatisfactory, yes."

"I'm flattered by the implication that I am not."

"If you are hoping for further flattery, you're going to be very disappointed. Don't dig for it from me, anyway."

I felt a swift color rise to my cheeks, and his laughter deepened it.

"Stop trying to flirt with me," he taunted. "Not that I dislike it, but there's a time and place for everything."

I could have hit him.

"Harriet was right when she described you as ill-mannered," I retorted.

He laughed even more.

"That sounds like a typical Harriet description, and since the good soul is naive enough to believe that manners make the man — or should I say gentleman? — I am happy that she should keep her illusions. You, too, if you share them, in which case this will only condemn me further." He kissed me swiftly and very firmly. "And if you weren't expecting that, my girl, you should have been."

His calm effrontery left me speechless. When I managed to regain my voice, I remarked icily, "May I remind you that we are on duty?"

"Not at that moment. Forceful type, aren't I?"

His smile mocked me. I wanted to snub him, but could think of nothing to say. At that moment the door opened abruptly.

My hands flew to my hair, a betraying gesture which Matthew Deacon, entering, did not miss. His glance went fleetingly from myself to the doctor and back again.

"My apologies for the interruption, but poor Harriet is worried about dinner. She has been waiting to serve it for some time."

I crossed to the door. Behind me, David said easily, "Don't trouble to apologize. Miss Conrad and I had finished our discussion."

"So it seems."

I sensed the doctor's amusement. He didn't give a damn for anyone, I thought.

Walking toward the dining room, Matthew Deacon continued, "I myself

153

would like a discussion with you, Harvey. I am concerned about Katherine. I saw the state she was in just now and it seemed pretty abnormal, to me."

Abnormal? "Crazy" was the word he had used earlier, and I couldn't forgive him for it.

"Any form of hysteria is abnormal, if one must use the word." David's tone was abrupt.

"It seemed more than hysteria to me. The woman's totally unbalanced."

"Anyone overcome by fear is temporarily unbalanced."

We had reached the dining room. Harriet, waiting to serve, said, "Excuse me, Doctor, how is her ladyship? I didn't even know she had been taken bad, until Mr. Deacon told me."

"She's all right now, or will be in the morning. She is sleeping and will continue to for a long time. That's all she needs just now."

I saw that Harriet had set three covers and the prospect of eating alone with Matthew Deacon, with my mother's empty place confronting us, caused me

154

to say impulsively, "Won't you join us, Doctor?"

After the incident in the morning room and my reaction, the invitation must have surprised him. For a moment I thought he was going to decline, but suddenly he changed his mind. Not because I urged him to remain, but because Matthew Deacon obviously wished him to go.

Matthew's face remained as bland as ever. "Of course you must stay; I insist. It would be a pity to waste Harriet's good cooking."

He turned the full battery of his charm on the old woman. I remembered her eulogy of him when we first met, and now understood. This was the first time I had witnessed Matthew Deacon's studied approach to Harriet.

David accepted, glancing at me a little quizzically. As we sat down I resolved to leave the conversation to the two men and to make my excuses as soon as the meal ended. The evening had already exhausted me, emotion crowding upon emotion and tension upon tension, and I longed for the solitude of my room. I wanted to make up my mind about Matthew Deacon, whose charm I mistrusted and whose voice held insinuations which might only exist in my suspicious imagination. The man might be all he seemed: amiable, courteous, and 'a real gentleman,' as Harriet put it. Possibly my own mistrust of him had made me notice undertones of doubt in his voice and his manner, but I couldn't forget my instinctive dislike of him before I even knew his identity. The well-tailored lawyer who walked unannounced into this house tonight had done nothing to alleviate my wariness, his apparent concern for Katherine being contradicted by his cruel reference to her insanity.

I became aware that he was speaking. I was eating automatically, scarcely aware of the food and even less of the conversation, but now his words echoed in my mind with the sharpness of stones dropped into a pool, sending out ever-widening ripples of challenge.

"I would like to know just why Gillian refused to let me see Katherine. She deliberately barred me from the room." He was apparently speaking to the doctor, but his eyes were on me. "In fact," he added, "she shut the door in my face. A new experience, I confess, and not enjoyable."

"Not if it is shut in one's face for a different reason," David answered with dry humor, "and most certainly not if it happens to be a bedroom door."

I seemed to detect an underlying reminder that I had not rebuffed his own advance half an hour ago. As if he had given me any chance to! The suddenness of that kiss had taken me by surprise, and he knew it quite well, I thought indignantly.

"No nurse would admit anyone but a doctor when a patient was passing through a crisis," I said briskly.

"Then you agree that poor Katherine *was* passing through a crisis. What sort of crisis? Come, you can speak frankly. I am very close to her and naturally concerned."

"It was an emotional crisis, a temporary one, no more." I was conscious that the doctor allowed me to answer although he was wanting to do so himself. Wanting to put Matthew Deacon in his place? I wondered. I was well aware that David resented the solicitor's interrogation.

"As Doctor Harvey has already told you," I continued, "Lady Katherine wakened to the storm and was overcome by fear."

"And yet, before the doctor arrived, you told me she would 'be herself again very soon,' as I would see when she came down to dinner."

"I was mistaken, Mr. Deacon."

"So it really was more serious? A mental breakdown, in fact."

David said sharply, "An emotional lapse, no more, as I've already told you. There's no need to exaggerate the situation and absolutely no reason to blame or cross-examine Gillian."

"But I blame myself," I said. "I meant to return to her much earlier and should have remembered her fear of the dark."

"No one is infallible," David pointed out, and I was grateful for his understanding.

Harriet returned and collected our soup bowls, placing a very tempting roast pheasant on the table. I noticed that she automatically set it before the solicitor to carve, as she would before the master of the house.

He carved meticulously, but pursued his questions the moment Harriet withdrew.

"Despite what the pair of you say, I want to know more about Katherine's condition. Don't forget, I am legally responsible for her and will shortly be involved in the dispensation of her father's will. Her state of mind is important. I must ask you not to withhold anything from me, although I know, of course, that medical people hang together, to protect one another, I suppose."

"I resent that," David said coldly.

The solicitor looked at him in pained surprise. "My dear Harvey, I cannot imagine why, but if you deliberately choose to misconstrue my remarks, I'll apologize if it will make you feel better."

"Don't merely apologize to me. To Gillian also."

"Really, I — "

"I said to Gillian also."

I sat there and waited, enjoying the moment. Deacon had cross-examined and grilled me earlier this evening, and I was more than willing to see the tables turned. His apology was surly, but I accepted it because even that was more than I had hoped for.

He remained truculent, however, returning to the subject of Lady Katherine. "I heard her crying," he persisted, "and she seemed deeply distressed, far more than merely frightened. At one time I even heard her accusing her companion of trying to steal something."

I went rigid. What was he leading up to? I was suddenly afraid of the man and even more frightened of the accusation he put into his words. I felt David's glance on me, so I turned to him and said levelly, "She had some terrible idea that I wished to steal her child."

Matthew gave a short, sharp laugh.

"That hideous doll, you mean? I said she was unbalanced, didn't I? I hope you reassured her."

"Naturally."

"But she didn't believe you."

"She was too frightened to even heed me."

The solicitor's assurance had returned. He sipped his wine and continued: "Of course, I've always considered it a mistake to indulge that ridiculous whim of hers. Letting her regard that doll as a human child is asking for trouble."

David answered curtly, "It gives her comfort. For the present, she needs it. You must allow me to judge what is best for my patient."

"But she is also my client. I have her interests at heart. How can I declare that her signature to certain documents is given in full possession of her faculties, unless I am sure that she *is* in possession of them?"

"As her medical adviser, that is for me to testify."

Matthew Deacon ignored that, and turned back to me.

"And *did* you try to steal the doll?"

"Of course not. Why should I?"

"Because you, like me, might consider it wise to take the thing away from her."

"I abide by the doctor's decision. Besides, she wouldn't let — "

Too late, I bit the words back.

"She wouldn't let you?" the man finished softly. "But you are stronger than she, surely? Couldn't you have taken it by force?"

"I didn't even try to," I replied coolly, and then I added impulsively, "She also believes that you wouldn't let me."

"I can hardly believe that."

"It's true. She said you would stop me, and so would someone else."

There was a brief and oddly significant silence.

"Did she, indeed?" the solicitor said softly. "And who do you think she meant by that?"

"Doctor Harvey, I imagine. Who else?"

I looked across at David and saw that he was watching Deacon intently.

"Who else, indeed?" the man said.

"That is up to you, isn't it?" David put in. "I urge you to hurry. The strain of waiting is becoming too much for her."

"I can't do more than I'm already doing. These things take time. The wheels of God and the Law grind slowly."

"So it seems. Too slowly. You could help by speeding things up."

"I'm doing my utmost and hope to have good news shortly. In fact, I am confident that I shall."

I glanced from one to the other, puzzled.

A tap on the door, and Harriet reentered. She moved methodically, clearing our plates away, and as she did so the conversation turned to generalities: the weather, the coming hunting season, and, inevitably, to horses.

"Do you ride?" Matthew asked me amiably.

I admitted I had never had the opportunity.

"We must remedy that, don't you agree, Harvey?"

David nodded, adding that I had been confined indoors too much since my arrival and that the exercise would be good for me.

"I understand the stables haven't held horses for years."

Matthew smiled at me, his earlier ill-humor forgotten.

"But my stables aren't empty, my dear. I'll be delighted to teach you to ride and you may rely on me to choose a gentle mount to start with."

His glance roved over me with appraisal.

"She would look well on a horse, don't

you agree, Harvey? Lithe and slim, and with those long legs . . . Yes, my dear, you must certainly allow me to teach you. An hour a day, starting from tomorrow. How about that? Can you spare her from her onerous duties for that brief time?"

"Of course, if the idea appeals to her."

It had to. I couldn't afford to reject any friendly overtures from a man who could be my enemy.

I thanked him as Harriet again withdrew, leaving a great bowl of fruit on the table. It was tempting, but I declined anything further because I was anxious to get away. I rose and crossed to the door.

"Until tomorrow then, Gillian? I take it that early afternoon will be most convenient? Katherine rests then, doesn't she, so shall we say three o'clock?"

I nodded, and thanked him again.

At the door, I looked back at the two men, both standing as I departed. The quizzical, amused glance still seemed to linger about the doctor's blunt features, but I refused to acknowledge or be disturbed by it. Nevertheless, I knew it mocked me, as if he were suggesting that I had made a conquest of Matthew Deacon. What nonsense, I thought irritably.

I opened the door, anxious to be gone, but Matthew's voice arrested me.

"By the way, Gillian, have you done any more sketching?"

I answered with a jerk, "No, no more."

"You didn't know she was a talented artist, did you?" he said to David.

The doctor admitted he did not, but added that having noticed my hands, he wasn't particularly surprised.

"My hands?" I echoed.

"They are sensitive and artistic. Very revealing."

"You must see her work sometime," Matthew said, smiling in a way which suggested nothing but the most sincere interest. "I wanted to see more myself, but alas, our first meeting was too brief." He turned back to me. "You could have had little time to spare between our chat and your arrival here later."

David looked puzzled.

"You are surprised, Harvey? So was I. I had no idea that the girl I nearly ran down in the lane outside was coming

165

here. Were you on your way at that precise moment, Gillian? I imagine not, since you had no luggage other than your portfolio. On the other hand, you could hardly have gone on a sketching expedition within the first hour or two of your arrival, not with a new employer to become acquainted with and the job of installing yourself in new surroundings, so you must forgive me for being curious. I noticed you had sketched the gates of Lyonhurst in detail — quite a task, since the wrought ironwork is very complicated — so you must have been there for a long time, or else you work very quickly."

"I do work quickly. Very quickly indeed."

He gave me a level glance, then said with a strange sort of significance, "You really must take a look at her drawings sometime, Harvey. I found them most interesting."

11

MY mother was herself again next morning, waking quite normally and not remembering a thing about the night before. I took breakfast to her room, and she greeted me with a smile and a yawn.

"I feel so sleepy," she murmured. "More than I usually do, first thing in the morning."

I didn't tell her it was the effect of an injection. I didn't tell her anything, except that the sun was shining and that after the doctor had been by I would take her for a walk in the grounds.

"Is he calling today? But why? He isn't due for a visit. He comes only twice a week."

"Sometimes more," I reminded her. "He often drops in when passing. He likes to see you."

"I am lucky in my doctor. Lucky in my friends. Harriet and Buxton and dear Matthew — and you," she finished, patting my arm affectionately. When her hand dropped to the coverlet again it fell upon her doll, which she had nursed throughout the night. She looked at it in surprise.

"Now what is Belinda doing here? She should be in her cot. I suppose she cried for me and you picked her up and brought her to me?"

I smiled, saying nothing, merely laying the doll aside and wondering if Matthew Deacon wasn't right, after all, when doubting the wisdom of indulging this obsession. It seemed to be increasingly necessary to her. When David arrived an hour later I made a point of mentioning this, but he merely answered, "Don't worry. The entire illusion will be dispelled shortly."

"But how? And when?"

"That depends on Deacon, who assured me last night that it won't be long now. Don't worry. When it happens it will mean only happiness for her, I can promise you that."

He gave me no chance for further questions, showing not the slightest desire for conversation with me apart from a

168

brief discussion about his patient after he had visited her. "No percussions at all," he announced with satisfaction. "Not that I expected any. A good night's sleep and a restful day today, and all will be well."

"I thought I would take her for a walk in the park."

"A good idea. A lovely day for it. Then a rest this afternoon, a leisurely evening, and early to bed. I'll look in again tomorrow."

Neither by word nor glance did he indicate that he so much as remembered a certain moment in the morning room, and it was absurd of me to feel disappointed about that.

After he had gone I felt oddly depressed, and the feeling was so alien to my nature that I was worried by it. I had been kissed before. I had even believed myself to be in love more than once, but my romantic experiences had been confined to art students, compared with whom David seemed a hundred times more adult. That brief contact with him had been emotionally bigger and more momentous than anything I had previously known, but to a man of his age and experience the incident had been entirely trivial. If I had any sense, I would regard it in the same light. I was disturbed to discover that my emotions seemed to be getting the better of me.

I was almost glad when Matthew arrived half an hour earlier than expected. I heard the sharp echo of hooves on the drive and, glancing from my mother's bedroom, where I was settling her for her rest, I saw him mounted once again on Rufus and looking as he had at our first meeting: self-confident and rather arrogant, but impressive. Riding clothes became him. Observing him now, I noted the breadth of his shoulders and the strong thighs, also his hands upon the reins. Why didn't I like his hands? They were large and well-shaped.

But, a brutal man's hands. That was the difference. That was the thing I disliked. David's were also strong and well-shaped, but there was a sensitivity about his touch which I had observed many times when he examined my mother. This gentleness was lacking in Matthew Deacon's. They were not hands which I should like to feel upon myself.

He had brought another horse on a leading rein. Despite my instinctive dislike of the man, I experienced a sense of pleasurable anticipation at the thought of learning to ride.

Katherine's voice, behind me, asked, "Is that dear Matthew? It must be, for he is the only person who comes here on horseback. The doctor rides very little — a pity, because he rides well, but he gets so little time with that busy practice of his. How nice of Matthew to call!"

She had joined me at the window and observed, "He has brought Patience, too — exercising her, no doubt. What a beautiful chestnut she is!"

I agreed, admiring the glancing sunlight on golden flank and shining mane.

"He has brought her for me to ride," I said. "Last night he offered to teach me."

"Last night! I didn't know he called last night."

"You were asleep, so naturally we didn't disturb you."

She gave me an affectionate smile.

"That was thoughtful of you, Gillian,

171

thoughtful of Matthew, too. My dear child, I am delighted that he should teach you to ride. You certainly couldn't have a better tutor. Hurry and change, my dear. It is such a lovely day; you must make the most of it."

"Unfortunately, I have no riding clothes. I should have told him, but I wasn't really sure that he would come. In fact, I wouldn't have been surprised if he had forgotten altogether."

My mother looked shocked. "Not *Matthew*! He would never forget a promise!"

Not so long as it suited him, I thought.

"It seems a pity that you should miss your first riding lesson just through lack of suitable clothes," she continued. "Ring for Harriet, will you, my dear?"

I obeyed. By the time the woman appeared I had helped my mother onto her bed and covered her with the faded chintz quilt. It was beautiful, badly in need of re-covering, but, like much of the furnishings at Lyonhurst, seemed likely to remain so.

My mother said, "Take Miss Conrad along to my old room, will you, Harriet, and let her choose a riding habit from among mine? They should fit her fairly well, I think. You'll find jodhpurs and jackets to choose from, Gillian, and if my old boots aren't the right size, wear a pair of stout walking shoes for your first lesson; they will serve well enough until you are more experienced." She stopped my thanks with a gesture and a smile. "I shall be delighted to see a young person wearing them again, for now."

I walked beside Harriet down the long corridor to the room my mother had occupied as a girl. It was not large, and I stood just within the door, looking at it, trying to recapture something of her early personality, for I knew that nothing reflected a person more than a room which was solely his or her own. My mother was no longer the girl with whom my father had fallen in love; she was a tragic and faded bloom which had long left behind the promising bud of youth. It was that bud which Pierre's love had brought to flower and which her father's relentless cruelty had destroyed. But here, in this abandoned room, was the heart of a girl called Kathy. For the first time, I met her face to face.

Harriet crossed to the large wardrobe, murmuring to herself as she did so, but I scarcely heard her voice, much less her words. My eyes roamed from the four-poster bed with its Victorian patchwork quilt, to the petticoated dressing table with its shield-shaped mirror, silver-topped toilet accessories and petit point tray. A hotchpotch of feminine articles lay on it, and it looked as if she had just left it and would very soon return, hurrying in to change, flinging her dress onto the bed, kicking off her shoes haphazardly. The room even had a faint perfume about it which gave it a lived-in air.

My silence attracted Harriet's attention, for she turned and looked at me.

"Come in, Miss Conrad, and shut the door. You look shy, but you needn't be. I keep the room just as it was, fresh as when she used it herself. No doubt, you've heard the unhappy story. The doctor, no doubt, would tell it to you, so that you would understand his patient better — the poor soul."

"I do understand."

But understanding alone was not

enough. My mother needed help and affection, and I experienced a sudden desire to make up for all she had lost, to help her to find compensation in reality rather than refuge in fantasy. I wanted to take her hand and lead her back to life.

Still talking, Harriet searched in the depths of the wardrobe. "Of course, when Sir Humphrey shut this room up he didn't know I had a key. I used to slip in here and keep it aired and dusted. That doll her ladyship is so attached to used to perch on the window seat over there. It was always her favorite, and even when she had outgrown dolls she kept this one around because it was the last present her mother gave her before she died. She called it Belinda because that was her mother's name and she used to say to me, 'Hattie, if I ever have a daughter, she will be called Belinda, too.'"

I turned away sharply, threatened by tears. The picture Harriet conjured up had a deep emotional effect on me. There was also a feeling I had never experienced before, that of being linked with my mother's family as well as my father's.

"What was Lady Katherine's mother like?"

"Look at the dear soul herself, and you'll know. Belinda Tredgold was a sweet woman and her daughter's life would have been very different had she lived. Lady Tredgold was the only person who could ever really handle Sir Humphrey, and doing that wasn't easy even for her. It was a tragedy for Miss Kathy that her mother died so young, because she was very protective toward her daughter. Perhaps she realized that the child needed a buffer against her father. She made me promise never to leave her. "She's going to need you, later on," she always said. Well, I did my best, but it wasn't enough. Not as much as a wife and mother could have done." The woman sighed and finished, "Ah, well, life goes on and we just have to go on with it. There now, try this for size."

She held a jacket aloft, inspecting it. "Good as new," she approved. "I knew it would be, of course. Clothes were made to last in those days, and although I do say it myself I've taken good care of Miss Kathy's things. Here are jodhpurs, too, and I must say I'm glad she offered them to you. I thought she'd be hanging on to all these things yet awhile. Of course, she's only lending them to you but — my word, that jacket fits like it was made for you!"

It did, and so did the jodhpurs. I was aware of pleasure tinged with sentiment because I was wearing something which my mother herself had worn.

Harriet stood back and surveyed me, then she whispered, "It's uncanny, that's what it is. I must find a shirt. There are plenty in a drawer over there."

Not until I was fully clad in my mother's clothes did I realize that, although I didn't resemble her in looks, I had apparently inherited her figure. Even her boots were the right size. Walking back to her room, I felt as if I had donned something of her personality, and as I walked along the corridor, I felt like the daughter of the house. Even my step seemed different.

But it halted abruptly outside the bedroom door, arrested by the sound of voices from within — my mother's and Matthew Deacon's. So he had let himself into the house and come straight up.

I opened the door and stood on the threshold, looking at them. Katherine was propped against pillows, and Mathew sat on the window seat, chatting with the ease and familiarity of a visitor who was more than a visitor, a privileged friend of the family.

I said nothing, merely looked from one to the other inquiringly. I saw Matthew's startled glance and couldn't understand why I was pleased by it, except that to discomfort him gave me satisfaction.

Harriet would have approved of the way in which he rose, bowing a little from the waist. In her eyes it would have been the act of a gentleman. To me it seemed to indicate a superficiality of manner which I disliked.

I closed the door and walked into the room, saying, "Please sit down, Mr. Deacon, since you are here."

"Meaning that you disapprove?"

"I left Lady Katherine to rest."

He turned to my mother. "Gillian is angry with me, Kathy. I'm glad you don't feel the same way." To me, he added, "Let me assure you that I am welcome here. In fact, I am welcome anywhere in this house, aren't I, Kathy?"

"Of course, Matthew dear."

My mother's voice trailed away weakly, and I realized that she scarcely heard what he said, for she was looking at me in stunned surprise. Even Matthew realized this. He looked from my mother to me, and back again, but apparently could see no reason for her shock, for he merely commented, "Lady Katherine seems surprised at the way you are dressed. Surely you asked permission for the riding lessons?"

His ability to patronize seemed unlimited. Even now he could not miss the opportunity to remind me of my place in this household, and that teaching me to ride was a concession, a favor for which I, a mere employee, should seek the proper consent.

I answered coolly, "A companion's time is usually her own when her employer is resting, which, I would point out, Lady Katherine should be doing right now. I left her lying down when I went to change."

"My dear, forgive me! Finding no one

downstairs I came straight up, assuming you would be here. When you were not, I waited, glad of a chance to assure myself that Lady Katherine had fully recovered from last night's upset . . . "

But I wasn't listening to him, for my mother's glance was still fixed on me in a disturbing way.

"What's the matter?" Matthew Deacon asked. "You look as if you'd seen a ghost, Kathy."

A ghost . . . The ghost of my father? Did I suddenly remind her of him, standing there dressed like a boy? I was twenty-three, my father's age at the time of their love affair. I was as dark as he, as French as he; my features resembled his far more than they resembled my mother's, but perhaps the similarity had not been noticeable until I appeared in tailored shirt and jacket.

"Lady Katherine is surprised by the transformation in me. I imagine I don't look a bit like a nurse-companion in these clothes."

"It — it isn't that." My mother's voice was almost a whisper. "It was just that, for a moment, you reminded me of someone. Someone I knew long ago . . . "

Her voice trailed away piteously. I saw her trembling hands grope for her doll and cradle it against her heart. "Suddenly, quite suddenly, there was a look of him . . . " Her voice died away, unhappy and uncertain.

"Him?" the solicitor echoed sharply.

"It is nonsense, of course," she continued with an effort, "because he was French and Gillian is so very English."

The solicitor moved impatiently. "What illusions will she be suffering from next?" he muttered beneath his breath.

"What are you saying, Matthew dear? I can't hear. Come closer."

I moved briskly to the bed, wishing the man had not come.

"You must rest," I insisted. "Doctor's orders. I'll be back in half an hour."

"Oh, no, my dear, take longer than that. You mustn't cut short your lesson on my account. Patience is a gentle horse and won't tire you."

"I wouldn't dream of encroaching on

Mr. Deacon's time," I said firmly, hoping this would make him realize that I no longer wanted his beastly riding lesson, but the only response to my remark was his usual bland smile.

12

THAT was the first of several riding lessons and became, from that afternoon, a regular daily occurrence. My progress was rapid, due to his excellent tutorage, but he gave all the credit to me.

"You are a born rider," he said when we parted the first day. "Are you sure you have never ridden before?"

"Only once, when I went to a charity fair at Hampton Court. There was a Donkey Derby and I entered for a bet. I didn't even finish the course; the donkey threw me clean over its head!"

"Well, Patience will have her work cut out to throw you, my dear. At your present rate of progress you'll be taking her over the jumps in no time."

We parted amiably. I was exhilarated by the ride and pleased with his compliments which, for the first time, seemed to contain no hint of flattery. Even I knew that I had acquitted myself well.

He retied Patience to the leading rein, which he had released within the first ten minutes, and turned her head around until it was neck and neck with his own horse. Beneath him, the fiery Rufus sidled and fidgeted, raking at the bits and blowing through flaring nostrils. I dismounted in haste, for close proximity with Rufus alarmed me. Matthew laughed and said, "You haven't got over your first reaction to him, have you? But I assure you that so long as I am astride him he is under control. I wouldn't let him hurt a hair of your head."

"It isn't my hair I'm worried about. He is strong enough to break every bone in my body."

"Don't worry, he won't. By the time you are ready to ride him, you'll be able to handle him well."

"Ride Rufus! Me?"

"Yes, you. I intend that you shall not only ride him, but take him over the jumps."

"Never!"

I was standing on the gravel drive, at the foot of the wide steps sweeping up to the impressive front doors of the manor, and I looked up at horse and rider with spontaneous admiration, for they made a striking picture, the stallion with the sunlight glancing off his rippling muscles, and the man sitting him so effortlessly. There was confidence in every line of his figure, plus a hint of ruthlessness which suggested that he knew just where he was going and would ride down anyone or anything in his way.

"Until tomorrow, then!" he called, and Rufus's rein tightened along his glossy neck as the rider's heels urged him forward. The stallion threw up his great crest, whirled around on his haunches, and Patience, startled, sprang to life obediently. Sunlight sparkled on gleaming hides and polished saddles as four pairs of hooves cantered away down the long drive. Sweat had gathered on Rufus's flanks when, after my riding lesson, Matthew had taken him for a furious gallop across the park while I sat on the docile Patience, watching as they leaped hedge and ditch with ease. They were a wonderful partnership, pitching mind against mind and muscle against muscle and reveling in the battle. But

185

in the end it was the man's mind which conquered and controlled and directed.

I remained where I was, watching their departure. Quiet Patience had difficulty in keeping up with the fiery Rufus. Dust spiraled from beneath the stallion's sledgehammer hooves and there was a certain viciousness in his plunging. Matthew Deacon seemed to enjoy it, for he flicked his crop encouragingly against the beast's gleaming flanks and then again, more sharply, against poor Patience, so that she whinnied in startled fright and plunged desperately beside them.

Until they reached the curve in the drive, Matthew let Rufus have his head, then wrist, heel, and body moved together in one imperative command and the great stallion came up to the bit, rearing and then standing still.

Matthew turned in the saddle, lifted his crop to me in a farewell salute, and called out again, "Until tomorrow, then!"

I waved good-bye and was about to enter the house when his voice arrested me.

186

"If you see David, tell him I shall shortly have news — good news. The news Katherine has been waiting for."

The air carried his voice to me so clearly that I glanced instinctively toward my mother's windows above. They were open, so she must surely have heard. Then I noticed that the curtains had been pulled back, which meant she had gone downstairs to the drawing room.

Matthew called reassuringly, "Don't worry, Gillian, I shall pick the right time to tell her. You can leave that to me. You can leave everything to me."

That was the moment when, for the first time, I felt I had seen Matthew Deacon somewhere before, that his face was familiar in a way I could not define. It was a strange illusion and a fleeting one, for suddenly it was gone and he was himself again, a man I had known for merely a few hours, who had never crossed my path until that morning in the lane, and who bore no resemblance to anyone I knew.

I entered the house by the side wing and went upstairs to change. Dark portraits of Tredgold ancestors watched my progress. I could feel their eyes on me as I mounted the stairs and the watchful, waiting glances of more from the landing above. They were shadowy figures, almost indistinguishable beneath the grime of centuries. Like the worn carpets and faded chintzes and curtains rotted by the sun, they would have to remain in their present state, neglected and beyond repair. I wondered idly if any of them were valuable and, if so, what price they would fetch. The sale of some of these musty, dusty pictures might well bring in much-needed funds.

I studied them as I passed. There seemed to be no recent ones, neither of my mother and her tyrannical father, nor of Prudence Tredgold, the immoral sister whose name was never mentioned. What had she been like, that unhappy woman whose appetite for sex had been insatiable? Had she been beautiful and vulnerable, or hard and ruthless? I would never know, of course. Nor would I ever know the identities of these shadowy men and women who peered at me darkly from their massive gilt frames. Some were no more than gloomy slabs of color upon a murky background, from which yellow features glowed dimly and unattractively. Katherine's loveliness had certainly not been inherited from any of these, so either she resembled her mother's family, or once in a century the Tredgolds yielded an accidental beauty.

The doctor called unexpectedly just before dinner. His arrival filled me with a pleasure which, caught off guard, I was unable to conceal. To my annoyance he laughed and said, "Not angry with me, then? I guessed that outraged pride of yours, last night, was merely assumed. Don't hope for a repeat performance tonight. I never distribute my favors too liberally."

When I tried to speak, and failed, he laughed outright, which increased my annoyance. At that he patted my shoulder and said, "Take heart. This is a duty visit and to kiss you now would be breach of professional etiquette. Be patient; sometime I'll be off duty again."

I was too infuriated to speak, and he had the audacity to laugh again.

"Now I've angered you, but what it

is due to this time — outraged pride or outraged virtue? My dear girl, your virtue will go unsullied, if that is what you wish. As for pride, it's a luxury in which only the most stupid indulge. Too often it is merely a screen behind which people hide under the fond illusion that others will admire them for it, but all that happens is that people don't even notice."

I answered frigidly, "I haven't the slightest desire to impress you."

"Of course you have. You're a woman and I'm a man. It's a natural feminine instinct to want to impress the male."

"And vice versa."

"Without a doubt — with the average male."

"And you are not average, I suppose?"

"Indeed not. Far above it."

"Well, you certainly have more than average conceit!"

At that, his mouth quirked with humor.

"You do rise to it, don't you?" he teased, and against my will I burst out laughing. We were friends again.

"And how did the riding lesson go?"

"Well. Very well, in fact. Which

reminds me, I have a message for you from Matthew. You can shortly expect the news for which Lady Katherine is waiting."

The effect on David puzzled me. He answered slowly,

"So he really has been working on it . . ."

"Didn't you believe he had?"

"I wondered."

"Why?"

He made no answer. My curiosity was whetted, but once before I had tried to find out just what the solicitor's mission was and why it was so important to my mother. I had failed then and I would fail now, for the doctor was not a man to betray a confidence.

I could see no reason why David should doubt whether the solicitor had been pressing forward with the execution of the will. It didn't make sense because there could be no possible motive for delay.

"I don't understand," I said. "If Lady Katherine's solicitor is entrusted with a legal duty on her behalf, he has to execute it."

"Yes."

"Well, then?"

"Well, then, we have nothing to worry about. Except yourself, of course."

"Why me?" I asked, surprised.

"Because, as Deacon must have told you, your employment here was to be only temporary, pending certain circumstances." David said quickly, "He didn't imply that the job was permanent, did he?"

I answered carefully, "No, but neither did he tell me of any circumstances it depended on."

The gambit got me nowhere, for he merely answered, "There was no need. They don't concern you."

That put me right back in my place again — a place which seemed to be suddenly insecure. During the last day or two I had almost forgotten that I was here under false pretenses and that the time available was limited by the conditions of my own life. In a couple of weeks Françoise would return from the Continent. She would wonder where I was, and I would have to let her know before she finally resorted to official inquiries. Apart from that, the College of Art was due to reopen in less than a month.

So I had little time in which to continue this masquerade, and now that I had pulled off the deception and feared no exposure, I began to wonder just what it availed me. I could get nothing out of this adventure. I would have to leave Lyonhurst under the guise in which I came, for to reveal my true identity suddenly would be a shock from which poor Katherine might never recover. Her reason was already poised perilously between sanity and fantasy. A revelation such as mine could drive her over the edge from which there might be no return. I could never do that to her.

The thought of departure, however, filled me with an inexplicable sadness. It would be a wrench to leave Lyonhurst where, in so short a time, I had put down unexpected roots.

My riding lessons progressed, and so did my friendship with Matthew, somewhat to my surprise. I had resolved to be on amicable terms with him because wisdom dictated it, but the possibility of actual friendship had seemed remote. However, our earlier sparring was overcome in the mutual enjoyment of riding. He was genuinely pleased with my progress, and I myself exhilarated by it.

I was conscious of nothing but the delight of a new sport. I had quickly advanced from trot to canter, from canter to gallop, and to race neck and neck with Matthew across the wild stretches of the park was not only an invigorating experience, but a shared delight. Not that I could keep up with him for long, but the challenge of it thrilled me.

Sun and wind and dappled light upon gleaming flank and tossing mane; thundering hooves and flaring nostrils and muscles straining beneath martingale and bit; gleaming metal and polished leather and the breathless, ecstatic plunge through long grass into darkening woods — these were the components of those enjoyable hours before happiness splintered like a fragile bauble on a Christmas tree.

13

"WE must give a dinner party," my mother announced one day. "Dear Matthew must come, and Doctor Harvey. I wish there were other young people of your own age whom I could invite, but alas, I have been out of touch with local society since my father's death . . ."

And long before that, I thought pityingly.

"It doesn't matter, Lady Katherine. A small dinner party will be more friendly."

She brightened.

"It will, indeed. Of course, I could suggest that Matthew should bring a guest. He has always been very popular." Her eyes twinkled. "I may be cut off from the world in this great and lonely house, but now and then I hear news from Harriet or Buxton. Village gossip, I suppose, but such tidbits are nearly always founded upon truth. He is both handsome and eligible. Indeed, I only wonder why he has not been snapped up long ago!"

I was rather surprised myself.

My mother looked at me a trifle archly and continued, "Have you any idea how splendidly matched the pair of you look when riding across the park, despite the difference in your ages? I said as much to David Harvey the other day, and he agreed."

"Did he, indeed?"

I had seen little of David during these last few days, apart from his brief professional visits. Even then, he had no time to spare for me. I knew he had forgotten that incident in the morning room which, even in recollection, disturbed me.

Like a child, my mother wanted her party immediately and nothing would satisfy her but that I should telephone David right away and invite him for the following evening. My delight because he was free surprised me, and in an attempt to combat it, I welcomed Matthew more warmly than usual when he arrived for my daily riding lesson.

"It's a wonderful day for a ride!" I exclaimed, lifting my face to the sun.

He answered, in a significant kind of

way which puzzled me, "A particularly wonderful day, Gillian."

I said, "Lady Katherine hopes you'll come to dinner tomorrow night. She told me to ask you the moment you arrived. Rather short notice, I'm afraid, but for her sake I hope you'll be free. Pleasures in her life are so few."

"I shall certainly come. Nothing would keep me away now."

"Why now especially?"

"Because I shall have a surprise for her. A splendid one. The matter was clinched this morning, but I can't reveal it until tomorrow, so a dinner party in celebration will be timely."

"If it is something she has been waiting for, is it fair to keep her in suspense?"

"It would be worse to let her spend a sleepless night through excitement. I will do things in my own way."

As I mounted Patience he caught hold of her rein, drawing her alongside Rufus so that we were saddle to saddle, knee touching knee.

"Don't spoil my surprise, will you?" he said softly.

My mother was as excited as a girl dressing for her first ball. "You choose, my dear," she said. "Belinda is already asleep, and in any case, she is too young to take any interest in her mother's clothes." Excitement had caused her mind to vacillate again, flickering between the present and the past, but evading the dark chapter in the middle. The doll, after being kissed and cooed over, had been placed in her cot and told to be a good girl and go to sleep at once. The mechanical eye-lids with their long sable lashes closed obediently, but the waxen lips still smiled with their stiff artificiality.

But having kissed her child good night, Katherine was happy and at peace, stepping from the past into the present again quite easily. She was ready for her little dinner party, ready to go downstairs and greet her guests.

The gown I chose for her was of rose brocade, with a deep collar of Brussels lace. It was outmoded, but became her well, its simple elegance enhancing the Dresden quality of her figure. "There should be music when you wear this gown," I said. "The music of a spinet . . ."

She laughed, pleased and yet a little aghast. "My dear, what age do you think I am? The spinet was in fashion long before my time!"

"You belong to all ages," I told her. "Your beauty is eternal." The words sounded flowery, perhaps, but I meant them. My mother's looks were indeed ageless. Despite premature lines which time and suffering had imprinted on her face, she had a kind of indestructible beauty. I wished with all my heart that I could call her Mother, instead of the enforced formality of her title, for I belonged to her and loved her. In so short a time the bond of our relationship had grown.

She smiled at my remark, pleased and touched.

"I mean it, Lady Katherine."

She studied herself in a long mirror, then sighed. "Perhaps it was true of me once upon a time, when I was young and happy, and loved. You may not believe it, Gillian, old maid as I am,

but I have known a man's love . . . "
She changed the subject abruptly. "You look very charming yourself, my dear, but then you always do. You don't need jewels or beautiful clothes when you have youth. And I like your dress. I have seen it before, haven't I?"

I glanced at the simple sheath dress into which I changed most evenings.

"Of course. It is the only one I brought with me."

"It is very simple, very chic, very good taste, and a very good cut. A model, surely?"

It was useless to pretend that I had bought this dress off the rack.

"I have a friend who works for a top Mayfair dressmaker, so occasionally I am lucky enough to be able to buy clothes after the models have worn them."

It was a lie, but only up to a point. Such slightly soiled dresses did come my way from time to time.

David was waiting in the drawing room, but Matthew had not yet arrived. David poured sherry for us while I settled my mother in her wing chair. Firelight danced on her rose brocade and pearls and fading blonde hair which tonight was swept high.

When he handed me a glass I had a sudden urge to tell David that, tonight, Matthew would end my mother's waiting and anxiety, but because of the stricture placed on me I remained silent.

I heard David speaking to my mother. His voice held that kindly note which he seemed to reserve especially for her and which I wanted to hear for myself. In truth I wanted more than that.

Disturbed, I jerked away from the thought. Firelight must be playing tricks with fancy, and perhaps I made an all-too-willing victim.

At that moment the urge to reveal my identity was almost overpowering. I wished I had never embarked on this mad escapade, setting a trap for myself and walking right into it. It would have been wiser to have marched boldly to the front door and announced myself openly and honestly. Knowing my mother as I knew her now, I felt she would not have turned me away. Of course, it would have been a shock to her, but after all the pain and misunderstanding of the past, we could have grown to know each other, not as employer and employee, but as two people who belonged together. I wondered if it were too late even now. Lulled by the warmth of the fire and friendliness, I stood on the brink of indecision, feeling confident that nothing could go wrong.

There was the sudden sound of car wheels on gravel and the roar of an engine which I knew well. It belonged to Matthew's powerful Mercedes. In an instant the atmosphere changed; the three of us sat listening. Why none of us spoke, I could never, afterward, understand. I was the only one who knew that Matthew brought news, and even that didn't justify my sudden apprehension.

Then he was standing in the doorway, looking across the room at the three of us. I could feel an excitement about him. I had a strange feeling that Lyonhurst itself seemed to hold its breath, and then the even stronger feeling that, although his glance was focused on my mother, it flickered momentarily toward myself and away again, so swiftly that I couldn't even swear that I had seen it.

He walked deliberately across the room to the wing chair, took Katherine's hands in his, and said gently, "I have kept you waiting a long time, I know, but it has been worth it. I have done what you asked me to do."

My mother gave an inarticulate cry and I saw David's arm go swiftly around her shoulders. I looked on, an outsider completely in the dark.

Matthew said softly, "There's no need to be nervous or afraid, Katherine. You will love her, I am sure of that." He turned to the door and called, "Come in, my dear."

A girl entered. She stood there hesitantly — shy, appealing, and extremely pretty. She had fair skin and blonde hair, an English rose.

My mother shook herself free of David's steadying arm and rose, trembling. She tried to take a step forward, and failed. I realized that I, too, had risen to my feet and was standing there, staring across the room, watching Matthew Deacon as he went to the girl and, taking her hand, said gently, "Come and meet your mother, Belinda."

14

I HEARD a splintering sound from a long way off, but didn't realize until later that it was a glass slipping from my fingers and shattering at my feet. Shock and incredulity stunned me. This wasn't reality. This was a scene set upon an unfamiliar stage, with unreal and unlikely characters making their entrances and speaking ridiculous lines.

I was staring at the girl, and at the man who had brought her into the room, but although his lips were moving, his words failed to register in my mind. Then someone spoke beside me.

"What's the matter, Gillian? Are you feeling faint?"

It took me some time to realize that it was David and that he was looking at me intently. No one else heeded me. Not the solicitor, nor my mother, nor the girl *who claimed to be myself!*

I was suddenly alert and angry, ready to do battle, ready to expose this girl as the fraud she was.

And expose myself as a fraud also?

"Her papers are in order," Matthew was saying. "Her birth certificate and all identification. There is no disputing the evidence, and I am satisfied with it legally."

My mother's face crumpled and in one swift movement the girl who called herself Belinda gathered her close. It was very touching — and very well timed.

I stood by, inarticulate and helpless, as Matthew Deacon produced a document which he handed to my mother. "Here is her birth certificate. Pierre Lemaître registered her birth after the event and later, as promised, gave her his name by deed poll. Of course you know all this."

"Yes. His sister told me in a letter. We kept in touch, or tried to, until the war severed communications."

I scarcely heard my mother's voice, for I was staring mutely at the paper in her hand. From where I stood I could not examine it in detail, but, if it was a birth certificate, it could only be a copy. It had to be, for the real one, my own, lay in the black deed box which Françoise lodged with her bank in London, along with all personal papers belonging to us both. That meant that I had to get to London at the earliest opportunity and gain access to the deed box, to which only Françoise held a key, and to whom no one but she would be given permission to open.

That thought pulled me up sharply against an impenetrable wall. Only Françoise could help me now, and where was she? Rome, Florence, or Paris — Hilda McClellan would know in which city the current shows were being held, but would she dare to contact her? Knowing Françoise, and knowing Hilda, I also knew that the secretary would never run the slightest risk of incurring the wrath of her employer, or run counter to her instructions. "Bother me when I am at the dress shows, at your peril!" I had heard Françoise say this a dozen times. All the same, I had to do so, I had to track her down quickly.

Katherine touched the girl's cheek with a trembling hand, saying in a tone of wonder, "Belinda, my child! *My* child, mine and Pierre's! Oh, Matthew, is it really true?"

"Really true," he confirmed. "Ask her to tell you all she remembers of her father. Find out for yourself."

I wanted to shout, "Don't be ridiculous! She can't remember a thing about him — *my* father! How can she, when I can't myself?" Although my lips opened, the words died before being uttered, for I had nothing to substantiate them. No proof. No evidence. Nothing. And she, apparently, had.

The solicitor continued briskly: "Everything is settled, everything certain. I have checked and double-checked." He gave an apologetic little laugh as he went on: "I'm afraid my thoroughness must have embarrassed Belinda. No one likes to have his word doubted and lawyers are tiresomely suspicious. That is why things were not settled so quickly as we hoped. You thought I was being dilatory, didn't you, Katherine? Certainly David did. But I assure you I was not. With so much at stake, I had to be absolutely sure. I checked on her entire history. Poor Belinda, you went through quite an inquisition, didn't you? And all this took time, even after I had managed to run her to earth."

"And where did you run her to earth, Deacon?"

It was David who spoke. His words brought the girl's glance around to him and despite my confusion I was aware that he caught her attention. He attracted her. I saw quick interest in her eyes.

Matthew Deacon saw it, too, and somehow I felt that he was displeased.

The girl said, "Please, ran to earth, what does that mean?"

Her English was good, with just the faintest suggestion of a French accent.

"To find a trace," David explained.

The girl's wide and innocent eyes regarded him in surprise.

"Where else could M'sieur Deacon find me, but at my home in France, where I have lived all my life?"

She sounded a little indignant, and immediately my mother said, "You must not tax her with questions, David, not at a moment like this. It is sufficient that Matthew has found her, that she is here. I have waited so long!"

The girl put an arm about her. "I

will let no one upset you," she declared. "That is why I'm here: to take care of you, to stay with you always. All my life, I've dreamed of meeting you and of coming here, to Lyonhurst."

David asked bluntly, "Then why haven't you done so, mademoiselle? You had only to get on a plane or boat, then take a train to Oakwell, and arrive."

"Without invitation, m'sieur?" The girl's large, lovely eyes registered astonishment. "I could not do that! I thought — I always understood — "

"What Belinda is trying to say," Matthew cut in, "is that she believed she wouldn't be welcome here. She told me so at our first meeting. It was a natural supposition in view of the fact that her mother had never tried to trace her — or so she believed." He looked compassionately at Katherine. "I have explained the reason for that. She understands now how desperately you wanted to and how you were prevented."

My mind was suddenly calm and I knew that if I spoke I should do so quite steadily. I kept silent for one reason only; I was determined to let this girl go right ahead and hang herself. She couldn't hope to get away with this masquerade. Sooner or later she would trip herself up, and when that happened it would be my cue to enter.

Besides, there was a lot I wanted to find out. A thousand questions clamored in my mind. Not so much who she was, but how she came to assume my identity — and, above all, *why*. She couldn't be here, as I was, solely out of curiosity. Producing a faked birth certificate was a criminal offense and only worth risking if the stakes were high.

My mother quavered pathetically. "But I did try, my child. Believe me, I did try to trace you."

The new Belinda answered gently, "Let us not talk about that, *Maman*. It distresses you, I can tell."

"But I want to. I want you to know just what happened. I wrote a letter without my father's knowledge and gave it to Harriet, who mailed it for me secretly to the last address in the Auvergne from which Françoise had written. Apart from that, there had only been a telegram — giving me news of Pierre's death. My father intercepted it and read it to me, when it came anonymously from London. Oh, yes, he let me see it. He seemed glad to do so, for, of course, he never forgave Pierre. The telegram had been handed in at Leicester Square post office, one of the busiest in London, where faces were unlikely to be remembered, and the name and address on the back of the original form proved to be nonexistent. That was a cover-up for the agent of the Maquis who had taken the risk of getting the news to me."

"But how did you find out all this, *Maman*?"

"Harriet did so. Before my father destroyed the telegram I noted the name of the post office and the time of dispatch, and on her very next free afternoon Harriet departed for London, telling my father she was visiting her sister at Maidstone. The telegram was traced and, bless her, she even persuaded the clerk at the post office to give her a copy of it, but apart from that the journey was quite unfruitful. I had to wait until the war ended, and then I wrote to Françoise at her old address in Mont-Dore, hoping against hope that she still lived there. Harriet mailed the letter for me, for I could never take a step from this house without my father's knowledge. But, alas, it found its way back, months later, marked 'unknown.'"

"And what did my tyrannical grandfather have to say about that, *Maman*?"

"He never knew, my dear, thanks to Harriet. It was her job to take the morning mail to my father's study each day, so it was perfectly simple for her to withdraw the letter and give it back to me. I have much to thank dear Harriet for."

"Your father was an obstinate and unreasonable man!" Matthew burst out. I was surprised by the intensity of his anger, but secretly shared it.

"That may be so," Katherine answered quietly, "but now is not the time to remember it. He tried to atone at his death."

"If you can call that atonement!"

"It was a great concession for a man of so strong a will."

212

"You should have appealed to my father," Matthew Deacon said. "He was alive in those days and had your interest at heart. He thought the world of both you and your mother."

"I know, but to enlist his help would have been a perilous risk. My father swore that he would never acknowledge his illegitimate granddaughter, so what would defiance have achieved? It would only have antagonized him further and, in anger, his punishment could be hard. If you think I was a coward, you are right. All I had courage to do was to wait, and hope, and pray, and when the will was read it seemed that all had been answered. You were to be found, Belinda, brought to Lyonhurst, and your future placed in my hands."

"Providing she qualifies," Matthew commented cynically. "Don't forget the stipulations."

"And don't forget that I am involved in them, too. I have authority now — more than I have ever had. I shall use it, but I shall also respect my father's wishes. Had he not been confident that I would, he would never have imposed them."

213

I had the extraordinary feeling that I stood outside the scene, a detached onlooker observing the players — my mother, tremulous with joy; the solicitor, listening and watching with satisfaction and a touch of human understanding which lifted him out of the cold legal rut; the doctor, quiet but alert, missing nothing, pleased because his patient's daughter had been found, but keeping a watchful eye for any adverse effect which excitement might have on her. And the girl herself — blue eyes, fair skin, blonde hair, all my mother's physical attributes which I so singularly lacked. But were these attributes so unusual? There were thousands of blue-eyed blondes in the world, and it must have taken more than her coloring to convince a shrewd lawyer that she was no fraud.

In all fairness to Matthew, I had to admit that he was not responsible for this girl's duplicity and couldn't be blamed for being taken in by her. Her identification papers were apparently in order. He had worked painstakingly for this moment, and not merely from a sense of duty. He had searched for

Katherine's missing daughter because it was tremendously important to her.

But why was it so important to the girl? Who was she, and why should she pretend to be someone else, arming herself with fraudulent proof to substantiate her claim?

There was a tap on the drawing-room door, and Harriet stood on the threshold, surprised and questioning. "Harriet, dear Harriet, she is here, my daughter! Mr. Deacon has found her!" Harriet took a few steps forward, then stood still, afraid to come farther, so that it was necessary for my mother to hold out her hand and say, "Come, Harriet, you must meet her! Just look at her hair! Touch it, feel it. Wasn't mine the same when I was young? Pierre always loved my hair and prayed that our child's would resemble it, but I used to say, 'I want our baby to be dark, like yourself.' But now I am glad that Belinda has my coloring, for that must have pleased her father."

Harriet was deeply moved, but the girl merely inclined her head in acknowledgment, saying, "How do you do, Harriet?" with distant courtesy.

With a clumsy gesture the woman seized the girl's hand and kissed it, holding it against her wrinkled face. The girl endured the impulsive demonstration, withdrawing as soon as she could, but only Harriet and myself were aware of her distaste. I saw a flush of embarrassment run darkly across the old woman's features as she said hurriedly, "I'll set another place for dinner," and bustled from the room. Somehow I knew that she was thankful to make her escape and that inwardly she was bitterly disappointed.

But my mother was not. She was too affected emotionally to be aware of anyone else's reactions, and far too taken up with her daughter. Little had I dreamed that she had been waiting for this, or that Matthew's quest had been in search of myself.

Katherine said tremulously, "I want to hear everything, my child!"

"About what, *Maman*?"

"Your life, of course. We have so much to catch up with. How many years? Twenty-three? To think that you have been in the world all this time, my own flesh and blood, living a life in which

216

I had no part! You can understand my desire to hear as much as possible and to get to know you? I have had to console myself with — with . . . " She became suddenly confused and her voice trailed away piteously. "I mean, I have had to console myself in other ways . . . "

With an imaginary baby, an imaginary child — the words were left unsaid, but somehow I knew that they shouted in my mother's mind with a terrifying impact. Shutters were unlocked, blinds drawn aside, and she was looking at reality for the first time since she had walked into her old room and picked up the doll with the waxen smile. Her glance now wavered from the girl to the solicitor, from the solicitor to the doctor, and from the doctor to myself, as if seeking confirmation that the thing she feared was not true and that only in her imagination had she cradled that stiff image in her arms.

I knew how important it was to let her think that nothing had been amiss. I read the same thought in David's eyes. From neither of us would Katherine ever learn of her mental lapse. It belonged to the past; it was gone and forgotten.

Then Matthew Deacon said briskly, "My dear Katherine, you must not think of that now. You are not going to delude yourself anymore."

I could have hit him.

"Delude myself?" my mother echoed. "My dear Matthew, what do you mean? In what way have I been deluding myself?"

"In imaging that hideous doll to be your child, of course; calling it by your daughter's name and believing it to be alive."

The girl with the innocent face and the wide blue eyes gave a high-pitched laugh. If she had slapped my mother's face, she couldn't have startled her more. The faded eyes jerked open in surprise, focusing on the girl in pain and disbelief. The girl promptly wiped the amusement from her face, assuming a smile of tenderness and understanding, rapidly and convincingly. Whatever she was, whoever she was, I had to hand it to her — she was a good actress.

Katherine's voice wavered again. "I — I

don't know what you mean, Matthew dear . . . "

David cut in swiftly, "Nor do any of us." His glance was fixed on the solicitor in warning, but the only effect on Matthew was bland surprise.

"My dear Harvey, surely *you* don't indulge in pretense, also?" The man turned back to my mother and finished, "Don't imagine that everyone didn't make allowances for your extraordinary behavior. We were all most sympathetic. You are not the first person to have become unhinged by shock, and after repressing your longing for so many years, a sudden release from it brought its own consequences. It was as simple as that. You had never got over the loss of your daughter. You had yearned for a sight of her, so when your father died, you seized on that doll and — "

"That's enough, Deacon!"

David's voice was sharp, but the solicitor's expression remained one of bland surprise.

"I am only explaining to Katherine how she came to — "

"Go out of my mind?" my mother

219

said quietly. Her voice was no longer uncertain, but calm with an acceptance which surprised me.

"I meant nothing of the sort," Matthew assured her. "If you had gone out of your mind, you would have been placed in a mental home."

"I doubt it," she answered calmly. "I have a very kind and understanding doctor."

This time Matthew really was surprised. If he had expected to shock or hurt poor Katherine, he appeared to have failed. Checkmate, I thought with relish.

What pleased me most of all was the unexpected strength my mother had revealed. Had she withstood her father's domination with the same calm acceptance, knowing herself unable to combat it, but enduring it with dignity and patience? I glimpsed a new aspect of my mother's character, hitherto unsuspected.

Somehow this whole scene, which had started as one of happy reunion, had become sharp with misconception and discord.

The girl made the first attempt to make

up by slipping her arm about Katherine's shoulders and saying, "Dear *Maman*, I have no idea what all this is about, but I am quite sure that M'sieur Deacon, who has worked so hard to bring us together, had no intention of hurting you."

My mother smiled and said, "Of course not, child. Matthew is like a member of the family to me."

For the first time, the words sounded like a chant, an oft-repeated lesson, a commandment learned by heart. I looked at Katherine with a new and inquiring interest. Who had drummed this lesson into her? Matthew himself? What could it gain him — a paltry legacy from a devoted client? That was all she was to him and all she could represent. Once upon a time the Tredgolds had been rich, but their depleted fortune could yield little benefit to anyone now. It could not even maintain Lyonhurst as it should be. The fate of the place was obvious. It would either go under the hammer or, as Mrs. Tracey at the village store had very sensibly suggested, be given over to the National Trust. Only that way could it be restored to its former glory and be handed down to posterity as a valued relic from the past.

I had thought of Mrs. Tracey very little since coming here, although I had taken good care to avoid the village as much as possible, and particularly the vicinity of her shop. I wanted no chance meeting with her, no awkward questions. Isolating myself at this great house on the outskirts of Oakwell had been easy, for shopping was done in Ockenbury, and on the rare occasions when my mother ventured forth, it was always in the ancient Rolls, chauffeured by Buxton. One Sunday, when she was feeling particularly well, we had gone as far as Canterbury for a cathedral service, and once I had walked down to the doctor's surgery to pick up a prescription, but although his house was situated near the center of the village, to get to it didn't necessitate passing Mrs. Tracey's shop. The likelihood of my coming face to face with her was small, and as time was now fast running out, there was little possibility of meeting her again.

Harriet was hovering at the door, unwilling to enter. Matthew saw her and said, "Harriet's well-cooked dinner is in danger of being spoiled. When you settle down at Lyonhurst, ma'am'selle, you must retain Harriet at all costs. She is a treasure. Besides, she is part of the place. It is her home, as it is now yours."

"For a trial period, did you not say, m'sieur?"

Matthew waved a negligent hand.

"A mere formality, my dear. A stipulation of the will and, I think your mother will agree, a very stupid one."

"I am sure my father had good reason for that clause, although I admit it may seem illogical," Katherine put in. "I believe it was meant as a test of myself, hence his stipulation about the part I am to play in it."

"And, as usual, *he* made the rules; *he* set the stipulations. Every decision had to be his, regardless of the wishes of others. You should have defied him, Katherine. But then, you were always weak, weren't you? Weak in every way."

His words brought a sharp protest from Harriet.

"Oh, *sir*! How can you be so cruel?

You, of all people! It isn't like you, Mr. Deacon. I've never known you to be cruel before." She stared at the solicitor in disbelief.

He was immediately penitent, switching on the charm with that unfailing ability of his. "Forgive me," he said, "but I can't help feeling indignant about Sir Humphrey's treatment of his daughter and the ridiculous stipulations of the will."

"But Kathy, dear Miss Kathy, why abuse her, sir? Hasn't she suffered enough?"

The woman was still shocked, still unable to believe that the man she regarded as a paragon could reveal a flaw. "Oh, Mr. Deacon, sir," she continued, "you couldn't possibly condemn Miss Kathy for falling in love!"

"Of course not," he said gently.

"I will not allow him to," said the girl called Belinda.

The right words uttered by the wrong person. It was I who should be standing there, defending my mother. Every instinct urged me to, but wisdom compelled me to remain silent. Wait, it said. Bide your time. Listen, and watch, and wait.

Matthew smiled at the girl with that potent charm which he had focused on myself more than once. But he wasn't aware of me now. I was merely an employee standing in the background, of whom no one was taking the slightest notice.

But a short while ago the doctor had. I suddenly remembered that he had stooped and picked up the pieces of my shattered glass, that he had looked at me in concern, that he had asked me what was wrong and I had given no answer. I looked at him now. I needed a friend badly, but just how much of a friend would this man be?

Matthew said briskly, "We are wasting time and I am to blame, I fear. This meeting has been one for which I have worked so hard that you must all excuse a natural excitement and a regrettable tendency to allow emotion to overcome self-control. A lawyer can't always be coldly logical. He can be as human as the next man — and, I suppose, as bigoted. As your solicitor, Kathy, my personal feelings about your father's will shouldn't have been betrayed, but as a friend may I be forgiven for being swayed by sympathy for you? The will was too exacting, but if you are satisfied with your father's motives, far be it from me to dispute them. And now, dear Harriet, if you would bear with us for just a few more minutes, I am sure that Mademoiselle Lemaître would like to freshen up after her journey."

My mother gave a little cry of concern.

"How very thoughtless of me! Harriet, she must have my old room, of course, but while it is made ready she must make use of mine."

The girl kissed her swiftly.

"Just a quick wash and a change, *Maman*. I am a little travel-stained and weary."

"Why?" David asked bluntly. "You haven't traveled from France today, have you? I understood that you had undergone a fairly long interrogation, a lengthy legal examination. Surely so much investigation couldn't have been accomplished between arriving in this country and being brought to Lyonhurst

226

on the same day, even allowing for the fact that the coast of France is merely across the channel from Kent and that planes take a mere twenty minutes from Le Touquet to Lydd?"

"What an inquiring mind you have, Harvey!" It was Matthew who spoke now. "But you are quite right. Belinda was brought to London a few days ago, direct from Paris. I went to meet and talk with her. When I was absolutely satisfied with the result of my searches, I arranged for her to come to Kent. In fact, I drove to town today to fetch her, bringing her straight here. Sixty-odd miles isn't an excessive journey, but quite long enough to make a fastidious young woman want to freshen up."

David merely lifted his eyebrows in acknowledgment. The girl looked at him, wide-eyed and puzzled. "You do not like me, m'sieur?" she asked in a tone of injured bewilderment. "You do not trust me?"

She was quite disarming, so I wasn't surprised when David smiled and said, "On the contrary, ma'am'selle, I find you very charming. And why should I mistrust you?"

She shrugged expressively.

"I have heard that Englishmen are suspicious of Frenchwomen. A little afraid of them — no? They think we are very wicked!"

Matthew laughed, and the sound eased the tension. My mother looked on indulgently and Harriet's face relaxed. I was the only one who was irritated; disappointed, too, for I had believed the doctor to be discerning, a man who could assess people. Apparently I was wrong. He could be deceived by a pretty face as easily as any other man. Any hope of having him as my ally died at that moment.

15

THE girl usurped my place at dinner. Normally I sat beside Katherine, but now I had been moved to the foot of the table. If anything could have emphasized my own relegation to the background, it was that.

Not that my unimportance in this household needed emphasizing tonight. From the moment the girl arrived I was overlooked, forgotten. It was inevitable, of course, and I was even a little glad, for in my present emotional state I wanted no one's attention. From behind a screen of anonymity I was able to watch and listen without anyone being aware, hiding my anxiety and bewilderment in silence. I was all too painfully aware that my position was that of an employee who would not be here much longer, for my services would no longer be required.

Now I knew why my engagement had been only temporary, and the circumstances upon which it depended.

With the arrival of a daughter to keep Katherine company, a companion was superfluous. All my mother required was the affection and companionship of someone belonging to her and, ironically, if anyone could have given her that almost from the moment of arrival, it was myself.

I realized now that dishonesty had been my worst possible course and, far from being clever, I had been incredibly stupid, with the result that this unknown girl, with her apparently conclusive evidence, was streets ahead of me. She was touching the winning post and I could not even come within challenging distance.

Time was the all-important factor. "*Time is a maniac scattering dust . . .*" I quoted Tennyson unconsciously, aware that beneath my attention to the conversation I was groping for the words which followed, and suddenly they leaped into my mind. " . . . *Life a fury, throwing flame.*" My determination had to be the same. I had to act, and soon.

Suddenly I remembered my father's Bible, locked in my wardrobe upstairs. It would be something to produce, but not conclusive evidence that I was Katherine Tredgold's daughter. A Bible in French, inscribed with the name Pierre Armand Philippe Lemaître, presented to him by his parents on the occasion of his confirmation at the Basilique Notre-Dame-du-Port, de Clermont, proved nothing without the support of my birth certificate and documentary evidence relating to the conferring of his name on me by deed poll, and all such evidence was locked away in a banker's vault in London, to which I could not gain access without the written consent of my aunt.

So the Bible alone was not enough. Anyone could come by a Bible bearing someone else's name — I had seen them, tragic memorials to the forgotten, buried on secondhand bookstalls in the Tottenham Court Road, and had no doubt that their French counterparts could be found among the bookstalls on the Left Bank, so my claim would have to be substantiated by something far more convincing than that. Infallible proof was what I needed, proof which would expose this girl's fraudulent evidence beyond a shadow of doubt, and only Françoise could provide me with that.

Always it came back to Françoise. Without her help, I was lost.

I glanced across the table at my usurper, envying her blonde loveliness and hating my own snub nose, dark hair, high cheekbones, and too large mouth. Long ago I had accepted the fact that I was not pretty and never would be, but Françoise had helped me over the awkward self-consciousness of adolescence, and the painful period when a plain-looking girl can suffer agonies, developing in me a flair for dress and the ability to choose clothes best suited to my type. Her taste was infallible, and in passing it on to me she had given me self-confidence, so that I no longer worried about my looks. "You are *distingué*, little one," she would say. "That is far more valuable than mere prettiness, because it can last a woman throughout her life, whereas prettiness offen fades rapidly."

Dear Françoise. She had given me more than the Tredgolds had ever done. She had opened the doors to life for me, and a good life it was, interesting, enjoyable, with an aim and a meaning. Her brilliant career had spurred me to make my mark as a dress designer and to work as hard as herself, so why should I sentimentalize over a great barn of a manor standing in the middle of nowhere, subjected to encroaching neglect and constant financial anxiety?

I became aware that, for the first time this evening, Matthew Deacon was speaking to me. Until now, he had spared me no more than an occasional glance. To him, I had no part to play in tonight's drama, but ever since his arrival there had been an air of suppressed excitement about him. I supposed it was understandable. He had been appointed to search for the missing daughter and he had succeeded. The search couldn't have been easy, for Françoise Lemaître had apparently disappeared into the blue with her brother's child, leaving no trace. Naturally, the solicitor would have begun his search in the Auvergne.

How then had this girl heard of his search and why had she thought it worthwhile to assume my identity? *And what had made her so confident that the real Belinda Lemaître would remain unfound?*

All this I intended to find out. For this I would remain silent, and listen and watch and wait.

★ ★ ★

"You could ride together," Matthew was saying. "Gillian is becoming quite expert. She is competent enough not to need my supervision."

For the first time the girl looked at me. Apart from a brief introduction, she had paid little attention to my presence. Now she smiled in the friendliest fashion and said, "I would like that very much, ma'am'selle, if you would."

I agreed. My voice was light and pleasant, exactly as it should be, reflecting no mistrust or animosity. Perhaps my own talent as an actress wasn't too bad, I reflected wryly.

Then she said, "For the short time you remain here, ma'am'selle, you must consider yourself free to make the most of whatever facilities Lyonhurst offers you. My mother will naturally need you very little with me here." The girl turned to Matthew. "When does Miss Conrad's employment terminate? If she has another appointment waiting for her, I think we should release her at once."

Before he had a chance to reply, David cut in. "Gillian will be released from her duties as soon as I think fit, and not before. Allow me to congratulate you on your excellent English, ma'am'selle. It is so fluent as to be almost perfect."

Her wide blue eyes met his quite calmly.

"And why should it not be, m'sieur?"

"For a French girl it is a little unusual."

"I do not see this. In your schools you teach French, do you not?" She shrugged expressively. "We are taught English in our schools."

"With such an excellent accent?"

"*Oui*, m'sieur. Besides, my aunt was always anxious that I should speak my mother's tongue fluently and had me well coached in it."

"Your aunt?" Katherine exclaimed. "How dreadful of me not to inquire after her. She was such a good friend!

But in the excitement of having you here — it is like a dream come true, you understand — ”

"Of course, I understand, *Maman*. And so would Françoise, I am sure."

"Surely she knows you have come? You met Pierre's sister, didn't you, Matthew? Surely she — ”

My mother broke off, looking from one to the other. Something in their faces, a quality of stillness, suggested that they were carefully controlling their reactions, silenced her.

"No, Katherine, I didn't meet her." Matthew shook his head regretfully.

"But why not? In the last letter I received from her she assured me that she would look after Belinda until I could rejoin Pierre. I have always believed, to this day — ”

"She kept her promise, *Maman*, for as long as she was able to." The girl's voice was tinged with sorrow. "I mean that she is dead, *Maman*. She died a few years ago."

Sorrow touched my mother's face. "Poor Françoise," she murmured. "Poor, dear Françoise . . . ”

A sharp and unexpected noise shattered the moment. I realized that I had dropped my fork in astonishment. This was the second time I had betrayed myself in such a way, and I saw David's eyes studying me.

"Are you all right?" he asked. "You've been looking pale all evening."

"Perhaps it's the heat," Matthew put in. "It's a sultry night. I think Gillian should go to bed, don't you, Katherine?"

My mother was looking at me in concern. In another moment she would be ringing for Harriet and asking her to look after me, and that would mean a tray in my room, banishment from everything that was taking place downstairs, exclusion from the conversation — the diabolically cunning tale of this girl who had apparently known about my aunt, but had no idea of what became of her. If the lie had not been so distressing to my mother, I would have laughed aloud. And so, I felt, would Françoise herself.

I protested that I was quite all right, and attacked my food with gusto to prove it.

"Poor Françoise," my mother said again. "She was a wonderful person and a friend to me and now she, too, has gone . . . "

"But I am here, *Maman*. You have me to live for."

"Yes, indeed!" My mother's voice lifted, touched with a happiness I had not heard in it before.

Very soon afterward dinner came to an end. We returned to the drawing room for coffee. David terminated the evening, however, by leaving early. As he rose, Belinda turned to me and said in a low voice, "Please do not wait up for my mother. I will put her to bed. We would naturally like to be alone together. We have so much to discuss."

It was a dismissal and I had no choice but to accept it.

Alone in my room I took the Bible from its hiding place in the wardrobe. The thin, faintly perfumed pages rustled between my fingers. I felt calm and reassured. Faith was indestructible if one held on to it.

★ ★ ★

I had no desire to go to bed. I was too alert, and too curious. Right at this moment Harriet would be preparing my mother's old room, and the thought of that impostor sleeping there filled me with a sense of outrage.

Something urged me to take one last glance at it before it was occupied by the girl with the innocent blue eyes. Without further thought I walked swiftly along the corridor, pausing on the threshold as I saw Harriet working busily within. Freshly aired sheets and blankets were ready to be put on the bed, and with Buxton's aid she was replacing the mattress with another.

"Oh, it's you, Miss Conrad; I'm glad. I thought for a moment it was Miss Belinda, and the room isn't ready."

"Couldn't she use a guest room tonight?"

"Yes, but her ladyship wouldn't like it. Nor would the young lady herself, I fancy. She certainly knows her rights, does that one."

"You sound as if you haven't taken to her, Harriet."

"Have you?" the housekeeper answered cryptically.

"I don't know her yet."

"Nor will you have the chance to, I'm thinking. Now that she's here there'll be no further use for you at Lyonhurst, mark my words. And I'll be sorry about that. That's all right, Buxton — I can manage now. Take the other mattress away to air."

The old man shuffled away and I lent a hand with the bedmaking.

"The radiator in this room isn't nearly hot enough yet."

"The room seems warm and well aired to me, Harriet."

"It isn't so bad," she admitted. "I've kept an eye on it all these long years, but there's always a disused feeling about unoccupied rooms." She tucked the sheets in firmly and added, "Well, and what do you think of her?"

"What do you?" I evaded.

"I'll reserve my judgment, as the saying is, but I'll admit I'm a bit disappointed. She's lovely, of course, but so was her mother as a girl, but beyond that — " The old lady sighed as she smoothed the counterpane. "I just don't know. I only hope she makes her mother happy. If she can wipe out all the years of loneliness and sorrow, then I'll take her to my heart, but I don't like the way she walked into this house all ready to take possession."

"Of what, Harriet?"

"She obviously considers it should be hers."

I said carefully, "According to her grandfather's will, I suppose you mean. But weren't there stipulations? Mr. Deacon referred to them."

"Aye, so there were. It wouldn't be like my late master to be generous without dictating terms."

"What are they, Harriet?"

She gave me a wry smile.

"There you go again, Miss Curious!"

"Why shouldn't I? I came here to look after Lady Katherine and, as I have already said to you more than once, anything that concerns her, concerns me."

"Not for much longer, I'm afraid."

"Doctor Harvey says I cannot leave until he releases me."

"Does he, now? Well, for once I'm pleased with him."

"Oh, come, Harriet, be honest and admit you really like him."

She gave a dry laugh. "I suppose I do, although he annoys me at times. He seems to like taking people down a peg or two."

"He likes debunking pomposity. He takes a kick at the Establishment whenever it needs it, and that I applaud. He is honest and fair-minded and puts his patient's welfare before anything."

Harriet glanced about the room.

"She has certainly brought enough luggage, hasn't she? That's a good sign. It shows she intends to stay. Of course, if she hopes to qualify, she has to."

"Qualify for what?"

"For what she considers should be hers by right, as I said before."

"This is where I came in," I retorted lightly. Harriet was unpacking a pigskin suitcase and the quality of it caught my eye, as did the contents. These clothes were expensive.

"Like mother, like daughter," Harriet quoted. "Miss Kathy loved clothes when she was young, and my, could she choose them! So can her daughter, it seems."

Her real daughter certainly could — Françoise had taught her to. But

242

who had taught this girl and where had the money come from?

"You can tell she's French all right," said old Harriet, impressed. "They certainly know how to dress. Just look at all this underwear!" She had opened another case and now took out some of the sheerest lingerie I had ever seen. Not a single item looked as if it had been worn. Likewise her shoes. Costly, elegant, French, and completely new. The entire wardrobe, suits, coats, dresses, underwear, and shoes, might have been an actress's wardrobe for a leading role.

She had certainly equipped herself well for the part. It would be interesting to know just where she had bought all this, and when.

"There now," said Harriet at length, "I've attended to everything. The room is ready for her whenever she wants to take possession."

It wasn't the first time Harriet had used those words. They seemed to hold a significance which I was anxious to have explained.

"Harriet, if you won't tell me the

details of the will, I shall ask the doctor to. Now that Lady Katherine's daughter is here, her arrival affects my future in this house, so surely I shouldn't be left in the dark any longer?"

"I'd rather her ladyship told you herself. Now that Miss Belinda is here there's no reason why you shouldn't know, so I expect Lady Katherine will take you into her confidence. There isn't time to talk right now. Miss Belinda will be coming to bed."

"Not yet. They were settling down for a long and intimate chat when I came up."

Harriet switched on a bedside lamp casting a soft glow, and I glanced around appreciatively. It was a pretty, feminine room, perfect for the daughter of the house. I felt a sudden lump in my throat and turned to the door abruptly, scarcely heeding Harriet's answer.

"Well, in that case," she was saying, "I dare say I could answer any questions you care to ask."

I couldn't speak, couldn't even see through a blur of tears. I stammered, "Not now, Harriet, I'm tired, and it's not important — "

"Not important to you, I admit, but very much so to my mistress and to her daughter. I only hope Miss Belinda will prove to be all we've prayed for."

16

NEXT morning, I took breakfast to my mother's room as usual. She looked rested and happy.

"You slept well."

"The best night I have had in a long time, my dear, and can you wonder? I have waited for years."

No need to ask for what. The whole situation had come flooding back into my mind immediately on waking, like a curtain rising on a scene one wished to forget. A girl had walked into this house, bearing my name, my identity, and assuming my place. And I had let her.

Not for long, however, I resolved. I would trace Françoise and get the counterevidence I needed, indisputable proof which would bring this girl's house of cards tumbling down about her head.

Today was Saturday. It had been too late to telephone Hilda McClellan last night, had I even known where to contact

246

her after office hours. The office of Françoise et Cie closed on weekends, so any contact with her secretary was out of the question until Monday, but if Katherine didn't need me tomorrow, I could get up to town for the day in the hope that an unexpected letter from Françoise might await me at the flat.

It was a forlorn hope, for I knew what a bad correspondent she was. Françoise preferred telephoning to letters, and not even that, unless in an emergency.

Any chance to question my mother about the possibility of freedom tomorrow was forestalled when she said, "Belinda wants to explore the house and grounds, my dear, and knowing it would be too much for me, she asked if you could show her around."

I was startled. Why me? Why should this girl want my company? She had scarcely spoken two words to me last night, and certainly had shown no sign of wanting to know me better. Quite the contrary. She had made it plain that I could well be spared.

"I was glad to consent," my mother continued, "for I know how familiar you are with everything. You have developed a great interest in the place, haven't you, Gillian? This has pleased and touched me, for I hardly expected anyone so young, and particularly a stranger, to take Lyonhurst to their heart as you have done."

I tried to murmur something about old houses being fascinating, with personalities of their own, but my lips moved stiffly and unwillingly. Katherine seemed not to notice. She was eating her breakfast with greater enjoyment than usual and, as she did so, chatted on happily.

"I'm delighted that Belinda wants to get to know her new home. She is very young and I wouldn't have been surprised had she regarded it as a musty old museum of a place. Her life has been so very different from mine, her background a complete contrast."

"I'll be glad to show her everything and to tell her what little I know of its history — all, that is, that I have managed to glean from Harriet and Buxton. I should have thought that Mr. Deacon was the person to tell her more."

To my surprise, my mother said almost

sharply, "Why, my dear? Why should he know more than yourself?"

"He is a native of Oakwell, born and brought up here, son of a local family which has had close connections with Lyonhurst for a very long time."

"That is true," Katherine acknowledged, and it seemed to me that she relaxed again. "But Matthew is a very busy man, with professional affairs to attend to, so he could hardly spare the time to act as a guide to Belinda."

He had spared plenty of time for my riding lessons, though, I thought, and as if sensing this Katherine continued, "He asked me to tell you that if you and my daughter wish to ride together, you can both borrow horses from his stable. I gather you have made great strides as a horsewoman."

I laughed. "Well, at least I manage to fall off less frequently!"

"Tomorrow is Sunday, so Matthew will be free and you can all ride together."

"I was hoping you might let me have the whole day free, Lady Katherine. I would like to visit friends in London."

"That isn't to be thought of!" cried a

voice from the door. "When am I going to have a chance to get to know my mother's companion? She was singing your praises so loudly last night that I know I can never hope to emulate you, but at least, before you leave Lyonhurst altogether, I hope to learn much from you, otherwise how can I take your place?"

I looked at her. She had entered without knocking.

"There will be no need for you to take my place, ma'am'selle."

"Meaning that you are not leaving?"

"Meaning that when I do Lady Katherine will no longer require a paid companion."

"In that case, I must get to know you as a friend," the girl answered with a smile. It was warm, spontaneous, and friendly, the sort of smile to which anyone would respond. I didn't want to, but forced myself to do so.

She stooped and kissed my mother. She had walked with a fluid movement which, I felt, was rather studied. I wondered where, and how, she had learned it.

"You cannot spare Mademoiselle

tomorrow, can you, *Maman*? I heard you saying just now that we could ride together and I should like that very much."

"Mr. Deacon will ride with you, mademoiselle," I put in. "He is a wonderful rider. I know, because he taught me."

"But I wish to ride with *you*. I need young companionship in this house."

I saw a fleeting shadow touch my mother's face. The girl might have charm, but she certainly had no tact. Katherine said hurriedly, "Of course you do, my dear; Harriet and myself are no companions for youth."

"I knew you would understand, *Maman*." The girl's voice was honeyed and she gave my mother a swift and affectionate embrace. "Miss Conrad's friends in London must be allowed to spare her, must they not? After all, it isn't much to ask, is it? No more than a kindly gesture to a stranger."

"It would be a kindly gesture to keep your mother company," I retorted.

"Gillian!"

Katherine's tone of surprise was tinged

with reproof, but I felt no guilt. I continued calmly: "I haven't felt the need for young companionship in this house. I have been content with yourself and Harriet."

"You have been paid to be," the girl reminded me sweetly.

My mother said pacifically, "Would it really be asking too much of you to forgo your trip to London tomorrow?"

You don't know how much, I thought wryly, but said politely that, of course, it would not and that I should be pleased to ride with her daughter. Then I picked up her breakfast tray and carried it down to the kitchen.

Harriet viewed it with approval.

"Her ladyship has eaten more than usual. That's a good sign."

"Yes, Harriet."

The woman looked at me.

"Is there anything wrong, my dear?"

"Nothing at all," I lied, thinking that nothing could possibly be more wrong. I was bound to this house — for how long? How soon before I could get to London, hoping for some word or message from Françoise; how long before

I could even contact Hilda McClellan and, when I did, how much could I tell her? Nothing. Hilda wasn't the kind of person in whom I could confide. I had to tread circumspectly. The only person whose help I could enlist was Françoise's.

When I returned to my mother's bedroom, I found she was already up. Belinda had run her bath and was now standing before the wardrobe, surveying its contents and saying, "And what will you wear today, *Maman*? Not this — or this! *Mon dieu*, we must see about new clothes for you! These are all outmoded!"

"They may be a little outmoded," I said, "but Lady Katherine wears them well."

The girl glanced at me over her shoulder, making a delicate little *moue* of distaste.

"Ah, but you are only accustomed to stodgy British clothes, Miss Conrad."

"On the contrary . . . " I began, checking myself sharply.

"On the contrary?" she echoed.

"On the contrary, we have many dress

253

designers in this country who are world renowned and we have beautiful ready-made clothes."

"I never buy off the rack," the girl said distastefully.

"You are lucky not to be obliged to, ma'am'selle. Only the rich are so fortunate."

She colored, realizing that she had made a mistake. She was not supposed to be a rich girl. She was the impoverished, long-lost, discarded daughter deprived of her life's inheritance. She added hurriedly, "I have always worked hard for my living, ma'am'selle. I have had to."

"Then you have obviously been very successful," I retorted. "At what?"

She made no answer. She had the advantage over me in being able to ignore an employee in this house should she feel so inclined. She flicked through my mother's clothes again and I went to her side, took down a lightweight mulberry dress which was one of Katherine's favorites, and said, "Lady Katherine has four morning dresses. She wears them in turn, so the selection is easy."

I closed the wardrobe, laid the dress

on the bed, and went into the bathroom to help my mother. I wrapped her in an enveloping bath towel and dried her gently. She sighed and said, "I shall miss you, Gillian, when you have gone."

"I shall miss you, Lady Katherine."

"But Doctor Harvey won't release you yet. He said so last night. I shall persuade him not to release you at all."

"I must go sometime soon."

"Why, are you tired of looking after me?"

"You know I'm not, but with your daughter to keep you company, you really have no need of me."

"We both have need of you. She was right about needing young companionship in this house."

"There are neighbors with daughters, surely?"

"Yes, and she must meet them all."

"In that case, she will not lack companions and I shall not be missed."

"I shall miss you. Harriet will miss you. Lyonhurst itself will miss you, for you have become part of it very quickly."

Her words gave me pleasure.

"And the doctor will miss you," she

added unexpectedly.

"That I don't believe!"

"Then you are not so observant as I, my child."

It was extraordinary, the way in which my pleasure promptly increased. When we went downstairs I found that all my previous despondency and irritation had vanished. I was able to face the pseudo-Belinda with ease. After settling my mother in her chair, I said, "If Lady Katherine can spare me now, ma'am'selle, I shall be glad to show you either the house or the park."

★ ★ ★

I took Belinda into the old part of the house, the shut-up, disused wing from which my mother had retreated after her father's death. Periodically Buxton opened all the windows and made ineffectual attempts to combat the gathering layers of dust, yet nothing could relieve the musty atmosphere of decay and age, emphasized by furniture shrouded in dust sheets and curtains which looked as if they were never drawn. They hung in rigid, dusty folds from immense scalloped and befringed pelmets.

It was cold, despite the summer sun penetrating the immense floor-to-ceiling windows.

We stood in the middle of the great, marble-floored hall and looked about us. The wide staircases, which swept upward from either side, were elegant and impressive, trod only by the footsteps of the dead. From the minstrels' gallery above I could almost hear the strains of forgotten music, but it was a desolate sound, sighing beneath the vaulted roof.

The girl shuddered. I made no comment, sensing her distaste. I led her through tall double doors with faded gilt moldings and beautiful crystal knobs, into high-ceilinged rooms where previous generations had dined and entertained and spent evenings of relaxation at spinet and embroidery frame, shielding their faces from immense fires with graceful Sheraton fire screens. Shades of the age of elegance, I thought rather wistfully. Echoes of a leisured past in which women were cosseted and waited upon and their menfolk led lives of their own. I didn't envy them, for in return for luxury and a life of ease, women of the upper classes were rewarded with loneliness and very often tyranny — an inheritance which my grandfather had perpetuated.

We had climbed the stairs and reached the long ballroom before the girl finally spoke.

"Well, this is one place which could be put to good use! Surely there cannot be one hotel in England which has a ballroom to touch this. Obviously, that is what I must do with Lyonhurst, after modernizing it, of course. Private bathrooms for all bedrooms. Decent public rooms and bars. A good restaurant and grill, and this ballroom with the best bands that money can buy. Tourists will flock here and I will be in the money then!"

"You wouldn't do such a thing!" I protested. "You couldn't."

"Don't be ridiculous. You don't expect me to inherit a monstrosity such as this and not get the best possible return from it, surely?"

"I don't see it as a monstrosity."

"As what, then?"

"As architecturally beautiful, even magnificent."

"And therefore admirably suited to become a palatial hotel. Personally, I prefer something more modern, but tourists, particularly Americans, fall for the period piece, providing all modern conveniences go with it."

"For someone who has lived all her life in another country, you speak very colloquial English, ma'am'selle."

She gave me a sharp look.

"Why shouldn't I?"

"No reason at all, if you have *not* spent all your life in France."

She smiled enigmatically.

"Who said I had spent all my life in France? English girls travel abroad. So do the French."

"From that remark, and from the way in which you speak English, I take it you have traveled a lot."

"Take it any way you like, Miss Conrad."

There was a note of challenge in her voice.

"Your idea of turning Lyonhurst into

an hotel would be contrary to your mother's wishes."

"And how do you know her wishes?"

"I don't, but I can imagine them. The thought of her home being turned into a plushy hotel would be distasteful to her, so if I were you I would put such ideas out of your head."

"But you are not me. Kindly remember that."

The girl walked slowly down the long ballroom, glancing at the paneled walls as she went. On these, as on the main staircases of the house, family portraits gazed down disdainfully — forbidding features, hawk-like noses, cold and expressionless eyes.

"They were an unattractive lot, weren't they?" said the girl. "The Tredgolds certainly never produced any beauties."

"They produced Kathy."

"Kathy? Oh, you mean my mother!"

"Who else? And what has happened to your French accent, ma'am'selle?"

I was satisfied to see a swift color rush to her cheeks. She took a sharp little breath, turned it into a laugh, and said, "Well, I have to relax sometime, haven't

I? My mother was expecting a girl with a French accent so how could I disappoint her? Mr. Deacon said it was important to play the part well."

"Play the part? Do you mean that you are neither French nor the real daughter?"

"I mean nothing of the kind. I am both. I teach English at an expensive girls' school just outside Paris. They come from all over the world, and to speak English with an English accent is one of the objectives. I had a natural gift for my mother's tongue and always wanted to speak it like a native, so after my earlier tuition at school I went to an Englishwoman who lived in Limoges. She taught me privately, helping me to overcome all trace of an accent, although I can assume it at will. It was my ability to speak English without error or effort which landed me the job at the finishing school. I am worth my weight in francs to them and well they know it! I have taught girls from all over Europe, plus practically every state in America, to speak English as it should be spoken — in the way which you yourself speak it, Miss Conrad."

"I am glad you think I speak it well."

That seemed to exhaust both our conversation and our tour of the ballroom. I led the way into the north wing of the house, which I had only explored once before. It was the coldest of all. The girl shivered and said, "Let's go outside. I'll see the rest another day."

I led her to the end of the long landing, to tall windows overlooking the park. The view from there was one of the finest. I opened the windows and stepped out onto the stone balcony. The view was breathtaking. She joined me and I moved aside to make room for her. The balcony was small, surrounded by copingstones carved by masons who had been artists as well as craftsmen. Similar balconies flanked other windows which stretched across the facade of the house, giving it an elegant symmetry of design.

"Isn't it lovely . . . " I began, then drew a sharp breath, my heart suddenly pounding and fear contracting my stomach, for as I moved aside to make room for the girl, I leaned against the coping and a sudden movement, accompanied by the sound of stone grating against stone, nearly catapulted me downward. For one sickening moment I leaned over, a hundred feet above the ground, seeing the gravel drive leaping up to meet me. My hands released their grip on the stone and a slab fell with a sickening crash. As it went, I dropped to my knees, bracing my arms against the supporting pillars at each side and so averting a headlong dive through the gap.

It was all over in a minute, but it left me sick and shaken. Only when the immediate danger had passed did I realize that my impostor had clutched me about the waist, pulling me back to safety.

I sat on my heels, looking up at her, unable to speak.

She burst out furiously, "What a ruin of a place! What a ghastly ruin! You might have been killed! Why, the building isn't even safe!"

Wordlessly, we stared through the gap in the balustrade. The copingstone had shattered into fragments on the ground.

I was shaking as I rose.

"Are you all right?" she asked in concern, putting out a hand.

"Quite all right."

"Let's get away from here."

She led me through the open window, closing it firmly behind her. My legs felt ready to buckle under me, but I managed to walk back along the corridor and through the door leading out of the north wing, back through the long ballroom beneath the cold, watching eyes of former Tredgolds, down the stairs, across the vast marble-floored hall and through the door beneath the minstrels' gallery which led into the occupied wing of the house. It was like reaching a haven of refuge — warm, quiet, familiar, and safe.

I began to feel better at once, but I was in no state to return to my mother. "Let's go outside," I said. "I need fresh air."

"You need a drink more."

"Not at this hour. Fresh air will be just as good and probably better."

By mutual consent we turned toward the rear of the house, away from the shattered copingstone lying beneath the front elevation. We emerged onto the terrace which flanked the southern side,

264

and the sun was warm on our faces.

"There's a little Italian arbor at the bottom of the rose garden," I said. "Let's go there."

"I hope it's safe?" she said sarcastically. "Or is it like the rest of the place, liable to crumble at a touch?"

I managed a laugh.

"One faulty balustrade can't be taken as an example of the entire structure."

"You are more tolerant than I, and with less cause. Personally, I think the place is a dump and the only sensible thing to do is to pull it down."

"Then you wouldn't have your luxury hotel," I answered lightly.

"I would build another in its place. There's money in demolition these days. The price of lead is fantastic and there must be enough in the roof alone to make a fortune."

She talks less and less like a French girl, I thought, becoming more and more convinced that she was not. But I said nothing. For one thing, I still felt shaken and in little mood for conversation, and for another I wanted her to do all the talking while I listened.

I led the way to the rose garden, along unkempt paths and then through a shubbery which was a wilderness of weeds and tangled undergrowth, through grounds which were now a jungle of encroaching neglect. We walked for a long time in silence. At length she broke it with an exasperated exclamation.

"It's all so terrible! How could the Tredgolds allow it to sink into such a state!"

"Perhaps they had no choice. Estates such as this cost a lot in maintenance."

"Surely the family has money? I naturally assumed . . . " She broke off, biting her lip.

"You assumed what?"

"That the lawyer told me the truth, of course."

"Which was — ?"

She wasn't to be drawn that easily, however. She cast me a shrewd, sideways glance. "Nothing you need worry about. Nothing which concerns you."

We had reached the little Italian arbor and I sat down on the lichen-covered seat. It was a charming little place — a trysting place for lovers, I thought romantically, but the girl didn't appear to share my view. She eyed the seat with distaste and the unswept paved floor equally so. "Doesn't anyone attend to anything around here? What is that decrepit old man paid to do, I wonder?"

"Buxton? He is handyman and gardener. He does what he can, but he can't cope on his own with grounds of this size."

The girl stood with her back to the arbor and looked around her. The park was rambling and immense, acre upon acre of neglected land. "Good building sites," she remarked briskly. "There's money in land, these days."

"You have a commercial head on your shoulders, ma'am'selle."

"I am glad you think so."

"I wonder how your mother would feel if she heard you. She loves Lyonhurst very dearly."

"I can't share her sentiment. The whole place gives me the creeps."

"I'm sorry to hear that. You won't tell her, will you? It would distress her."

"Perhaps she should be made to face reality."

"Perhaps she has faced it enough."

"And retreated from it, apparently."

"If you are kind, you'll forget what you heard last night. It was thoughtless of Matthew to refer to it."

"I'm glad he did. It let me know what I'm likely to be up against."

"What do you imagine that to be?"

"Need you ask? After all, you are her nurse-companion — that is why I want you to stay until she can be taken proper care of."

"What do you mean?"

"What I say, of course. You don't imagine I want to be left alone with a lunatic, do you?"

"She is perfectly sane!"

"Is she? It doesn't seem so to me, nor, I suspect, to that shrewd solicitor of hers. I'm surprised at you, Miss Conrad. You strike me as being far too sensible to pretend that a woman who plays with dolls can actually be normal."

"She *is* normal. You saw her yourself, this morning. Could anyone have been more rational?"

"But she jumps from the rational to the irrational, I understand."

"Who told you that? Matthew Deacon?"

"He warned me what to expect. It wouldn't have been fair to bring me here without full knowledge of the facts."

"What facts?" I demanded bluntly. "And don't try to sidetrack by telling me again that it's no concern of mine."

She looked at me for a long moment.

"You seem to have an exaggerated sense of responsibility toward a woman who cannot possibly be more to you than just another employer. Isn't this unusual, even in a companion with a strong sense of duty?"

"Not in the least," I answered calmly. "Many companions become devoted to their employers."

The girl moved restlessly. The quietness, the wildness of the grounds, the sense of isolation seemed to irk her.

"If you're feeling better," she said, "let's go back to the house."

"I'm feeling fine now. Thank you for your presence of mind. If you hadn't seized me so swiftly I might have — "

"Don't think about it!" she said sharply. "You would have reacted in the same way had I been in danger. In any case, you grabbed the balustrade just in time. Someone will have to do some repairs around here soon or the whole place will be toppling about our heads."

"I don't think that's likely," I said, walking down the steps of the arbor. "Lyonhurst has stood for hundreds of years and will stand for hundreds more. A building can't be condemned because of one faulty copingstone."

"All the same, I shall speak to Mr. Deacon about it. He must have authority to release some funds for immediate needs."

"Speak to him if you wish, but not to Lady Katherine, please. I don't want her to hear of the incident. It would upset her."

"Don't worry. I won't tell her a thing. Nor will I let her know what I think of this ancient dump."

When we reached the terrace, the girl turned and looked back. "All this emptiness!" she murmured. "Mile after mile of it, nothing but trees and shrubs and grass! No life. Nothing. It's depressing. Don't you find it so?"

"No. I find it beautiful. I like it."

"Perhaps we should change places," she said with a little quirk of a smile. "What a pity we can't! But I was born to this inheritance and I intend to have it. What I shall do with it when I get it is another matter."

"Are you so sure you will get it?"

"Of course. That's what I've come for. At least my grandfather remembered me on his deathbed! Since he deprived me of so much during his lifetime I shall damn well extract the most now. And *she* won't stop me."

"She? You mean Lady Katherine? How could she stop you if Lyonhurst has been bequeathed to you?"

I tried to keep curiosity out of my voice, but it was difficult, for at last I felt that I was on the brink of learning things at which both Harriet and the doctor had hinted, things which had disturbed and puzzled me. One by one the pieces were dropping into place; slowly a pattern was evolving; bit by bit I was learning all I wished to know, and I blessed my foresight in remaining here and in keeping silent. Had I challenged this girl last night, where would it have got me? Out on my ear, if she had her way. And she would have had her way, with so much proof to back her up, proof which would have countered my own insubstantial claim. Any protests or declarations I uttered would have been dismissed as fabrication. I might even have been accused, as my mother was, of being slightly unbalanced, my word unreliable, my imagination running wild.

According to this girl, Katherine was more than slightly unbalanced. She was a lunatic who would ultimately have to be 'taken proper care of.' The words had a sinister sound and meaning.

17

THE girl turned and entered the house, not answering my question. I followed her, feeling faintly satisfied. To have stymied a person who had so many ready answers was pleasing. Until this moment she had produced a comeback for everything.

She had either been lying, or had said too much, and somehow I was convinced that she had *not* been lying. A very strong reason brought her to Lyonhurst and that reason could only be the one she gave — that Sir Humphrey had at last made a gesture of recompense to his daughter's child, on certain conditions. I was curious about these conditions. Last night, a trial period had been referred to, but I guessed there were other stipulations involving Katherine herself.

"You are going to be generous to me now, *Maman*?"

"I am indeed, my dear."

The words echoed in my mind, stirring

273

up doubt and alarm in a vague and troublesome fashion. In what way, and to what extent, could Katherine make up to her daughter for all she had missed, apart from giving her a home in this beautiful but rapidly deteriorating old house? The inference was that there was money behind the scenes. If so, just how much of it was this girl out to get? And if she was dissatisfied with her portion, what then? Would she bully, cajole, or threaten poor Katherine for more? Would she demand the absolute maximum, exercising a relentless blackmail until my mother was bent to her will, as she had been bent to her father's?

If Katherine proved unexpectedly stubborn and the girl's ambitions were unsatisfied, what would the next step be? To claim that my mother was of unsound mind, incapable of making rational decisions, a woman from whom all responsibility should be removed and vested in her daughter?

A chill ran through me. I stood still, watching the girl walk ahead. I suspected that she would stop at nothing to gain her ends, and that if a decision of my mother's seemed likely to undermine her schemes, she would fight back in a cold, calculating, and merciless way. She would need medical support for that, and I felt sure David would not only refuse to give it but, if she appealed to another doctor, would fight — and hard. The thought was reassuring.

The girl paused at the door of the morning room and looked back at me.

"Coming?" she said, holding the door open for me to follow. I let her hold it, and said, "You didn't answer my question."

For reply, she released the door and let it slam in my face. I wasn't annoyed. I was pleased.

★ ★ ★

Matthew Deacon had telephoned. He was off to Canterbury tomorrow, so couldn't join us for the promised ride, but was sending his stable boy after lunch with mounts for the two of us.

The horses proved to be Rufus and Patience, but when I automatically went to mount Patience, the boy said, "Sorry,

275

miss, Mr. Deacon says Rufus is for you and Patience for the new young lady."

"But I've never ridden Rufus! I'm not experienced enough."

"I'm to ride with you, miss, and Mr. Deacon says I'm to make sure the other young lady has Patience."

I stood aside.

"In that case, I'm afraid I can't ride at all. Rufus is far too fiery for me."

"I'm sure Matthew wouldn't let you ride him if that were true," the girl put in. "He gave a glowing account of your skill last night."

"What skill I have isn't sufficient to cope with a horse like Rufus. Take Patience by all means, and I'll forgo the ride. Believe me, I shan't mind."

"But I shall. Besides, you made a promise both to myself and my mother. I'm sure Lady Katherine would be disappointed in you if you broke it. She wouldn't wish me to ride alone. Until I'm familiar with the countryside I might get lost."

"You can stick to the park and Jim will be with you."

She had already mounted Patience,

seating her well. Obviously, she had ridden before. "Do hurry!" she urged. "The day is too lovely to waste. Where are you taking us?" she asked Jim, who was standing beside Rufus, waiting to help me mount. "For a good canter, I hope?"

"That I can promise, miss. The park offers good riding."

"And afterward we visit Mr. Deacon's field for some practice jumping, no? He told me we could."

"That's right, miss. He told me, too. He has two brush fences, a stile, and two gates in the field alongside his stables. He practices there."

"Splendid! A good gallop across the park, and after that, the jumps." She turned Patience's head, saying eagerly, "Do hurry, Miss Conrad!"

The stable boy cupped his hands. "Up you go, miss. Don't worry, Rufus only goes wild at times."

"That's comforting," I murmured ironically as I placed my foot within his clasped palms and sprang into the saddle.

To my surprise, Rufus was quite docile.

We trotted at first, getting to know each other, progressing into a canter when reaching the open stretches. The girl was streaking ahead on Patience, riding confidently and well. When she broke into a gallop, the stable boy grinned and raced after her, forgetting me. For that I was glad. Quiet as Rufus was proving to be, I was nervous and had no desire to give him his head, but the sight of two horses racing ahead spurred him to action and he broke from a canter into a gallop with an abrupt transition which nearly unseated me.

Somehow I held on, knees gripping, thighs braced, tightening the rein at first in the hope of checking him, then letting him have his head because he was determined to. Thwarting a horse like this could be a mistake and I would be the one to suffer for it.

Despite my fear, that wild gallop was invigorating, with the world and the wind flying by like all the furies. It was challenging and stimulating and exciting, too. I had almost caught up with the others when the girl turned her head and cried, "I'll race you to that copse over there!"

Rufus won. It was his doing, not mine. How I kept in the saddle was nothing short of a miracle, but both the girl and the stable boy were generous in their praises.

"You see, Miss Conrad, Mr. Deacon was right about you. You are a born horsewoman. I was sure he wouldn't let you ride Rufus unless he thought you could."

"She's right, miss," Jim added. "Mr. Deacon's as good a judge of a rider as he is of horseflesh."

I was human enough to be encouraged by their praise. It worked wonders for my ego and I allowed myself to be lured to the jumps without much resistance, although I had only visited Matthew's field once, and on that occasion the jumps were lowered for me. Now they loomed large and formidable.

Seeing my hesitation, the stable boy said again, "No need to be nervous, miss, not if you can ride Rufus the way you did just now."

"That was Rufus's doing, not mine."

"Then all you have to do is let him take you over the jumps the same way," my imposter said.

It sounded logical; how could I argue against it? But when I realized that I was to jump first, all my apprehension returned.

"Rufus should go first, miss," the stableboy said. "He's a temperamental beast and it's no use thwarting him."

"Couldn't the jumps be lowered?"

He looked dubious. "Not without Mr. Deacon's permission, miss. It'd be more than my job's worth. He hates to have the jumps mucked about with."

Rufus was raring to go. I could feel him tense and restive beneath me. I held him tightly on a short rein, fighting for control, not realizing that the mere sight of a jump was an irresistible challenge to him. A moment later he was streaking down the field like unchecked lightning. I had no choice but to give him his head unless I wanted to crash the first fence.

He soared over it like a bird, and relief vied with a heady sense of triumph as I felt myself carried with him. The girl was right. Matthew was right. Rufus was right. They were all right, but me. The horse was magnificent and all I had to do was trust him.

Over the second fence — a gate — and then another, higher than the first. Somehow I stayed in the saddle, but the horse was in control, not I.

The fourth fence was approaching and beyond that lay the stile. It was deep and, as it drew nearer, seemed even more so. My eyes were fixed on it in mesmerized horror, so that the oncoming brush fence didn't even exist for me. I had already taken a brush fence, so had nothing to fear from this one. It was the last jump, the final challenge, which terrified me.

I was only aware of Rufus gathering to leap, of thudding hooves beating a swift accelerando, of creaking leather and straining bit, of the great heaving body beneath me, of flaring nostrils and gigantic breaths and muscles rippling like fluid steel — and then the leap, accompanied by an abrupt cessation of sound, with nothing but the rush of wind in my ears.

There was something else, something which registered only remotely. The roar of a car in the adjoining lane.

After that, I heard nothing. At the peak of the jump Rufus checked with a jerk, as if suddenly, viciously struck. I shot from the saddle, and as I hit the earth I felt the vibration of his massive body falling beside me. And then pain was drowning in darkness, taking me with it.

18

IT was a long climb back. Slowly and laboriously I struggled upward from oblivion, aware that I was not doing it alone. Someone was helping me. Hands were lifting me. There were voices, among them one I knew but could not identify. Despite what seemed to be enormous pressure on my eyelids, I opened them and saw David Harvey looking down at me. His mouth was a tight line of anger and concern.

Someone murmured, "You don't look the least bit attractive like that," and I didn't even realize it was I.

"Good. That sounds more like yourself."

I let my heavy eyelids fall again, not bothering to answer. Now that I had placed the unidentifiable voice I felt more than content to relax against the owner's shoulder, which proved to be obligingly near. Then David slipped an arm about me and said, "Let's see if you can sit up."

"Anything to please," I murmured with an attempt at facetiousness.

"Shut up, you little fool."

Propped against his arm, I opened my eyes again. Shapes and figures swam into focus: a brush fence leaning drunkenly to one side; Jim, the stable boy, white with shock; the girl who called herself Belinda looking down at me with a concern which, I felt, bordered on fright; and a few yards away an inert hulk on the ground. Rufus.

I closed my eyes with a groan. Pain seemed to be splitting my skull. David was saying something, but this time I couldn't take it in. Something was shouting in my brain, "Look again! *Look!*" and I knew that I had to, for in that dizzy, uncomprehending glance something had registered, something horrible from which I had retreated, but which I knew I would have to face.

David lifted me carefully. "Rufus," I muttered. "Rufus — "

"Forget about Rufus. Relax."

But I couldn't forget him. I had to look again. David was carrying me away and I forced myself to open my eyes and look back over his shoulder. The animal's huge frame lay in a pool of blood and I knew at once that he was dead.

Shock ran through me, intensifying the pain in my head. From a long way off I heard David's voice saying peremptorily, "Ride back to the house at once, mademoiselle, and tell your mother I'll bring Gillian home later, but whatever you do, don't alarm her."

"She — she isn't . . ." I spoke thickly, stupidly, and tried again. "Her name isn't Lemaît . . . " but the sounds were incomprehensible even to my own ears, blurred mutterings without meaning or sense. I gave up, submitting to my aching head and praying for oblivion which failed to come again. Not even when David laid me on the back seat of his car did unconsciousness take over. I lay with my eyes closed, suddenly wanting to cry and finding it impossible. Everything was too horrible. Rufus was dead, and I had killed him.

"I killed — "

"Be quiet," David said. "Just be quiet, my sweet."

His voice was different. The concern

was still there, but it was no longer sharp and angry. It was warm and gentle, comforting me like a caressing hand. I opened my eyes and looked at him. He smiled and said, "Shut them again and relax. Everything is going to be all right. You'll see."

I wondered how he knew that everything was all wrong, and what he would think if he knew just how wrong, that things were far more serious than a cracked head and broken bones. In a woolly-headed sort of way I felt that I had both, but I had survived. Poor Rufus had not.

"Matthew will be angry — "

David cut across my words. "I'll deal with Deacon. Forget him. Forget everything. Do as the doctor orders — relax and keep quiet."

I obeyed gladly. He got into the driver's seat and started the engine. I wanted to ask where he was taking me, for although my senses were too hazy to observe the route, I sensed that it was not in the direction of Lyonhurst.

It wasn't long before the car slowed

down, stopping before David's house.

"Don't move," he commanded. "Stay right where you are." He lifted me with gentleness and painracked as I was, dizzy as I was, I loved it.

He laid me on the couch in his surgery, then brought me a glass of water and some tablets. Obediently, I swallowed. His hand pressed me back against the pillow as he said, "You've no broken bones, but you've taken an almighty crack on the skull, with slight concussion as a result."

"Slight!" I gasped. "You ought to sample it!"

"I know," he smiled. "Feels like a sledgehammer, doesn't it?"

"Make it plural and I'll agree."

"I can tell from the way you're talking that a rapid recovery has already begun." He covered me with a blanket and finished, "I'll come back in an hour or so. You're going to sleep meanwhile."

I murmured drowsily, "In that case, why didn't you take me back to Lyonhurst?"

"Ulterior motives," he replied darkly. "I have designs on you."

I wanted to laugh, but was half asleep already. Only vaguely did I hear him speaking on the telephone and realized that it was to Harriet.

"She had a miraculous escape. You can tell Lady Katherine not to worry. She's resting now and I don't intend to move her until she wakens."

I slept for a long time. I could tell from the rays of the setting sun when I wakened. It had been midafternoon when we reached Matthew Deacon's field, and only a few minutes later . . .

I was suddenly wide awake, remembering everything, seeing Rufus's inert body humped in a pool of blood, and the stable boy's face, white with horror, and David's tight-lipped anger and concern. But why should he be angry? I hadn't muffed that jump deliberately! I flung back the rug and stood swaying. The sledgehammers were still working, though less violently.

The door opened and David's voice said crisply, "Get back on the couch. You're not ready to walk yet. Here's some tea to speed recovery."

It was hot and sweet and strong. "Just

right for shock," I said mechanically, remembering my St. John's Ambulance course.

David tilted an eyebrow and replied, "So you do know something about nursing, after all?"

The cup was halfway to my mouth, and remained there. "I don't know what you mean," I said carefully.

"Don't worry. You will. When you've drunk that tea."

At least it gave me time to marshal my thoughts. I sipped it slowly — too slowly, apparently, for David said, "There's no need to stall, my girl. You can have another cup, if you wish, and I'll save all my questions until then."

I finished the tea. "I'm ready, Doctor. You can ask your questions while I drink that other cup."

"There's no hurry. My questions will keep."

"But my curiosity won't."

A corner of his mouth tilted in amusement. His anger and concern had gone. Had there been a moment when he called me "my sweet"?

"All right. Question one. How in the

name of heaven did you come to be riding Rufus?"

"Matthew's orders. He sent Jim, the stable boy, over with mounts for — for Lady Katherine's daughter and myself. Patience for her, Rufus for me."

"But I thought you always rode Patience?"

"Until this afternoon. Jim said Matthew insisted that Patience was for Mademoiselle."

I couldn't call her by name. Not my name.

Watching me, David's face was expressionless.

"I suppose he wouldn't have sent Rufus for me if he wasn't confident that I could manage him. And I did manage him," I added defensively. "I even galloped him — right across the park, beating the pair of them."

"And that, I suppose, went to your head so much that you decided to put him to the jumps."

"I did not!"

"Don't fly into a temper. It will make your head worse. Is it still aching?"

"Yes; not as badly, though. Thank you for the tea."

He took my cup and laid it aside, then sat on the side of the couch. If I had wanted to get up, he barred the way. But I didn't want to, not even to avoid his questions. The pillow was soft beneath my head, the room was quiet, and David was near. I was content.

"Then who suggested the jumps?"

I couldn't remember.

"It doesn't matter. What does is that you were fool-hardy enough to try." For a moment his large hand touched my own, then he rose abruptly and walked away. With his back to me he said a little gruffly, "I suppose you realize you could have been killed?"

I answered slowly, "Instead, it was Rufus . . . "

"Exactly."

Something about his voice compelled me to say, "What do you mean?" When he made no reply I added, "How did he die?"

"His neck was broken."

"But there was blood — "

"Yes."

"That wasn't from a broken neck. There was too much."

"His forelegs were cut clean across."

"But *how*? A brush fence — "

"A brush fence," David said slowly, "isn't usually wired."

"Wired?" I echoed stupidly.

"Very simply. Very ingeniously. Tight and taut, in the precise position to trip your mount, catapult you over his head, and break your neck. Fortunately, you're young, and resilient, and, even more fortunately, the wire acted almost as a brake, checking Rufus's flight and therefore the force of your own. But it couldn't check his violent reaction to his wounds. You were scarcely out of the saddle before pain enraged him; he fell violently and broke his neck. It was over in an instant. I saw it all."

I couldn't speak, couldn't move. I felt horror rising and fought it down. I put both hands out blindly toward David's.

"But who?" I whispered. "*Who?*"

"That's what I mean to find out. Only a murderer would have done this."

19

HIS words echoed in the quiet room. After a while I asked tensely, "*What do you mean?*"

"Precisely what I say. Someone wants to get rid of you."

I tried to speak and failed. *Who wanted to kill me?* And why? The questions answered themselves. The only person with a motive was the girl pretending to be myself, and the only motive — I stood in her way. Which meant that she knew who I was.

I couldn't work this out alone anymore. I took a deep breath. "I need your help, David. I'd better tell you the truth."

"It's about time, my child. I was wondering when you were going to. Frankly, I'm tired of waiting."

"I am not a child!"

"Then stop behaving like one, which is what you've been doing ever since you arrived with your cock-and-bull story about being Gillian Conrad, whose

293

current employer needed her one moment and not the next. You should have thought up a more convincing story than that. What made you imagine you could get away with it?"

"But I did!"

"What makes you so sure?"

He crossed to his desk, took out a file of correspondence, and handed it to me.

"Read that," he said. "There are only one or two letters, but they'll suffice. The first is a copy of mine to Miss Conrad, following her telephone conversation with Matthew Deacon. You'll see from it that I approved her engagement and went on to outline Lady Katherine's condition and needs. The next is her acknowledgment and promise to arrive as soon as released from her current job in a fortnight's time. Then came her telephone call, telling my secretary of her sudden departure for Majorca. All cut and dried up to that moment and then you appeared on the scene, presenting yourself as Gillian Conrad and telling a very obvious pack of lies."

"Then why didn't you challenge me?"

"I did, whereupon you revealed both audacity and ingenuity and, I must say, courage. I admire a fighter. Besides, I was intrigued and amused. Not that I would have let you remain solely for those reasons. There was another, a much bigger one."

"Which was?"

"That Katherine Tredgold had taken a liking to you and that you had shown a surprising and rather touching response, plus an understanding which I hardly expected from one so young. A sensitivity, I might add, which her own daughter has not revealed, yet."

I let that pass. I would speak when he had finished and not until then. I needed not only time, but all of his facts, knowledge, and reasons. Armed with these, I would know just how much to confess and how much to conceal.

With that uncanny perception of his, he continued, "In case you are thinking of hiding more, let me warn you not to try. I'm giving you the whole truth from my side, after which I want it from yours. And I'll get it, what's more. I always get what I want."

"I'm aware of that. A straight line to any given point — that's how your mind runs. Please go on."

"So, I let you remain. It suited my purposes. I needed someone to care for my patient. I was worried about her for reasons which I needn't touch on now. It was important that she have a companion who would not only humor her, but understand her, and you seemed to do both very quickly. There was a sort of kinship between you which pleased me. The need for her to have the close companionship of someone like yourself was imperative, someone who could be with her more constantly than Harriet, someone who could protect her."

"Protect her?" I echoed. "Why didn't you mention that to me?"

"Because I didn't want to draw attention to the need for it. You'll see from my original letter to Gillian Conrad that I merely stated that my patient was frail and, as a result of prolonged unhappiness, tremendously vulnerable."

"Vulnerable to what, Doctor?"

"Please keep calling me David. Informality makes for greater ease between one person and another and from now on that is going to be important between us. There must be no professional barriers now. I can't call you Gillian, because that isn't your name. Tell me your real one."

"Tell me how you found out that it wasn't."

"It's all there, in front of you. Gillian Conrad followed up her telephone call with a letter of apology and explanation, and so did Marlborough Bureau. They immediately sent me particulars of three other candidates. Those letters are also in the file, likewise copies of my replies to both. Read them."

The top one was to Gillian Conrad.

Dear Miss Conrad,
Thank you for letting me know why you were prevented fom fulfilling your engagement. Naturally, I understand the circumstances and have taken immediate steps to replace you. I am informing the Marlborough Bureau accordingly.

I turned to the other which he had written to the bureau.

Thank you for offering to replace Miss Conrad. I have to inform you that this will not be necessary as I have obtained the services of another nurse-companion who has already taken over.

I closed the file and looked up at him.

"Why did you do this?" I asked.

"I'd like to say that it was for love of your beautiful dark eyes, but that would be lying. I didn't notice how lovely they were until the night I kissed you." He continued briskly: "I did it for more practical reasons. As I said, you suited my purpose. Also, you were on hand and I was averse to further delay or the chance of Katherine being exposed to Deacon's schemes."

"Matthew's?" I echoed, surprised. "What schemes could he have?"

"Plenty. In particular, that she should be so preyed upon that she would indeed go out of her mind, in which case she wouldn't be considered fit to sign important documents or capable of making decisions when the time came.

Better still, she might be more easily persuaded to sign certain papers in a moment of extreme vulnerability. Haven't you noticed how he continually harps on her disturbed mental condition, insisting that her obsession with that doll was so abnormal as to be dangerous? Even so, I think he would like her to become obsessed with it again."

He came back to the couch and looked down at me.

"Suppose you tell me who you are."

"I'm surprised you haven't guessed. I'm Belinda Lemaître. The real one."

His astonishment was satisfying. I smiled and said proudly, "So I actually didn't give myself away — even to you!" Then I realized that the expression on his face was something more than astonishment; there was comprehension, coupled with alarm. "What's the matter? Why do you look like that?"

"Because although you didn't give yourself away to me, you obviously did to someone else."

"I don't understand." I put a hand to my forehead and brushed back my hair. My head was aching badly and bewilderment only seemed to make it worse.

"You *must* understand!" he said urgently. "If you are the real daughter a tremendous amount hinges on it."

"I know. At least, I've gathered so. My grandfather had a change of heart, didn't he, and bequeathed Lyonhurst to me?"

"Not exactly. His granddaughter is to share it with her mother, and everything else besides, providing she agrees to settle here forever, to adopt British nationality, and to toe the traditional Tredgold line in every way. Of course, respectability was to be preserved by some trumped-up story about his daughter's youthful marriage, tragically severed by the war. Even to the last, when trying to make restitution for his cruelty, he was anxious to preserve his good name."

"You're a cynic, David."

"Sometimes, perhaps. Show me a doctor who isn't. We see enough of life beneath the surface to recognize the real from the sham. What is a cynic, anyway, but a disappointed idealist?" He gave me a wry, but gentle, smile. "Funnily enough, we tend to cling to

300

our ideals like hell. But to get back to the daughter, she is to be taken into Lyonhurst more or less on probation. A trial period, the old man stipulated, to put her to the test, to find out just how well she will 'fit in.' If she settles down, all well and good. If not, she will receive a small annuity which would be no more than a pittance in comparison with a half-share in her grandfather's estate. The only Tredgold left to finally decree just how well she qualifies or just how much she is to receive is her mother. After a lifetime of being ruled by her father, poor Katherine now holds the reins — unless they are jerked out of her hands."

"By my impersonator, you mean?"

"Yes, for one. Don't take Lyonhurst at its face value. Don't be deceived by the general air of neglect. Far from depleted, as people imagine, the family fortune is more than intact. Sir Humphrey became a miser in his old age, so there it has remained, increasing steadily, gathering good financial moss because he was shrewd and clever, speculating well on the Stock Exchange. Gambling in shares became an obsession, his sole interest in life, but he wasn't interested in spending, only in amassing more and more. So if someone could get his hands on the lot, it would be well worth his while."

"I've got to take this in," I said slowly. "I wish my bead didn't ache so much."

He touched my forehead gently. "We can leave things until later. Tomorrow, perhaps."

"No. It's important that I know everything and understand everything."

He raised the end of the couch and propped me against it, putting the pillow behind my head. He brought another glass of water and told me to sip it slowly. It was cool and refreshing, making me realize that my throat had been parched from apprehension and fear. His statement that my life had been deliberately threatened had shaken me badly, I hadn't believed it because I saw no reason for it before.

"Why the devil did you keep quiet about your identity?"

"Originally I had no intention of even visiting Lyonhurst. I read of my grandfather's death and was curious, no more than that. I wanted to see my mother's birthplace, but I had no desire whatsoever to meet her. You see, I always felt that she, like my grandfather, had rejected me."

"Because she apparently made no attempt to find you after the war?"

"Yes."

"But now you know the truth about her wretched life, surely you understand and have some sympathy for her?"

"I have — now." I handed him the empty glass and went on: "I suppose you want proof of my identity? Well, I can't produce it. Yet."

"The mere fact that someone wanted to kill you is proof enough for me. But why can't you prove it?"

I told him everything. "So until I can contact Françoise," I finished, "all I can produce is my father's Bible. That is locked in my wardrobe, but in itself it isn't final proof."

"No, but useful. Before I take you back, I want to know just one more thing. How did you get the opportunity to impersonate Gillian Conrad?"

"I was lodging at Mrs. Tracey's store. I'd been there for three days, pretending to be on a sketching holiday. I'm an art student studying dress design, not a nurse-companion."

"I knew you had no nursing experience, particularly when faced with that hypodermic."

I said rather shamefaced, "I remember. Well, to get back to Mrs. Tracey. One day, a woman came into the shop, Gillian Conrad's aunt, to deliver a letter to Lady Katherine explaining why Gillian wouldn't be coming. I offered to take it to Lyonhurst. It was terribly easy, absolutely dishonest, and I'm not in the least sorry. I destroyed the letter and took the girl's place. I don't know what made me, except that it was a challenge."

"Your sense of adventure needs curbing, young woman."

"It was more than that. Every day I had visited Lyonhurst and got no farther than the gates. They frustrated me. They *dared* me. Do you understand?"

"Yes."

"I thought you would. You have a sense of adventure, too."

"I don't go swaggering off alone into situations which could be dangerous."

Don't you? I thought, remembering his solitary penetration into perilous jungle terrain in search of a lost comrade. Aloud, I answered, "You are wrong about one thing — that at some time, somehow, I gave myself away to someone. I couldn't possibly. For one thing, I've been too careful, and for another, I have carried nothing identifiable about with me — "

"Except your father's Bible."

"Which has been well concealed. Perhaps," I said hopefully, "you're making a Grand Guignol affair out of nothing and my riding accident *was* an accident."

"Was a wired brush fence an accident? I'm too practical to go around looking for melodrama, but when I think of what could have happened to you!"

He gathered me close. After a breathless moment I relaxed with a sigh, making no effort to free myself.

From the depths of his shoulder I said, "There is only one person who would want me out of the way — the girl herself."

"It would seem so." David brushed his cheek against my hair thoughtfully.

"You sound doubtful."

"I am — "

"It's so obvious! Whoever she is, she is here for one reason, to claim an inheritance which should be mine. She has even produced documentary evidence which staggered me. But on two points she revealed complete ignorance — first, about Françoise, who is not dead. And second, she obviously doesn't know that Belinda Lemaître is already a British subject. Françoise took out naturalization papers for both of us as soon as she could. It was Pierre's advice, should she manage to escape to England with me."

"Well, this girl certainly checked on the essentials. Had she any opportunity, since her arrival and the time of your ride today, to plan your death, to go to Deacon's field and fix the jump? I doubt whether a woman could have tied that dangerous wire so tightly. No, Belinda, it all adds up. It is staring you in the face. Can't you see it?"

"You mean Matthew."

"Of course. They are in it together. He brought her. He found out who you were. Up to that point I doubt whether he had any intention of searching for the missing daughter."

"Why not?"

"As I said before, I have my suspicions. They were temporarily lulled, but now they are active again. When I'm more certain, I'll tell you. Trouble is, they're going to be the devil to prove."

"I'm not completely obtuse, David. Matthew has dug himself in at Lyonhurst, assuming the role of man of the house so effectively that my mother has accepted him as such. He has his own key and she frequently refers to the fact that he is like a brother to her, so I suppose you mean that he might persuade her to provide for him as such."

"Something like that," David answered noncommittally.

I sighed and said, "So what do we do now?"

I was leaning back against the pillow again. His head was close to mine and his arms, still about me, tightened. "For a man of my temperament," he said rather unsteadily, "that's a leading question. I find myself remarkably single-minded at this point."

He released me abruptly, smiled down

at me, and said, "Forget it, my sweet. Remember that I am a man, and that although the spirit may be willing the flesh is weak, so don't tempt me."

I felt the blood surge to my face and was glad of the shadowy room. The sun had long since set, but neither of us had been aware of it. Now David said briskly, "The next thing is to get you home. Think you can walk now?"

I put my feet to the ground. It was much firmer than before. Apart from a dull throbbing in my head I felt quite wonderful. Faintly delirious, in fact.

As he turned his car through the gates of Lyonhurst, he said, "As your medical attendant, Belinda, I insist on hot milk and a sleeping tablet tonight. I'll come to see you again tomorrow and while I'm with you I'll take a look at your father's Bible, if I may."

"I'll be glad to show it to you. But you mustn't call me Belinda."

"I'll remember that, Miss Conrad."

My mother was waiting up. She came to meet us rather shakily. The girl was with her, displaying every appearance of friendly concern for me.

"*Maman* has been so worried, wanting to telephone the doctor every moment to see how you were, but I assured her that you were in good hands — "

My mother said a trifle testily, "My dear Belinda, I was well aware of that. I know Doctor Harvey a great deal better than you do!"

We were all surprised by her outburst. Katherine was not usually so spirited and certainly never sharp-tongued. Could it really be concern for me? It seemed so, for the way in which she put her arms about me betrayed a very real anxiety.

"She must go to bed at once," David said. "Give her this sleeping pill with a glass of hot milk . . . "

He broke off, and I followed his glance. Standing aside, like a spectator, was Matthew.

"Are you all right?" he asked, coming toward me. "The news was a terrible shock. I went to Canterbury this morning to attend matins in the cathedral, and didn't return until after dinner this evening. So I didn't hear the news until I got back."

I found it difficult to speak, but finally managed to say, "I'm sorry about Rufus . . ."

I saw that the mere mention of his horse Rufus caused him pain.

"I am dreadfully sorry," I reiterated helplessly. He turned away from me.

My mother put an arm about my shoulders and said, "It is a tragedy, of course, but it would have been greater if you had been killed."

Matthew spun around.

"Why?" he burst out furiously. "*Why?* Rufus was a wonderful horse, a magnificent animal. His life was just as precious!"

Harriet said to me, "Come, my dear, I've turned back your bed. You must do as the doctor says, get into it right away."

Her words and tone terminated the scene. I followed her upstairs obediently and as I did so I heard the girl say, "I will help you tonight, *Maman*." My mother answered a little tiredly, a little fretfully, "There's no need! If I can manage without Gillian's help, I can manage without anyone's."

"But not without mine," the girl

310

insisted, urging her upstairs.

At the door of my room I turned to say good night to Katherine. The girl held her with an air of possession which I resented. I wanted to thrust her aside. Instead, I controlled myself and let Harriet fuss over me like a mother hen with a chick.

"I'll get your dressing gown," she said, and before I could stop her, her hand was on my wardrobe door. I fetched my handbag and opened it to take out the key, trying to think of some excuse for the wardrobe being locked. I could think of nothing.

"That's funny," said Harriet, "the lock is broken . . . "

My head jerked up. She was standing there, the door agape. She was fiddling with the handle, which jerked about loosely. "Now how could that have happened?" she said. "You didn't tell me. I'd have had Buxton mend it at once . . . "

"I — I forgot."

"Never mind. I'll have it replaced tomorrow."

I thanked her and then said. "I'll get

ready for bed while you heat the milk, Harriet."

I listened impatiently for the sound of her footsteps retreating downstairs, then seized my rucksack from the shelf. The Bible was gone.

20

MY sense of defeat was almost overwhelming. The one tangible link with my birth had vanished. Now, without a shadow of a doubt, the girl knew my identity. She had the advantage over me in being able to anticipate and forestall any movement I tried to make, any statement, any claim. All I had to rely on were words, which could not be substantiated without the help of Françoise who, first thing in the morning, I would have to start trying to trace. There was no time to be lost now. I had wasted enough.

I closed the wardrobe and prepared for bed. The broken lock would not fasten and the door swung open on its hinges. Harriet returned with the milk, insisted on my taking the sleeping pill, hovered over me for a while, then left. The dark cavern of the wardrobe yawned at me from across the room. I switched off my bedside lamp and lay in darkness, fighting sleep, putting up a determined resistance against the drug David had prescribed. I had to think, clearly, constructively, and fast! I had been a fool to imagine that I could pull the wool over David's perceptive eyes, and equally so to overlook the obvious steps that Gillian Conrad would take. A letter of apology and explanation would naturally follow her telephone call, and she would naturally contact the employment bureau to explain why she had failed to take up the appointment, otherwise she was liable for their commission and the first fortnight's pay, and no companion-help could afford that.

And what of the solicitor, the man who had remembered her, recommended her, and engaged her? He, too, she must have notified, so he had known me to be a fraud all along. And yet he had let me get away with it — or let me believe that I was doing so.

Drowsiness threatened — the heavy, unnatural drowsiness of artificially induced sleep. I fought it back. I went to the bathroom, splashed my face beneath the cold tap, and felt the threatening cotton-wool clouds recede, then I returned to bed, refusing to look at the gaping wardrobe, refusing to do anything but marshal my thoughts in some coherent order.

Something tugged at my mind, some memory, some important loose end which I had overlooked. Something had happened to put Rufus off balance, so that he took the jump badly.

The sudden roar of a car engine — David's car, driven in that forceful, direct way of his. Mingled with the rush of wind in my ears I had been subconsciously aware of that unexpected sound, and so had Rufus. It had startled him, making him take the jump at such an angle that he was not merely tripped, but savagely wounded.

This was the unexpected contingency which the murderer had not anticipated. Who would? Who would expect a disturbance from that quiet lane on a sleepy Sunday afternoon? But chance had brought David along at the critical moment and saved my life.

The thought of David lulled my

agitation, reminding me that I was no longer entirely alone. I had an ally, so there was no need to panic, no need for fear. His logical mind would rationalize and clarify everything. Yet, I couldn't lean back and leave it all to him.

The cotton-wool haze began to descend again and this time found me unresisting. I welcomed it, but suddenly another question jerked my brain into action again. If Matthew's job was to trace the missing daughter, and if, unbeknown to me, he had somehow stumbled on my identity, why had he accepted the forged identification of this unknown girl as the real Belinda Lemaître?

A heavy haze fell over my eyes, smothering my senses.

I awakened to see Harriet and David looking down at me. For a moment recollection was lost in an abyss. I began to speak, but David forestalled me by thrusting a thermometer in my mouth and saying, "Something light for breakfast, Harriet."

I mumbled forcefully, "Something solid, a side of ham or a steak will do to begin with!"

"Be quiet, Miss Conrad. I'm taking your temperature."

His fingers were on my pulse, strong and compelling.

Harriet beamed and said, "How about an omelet, Doctor, with toast and coffee? She's in fine fettle, you can see."

David's lower lip was outthrust and his brows were creased. I snatched the thermometer out of my mouth. "Make it a big omelet, Harriet, and to hell with the doctor's orders. I'm the one who missed dinner last night."

She departed with a chuckle and David said, "You're good friends you two. She likes you."

"I like her."

"But Mademoiselle doesn't. And the feeling is reciprocated. I arrived just when the girl was complaining to Harriet about breakfast not being sent to her room."

"What did Harriet say?"

"That Lyonhurst wasn't an hotel."

Yet. I thought.

He put the thermometer back in my mouth. I began to mutter, "You know perfectly well I haven't a temp . . . " But he cut me short.

"It's the only way to keep you quiet. Either that, or by kissing you, and although the latter course appeals to me more, I think you'll agree that privacy is essential. Someone could walk in at any moment. Your mother, for instance. Or your other self."

My mother. For the first time I heard someone else in this house call her that. David put his large hand over mine, sensing my emotion just as he seemed to sense so much about me.

"David, it has gone!"

"Normal. Absolutely normal," David said, shaking the mercury down.

"*No, not my headache, the Bible!* Someone forced the lock of my wardrobe and took it. See for yourself."

He crossed the room swiftly. "You're right," he said, examining the lock, "and we can guess who did it, and when. She had plenty of opportunity when you were at my house yesterday. It must have been her. Deacon was in Canterbury and you may be sure his alibi is watertight."

"David — "

"Yes?"

"If Matthew really does know who I

am, why should he accept this girl in my place?"

"He didn't accept her. He produced her. I've already told you that until you arrived, or until he discovered your true identity, I believe he had no intention whatever of finding you."

"As the family solicitor, he had to."

"And as solicitor, he could easily announce, after a suitable lapse of time, that the search was fruitless, that you were untraceable, and who would dispute his word? Certainly not Katherine.

"And then," he said slowly, "she would probably have gone completely out of her mind."

"Do you *really* think that was what he wanted?"

"I believe it would suit his plans well, but, as I said last night, I can't prove a thing. My only hope is that he'll betray himself in an unguarded moment."

"As, apparently, I did. David, I've gone over and over every action of mine since I came here, and I was absolutely convinced that for anyone to guess my identity would be impossible, until my Bible was stolen. That would point to the truth, although it *could* be claimed that I came by it unlawfully. But since I am absolutely certain that I never betrayed myself, that confounds your murder theory by removing the motive."

He came back to the bed, dropped a kiss on the tip of my nose, and said stubbornly, "Nevertheless, you *did* betray yourself, Belinda. Somehow. Sometime. Somewhere. Not to me, but to Deacon." The second kiss landed on my mouth and I said a trifle shakily, "I thought this was a professional visit, Doctor."

"I find myself increasingly tempted to mix business with pleasure these days. I'll try to keep my distance for now. No distractions permitted until the important things have been attended to. I'll begin tracing Françoise immediately. If I fail, then legal pressure must be brought on the bank to yield up her deed box. It can be done but could take time. I'm going to London today."

"What about your patients?" I asked.

"I've arranged for urgent calls to be put through to Halliday in Canterbury."

Harriet entered at that moment, bearing

my breakfast tray, and behind her came my mother, accompanied, as usual, by the girl, whose arm lay affectionately about her shoulders.

She met my glance with a friendly smile, a smile without artifice or guile and certainly without embarrassment or guilt.

David prepared to take his departure, saying something about Miss Conrad having a skull made of rock and bones of India rubber. "She's unbreakable," he said cheerfully.

The girl's laughter was spontaneous. "I will mount guard over her, m'sieur, for my mother's sake! You do not wish to lose your favorite companion, do you, *Maman*?"

The atmosphere was friendly, tinged with relief because my accident had not been serious. "You had a miraculous escape, Miss Conrad," she continued. "I saw the whole thing and, believe me, I was paralyzed with fear, even more than when the copingstone gave way."

David, at the door, said sharply, "What coping-stone?" and my mother gave a little cry of alarm. The girl's hand flew to her mouth.

"Oh, dear! Miss Conrad told me not to mention it to anyone, particularly my mother! She didn't want her favorite patient to be upset."

I was irritated by the words, which seemed to contain a hint of sarcasm. Her expressions seemed not only unnecessary and exaggerated, but to contain a sneer.

David demanded an answer. I responded casually for my mother's benefit, "Merely a broken one on the north wing — a balcony balustrade. It was loose and I leaned on it and down it went — "

"Buxton told me about it!" Harriet exclaimed. "He found it smashed in the drive and wondered how it fell. It didn't occur to either of us that someone had leaned against it."

"It was my own fault. I wanted to show Mademoiselle the view, so I opened the windows and stepped out. The balcony is small and in making room for her I leaned against the coping, dislodging the stone. That was all."

David said a shade too sharply, "Don't go near that balcony again!" He recovered himself and added, "For everyone's sake, Lady Katherine, that parapet should be seen to."

"It will be. Buxton must fetch a builder from the village as soon as possible, Harriet."

"I'll see that he does, your ladyship."

The girl said, "I hope you are not accident prone, Miss Conrad?"

"Why? Are you afraid there may be some truth in the saying that things always go in threes?"

"In France we do not know that saying."

"My dear Gillian, you mustn't talk like that!" Alarm fringed the edges of my mother's voice, and I was immediately penitent.

"Miss Conrad should stay in bed today," Harriet advised, picking up my tray and moving to the door.

"Miss Conrad will do nothing of the sort," I retorted, "and if anyone tries to make me, they are wasting their time."

"No one is going to," David said. "You can get up by all means, but keep an eye on her, won't you, Lady Katherine?"

"Why should she be watched, *M'sieur le Docteur?*" the girl asked innocently.

"Knowing Miss Conrad, she will overexert herself, and following shock it can be a bad thing."

"She will stay right by my side," my mother assured him. "She can take a gentle walk with me this morning, and rest this afternoon."

"I'm not an invalid," I protested.

But that was my program for the day, rigidly adhered to by Katherine. It was beautiful outside, clear and sunny and warm, but inwardly I chafed for action. I wanted to get to the telephone, ring up Hilda McClellan, and ask for news of Françoise. With luck, there might even be a letter for me, awaiting my return. Access to the telephone was frustrated, however. It was too public, there in the hall. I had to wait for a moment when no one would be about, and the morning was no such time.

My mother, the girl, and I went out of doors, walking to the rose garden, sitting for a while in the little Italian arbor, then strolling back to the terrace for morning coffee. The atmosphere was easy, lightened by relief on my mother's part because I had not been injured by the fall. "You are lucky," she said more than once. "Your guardian angel must have been watching over you."

"If my guardian angel was responsible for sending Doctor Harvey along at that precise moment, I'll offer up a prayer of thanks."

"What puzzles me is how the accident happened," Katherine continued. "Rufus is an experienced jumper. He goes over those fences many times a week."

"It was Mademoiselle herself who took the jump badly, *Maman*. You made the wrong approach, Miss Conrad. You should have tightened the rein on the run, then timed the release at the precise moment for him to leap."

"I expect you are right, ma'am'selle, but never having jumped Rufus before, nor even ridden him, all I could do was let him have his head and hope to stay in the saddle. If Rufus was so familiar with the jumps, I'm surprised he mistimed that one. He was a highly intelligent horse."

"Then what went wrong?" my mother

asked. "Something must have upset him."

If the girl had seen that murderous wire, she obviously intended to ignore it. If she could put the blame on me, she obviously intended doing so. Now she said, "I think you were wonderful to stay in the saddle at all, ma'am'selle. And Mr. Deacon is not blaming you for the loss of Rufus. You have nothing with which to reproach yourself."

"I am not reproaching myself. The accident was none of my doing."

I could tell that my mother was aware of the underlying antagonism between us, despite the surface goodwill. I knew this distressed her, so changed the subject.

"Your new library book arrived by this morning's post. Would you like me to read to you?"

"*I* will read to *Maman*," the girl said, and jumped up to go indoors. The minute she was out of earshot, Katherine leaned forward and said in an anxious voice, "Gillian, tell me honestly, are you happy here now?"

I was so surprised that, for a moment, I could not answer, then I echoed carefully,

"Now, Lady Katherine?"

"Since my daughter came."

"Why should her coming make any difference? I am an employee here. I have a job to do, irrespective of your relatives or friends."

"By friends you mean Matthew Deacon, I suppose? You don't like him, do you? I've known that all along, and am sorry about it because Matthew — "

" — is like a brother to you," I finished automatically.

"He is indeed, but I want you to be happy, and if my daughter's coming has made you feel out of things, I am sorry. I am also anxious that you should remain. I want both of you to be happy at Lyonhurst."

I assured her again that I was, adding that I had felt at home very quickly.

"I felt that, and was pleased. I wish it were so with Belinda."

"She has been here such a short while," I said helplessly, aware that although this was an opportunity to sow a seed which would not be in the girl's favor, for my mother's sake I couldn't do it. I felt that she was perturbed already.

"I am very anxious for Belinda to settle down here. So much depends on it."

"How much, Lady Katherine?"

"Her whole future. And the burden of it rests with me. My father made certain stipulations in his will. The long and the short of it is that, if I choose to, I can share everything with her, and that amounts to a great deal, or I can give her the larger share, which amounts to a great deal more. Or, on the other hand, I can withhold it all — not that I would do such a thing, but I am troubled, even so."

"About what?" I asked gently. "Tell me. If you are worried, perhaps I can help."

"I just cannot imagine a girl like Belinda settling down here. She is temperamentally unsuited for such a quiet life. You think I am hasty in my judgment? Mothers have an instinct about their children, and are rarely wrong. After six months, what would Belinda do? Turn her back on Lyonhurst, sell it, get rid of it?"

"She couldn't do that, unless she had sole ownership."

"That is true, but already she has decided that the place is a burden as it stands and that I — we — would be wise to turn it into money. Those were her very words."

She hasn't wasted much time, I thought grimly, but aloud I said, "In what way did she suggest it?"

"In no specific way, but the obvious inference is a sale."

"To which you wouldn't consent, so aren't you worrying unnecessarily?"

"Very possibly, yet the thought and the fear are there, also the awareness that if Matthew supported her idea I would be no match for them."

I said urgently, "No one can persuade you to part with your home unless you wish to."

She smiled.

"It is you who sounds like the older and wiser one, whereas it should be I. You must understand that there is nothing I wouldn't do to make my daughter happy. I have so much to make up to her, so much for which to atone."

"Not that way!" I cried.

Further conversation was cut off by approaching footsteps, and a moment later the girl came out onto the terrace again. She carried something in her hand and she was smiling. She pulled a chair close to my mother and said, "I will read to you from this, *Maman . . .*"

I froze. She held my Bible toward Katherine, open at the flyleaf. "My most treasured possession," she said proudly. "I have never been parted from it."

21

THE sun went behind a cloud at that moment and the world became suddenly gray. The tragic immobility of my mother, looking at the Bible as if seeing a well-loved face after many years, struck me. I remember the girl's smile, full of tender pride, and the note of reverence in her voice, and her long fingers touching the morocco binding as if it were sacred.

"I have drawn comfort from this for many years, *Maman*, as my father did."

I wanted to snatch the Bible from her, denounce her. She was diabolically cunning and unscrupulous. She would stop at nothing. She would use every weapon, *any* weapon, and I possessed not a single one.

My mother uttered an inarticulate cry.

"Pierre's Bible! We took it to the little church in Mont-Dore and laid our hands on it as we exchanged vows. I would know it anywhere! I remember that inscription from his parents on the flyleaf — *Pierre Armand Philippe Lemaître . . .* "

To my astonishment I heard myself demand, "Where did you get that, mademoiselle?" The girl looked at me with an expression of mingled surprise and reproach.

"From my father, of course. He left it to me. It has been with me since the day he was killed."

"*That's a lie! It's mine! Give it to me!*"

I tried then to take hold of the Bible, but she withdrew swiftly, clutching it to her and crying piteously, "*Maman!* What does she mean?" To me she said harshly, "Get away from me, do you hear?"

She jumped to her feet, overturning her chair. It fell with a crash on the flagged terrace and the noise was echoed by a distant roll of thunder. The atmosphere was suddenly hot and breathless. Not a breeze fanned the air and the tall trees of the park stood rigid, like frescoes carved against the sky.

I cried, "*You stole it! You stole it from my room!*"

332

The girl looked from me to my mother in bewilderment, but I didn't even glance at Katherine, for nothing could stop me. I wasn't going to allow this girl to get away with another thing.

All of a sudden she said pacifically, "You are still suffering from shock. The doctor shouldn't have allowed you to get up. *Maman*, dear *Maman*, don't look so frightened! She cannot harm you. I'll not let her harm you. She may have gone mad, but it is only the after-effects of her fall. That blow on the head has caused it. Harriet must get her back to bed at once — "

"Stop!" I cried. "Be quiet! *Let me speak!*"

I saw my mother rise uncertainly to her feet. She was pale, but quite calm.

"Yes," she said gently, "you must go back to bed, Gillian. We will send for David Harvey and I know he will come at once. You are not yourself, my dear, but when you have slept you will feel much better and we will forget all about this dreadful moment."

I was shaking uncontrollably.

"But it's true, *true!* Believe me! Please

believe me! That Bible is mine. It belongs to *me*."

"Come, my dear, you cannot expect me to. It belonged to my dear Pierre and no one could possess it but his daughter. *My* daughter. Ah, Matthew — thank God you are here! Be so good as to telephone the doctor and you, Belinda, please call Harriet. This poor girl must be put to bed immediately."

Three against one. They stood there, lined up against me, with mingled expressions of pity, annoyance, and anger. Anger glinted in Matthew's eyes, cold and hard. I had not heard him arrive, but now I was glad he had come. I pointed an accusing finger at him and declared, "It was *you* who wired that brush fence!"

"Miss Conrad has gone out of her mind," he snapped.

"She cannot help it, m'sieur." The girl's voice was as sweet as poison in a perfume. "Please, understand. It is not her fault. It is the result of her accident. I will fetch Harriet at once."

"You're a clever actress," I flung at her. "I'll hand you that."

But my voice was trembling, betraying

my fear. This did nothing to encourage either belief or confidence in me, but it did achieve one result. It brought the girl to a standstill. "What do you mean?" she demanded. "I have never acted in my life."

"Then you're giving a superb performance!" I retorted, and promptly burst into tears.

"She's hysterical," Matthew said. "Don't worry, Katherine, I'll handle this. I'll call Harvey at once."

At that, I burst into laughter mingled with sobs. I wanted to shout, "You won't get him! You can't reach him! He's gone to London to help me, to ruin your diabolical plans!" But even in my present emotional state something cautioned me to silence.

Matthew came over and slapped my face. The sudden impact jerked my head and pain stabbed like a knife. I heard my mother utter a protesting cry and my hand went up to my stinging cheek.

"You see?" he said. "That has silenced her. It is the only way to deal with hysterics. Here is Harriet. She'll take charge of the girl for now. When Miss

Conrad has rested, I suggest you send her packing. We can't employ persons who don't know how to behave. You'll take your money and get out of this house, Gillian Conrad, at the earliest opportunity. If I had my way, you would leave now."

I wanted to tell him that he hadn't a hope of getting his way, that David would stop him, and that pretty soon the game would be up. Suddenly I was too spent to argue. My mother was looking white and shaken and I had been responsible for that. I had created an emotional scene which had shocked her deeply and it was the worst thing I could have done. One moment I had been quite calm and the next I had been making wild accusations. How was my mother to know that the sight of that Bible had snapped the last link in my self-control?

I passed a weary hand through my hair. A feeling of hopelessness had me in its grip and it was almost with relief that I saw Harriet's kindly face. She looked concerned. She came toward me, saying, "I hear you're upset, my dear. Miss Belinda says you're not yourself.

Didn't I say you should have stayed in bed?"

"I'm perfectly all right, Harriet — "

"You'll be all the better for a rest, Gillian." It was my mother who spoke and her voice was tinged with very real concern. "Forgive Matthew's anger. He didn't mean to be unkind."

"Unkind or not, my dear Katherine, she must go."

"And *I* say she must not. I won't part with her just because she is a little distraught."

I saw his lips tighten. Harriet put a maternal arm about my shoulders and I allowed her to lead me indoors. The house was cooler than outside and certainly less oppressive. As we stepped into the drawing room another roll of thunder sounded menacingly overhead. Behind me, my mother's voice said, "I hate storms — "

"I know you do, Katherine. The last one had a very adverse effect on you. Remember?"

"No, I don't . . . "

She sounded surprised and bewildered. I looked back over my shoulder and saw

337

them standing where I had left them, face to face. My mother looked diminutive beside the tall, thickset man, but she was erect — more erect than when I first came to Lyonhurst.

Harriet said to me, "Come along, my love — "

"I shouldn't indulge her if I were you, Harriet, or it may be the worse for you."

It was the girl who spoke and her tone was sharp. She had followed us from the terrace, but I paid her little heed, for I was straining to hear the conversation between my mother and Matthew. I could hear him saying, "Surely you remember? You were terrified. Screaming. Clinging to that comical doll as if to defend yourself. Only it wasn't the storm you wanted protection from, but Gillian Conrad. You insisted that she had stolen something."

I called out, "It isn't true! Don't believe him!"

"There she goes again!" the girl said wearily. "For pity's sake, Harriet, get her to bed or she'll be making all sorts of accusations again."

"Miss Conrad making accusations,

338

Miss Belinda? I don't believe it!"

"No? Then let me tell you that she accused me of stealing my father's Bible from her room."

"I don't believe it," Harriet repeated stubbornly.

"Ask her, then."

Harriet said to me, "Come, my dear."

But I said urgently, "Harriet, remember last night, when you went to my wardrobe, you found the lock broken?"

"Yes, dear — "

"A broken lock proves nothing. Take her away, Harriet."

She was right, of course, that proved nothing. I allowed myself to be led upstairs, but once inside my bedroom I pleaded, "Harriet, help me!"

"I'm trying to, dear. Let me get you to bed."

"I don't want to! I just want you to know the truth."

She stroked my hair maternally.

"There, there, child. That fall you took must have been a terrible one — "

I brushed her touches aside impatiently. "You heard what Doctor Harvey said this morning. My skull is hard as a rock. There's nothing wrong with me, Harriet, only no one will believe me . . . "

I saw in her face the patient indulgence with which one humors a sick person. She unzipped my dress, urging me to lie down, and I jerked away angrily.

"Harriet, listen! Someone has *got* to listen! *That man is a murderer!*"

Shocked, she scolded, "Now pull yourself together, my dear! You don't know what you're saying!"

"I most certainly do. *He* wired that brush fence. *He* made me ride Rufus to make sure that I jumped first. Rufus would never let another horse go before him, so whoever was mounted on Rufus was bound to be thrown."

"My dear," the woman said patiently, "who are you talking about?"

"Matthew Deacon, of course."

She stiffened. I had lost her sympathy. In her eyes, Matthew Deacon could do no wrong. I had forgotten that.

"You don't know what you're saying, my girl. I'll forget all about it, I promise, only don't let me hear you say such things about Mr. Deacon again."

340

"Oh, Harriet, not you, too!" I said wretchedly.

"I don't know what you mean. I won't hear a word against him. He's been very good to my dear mistress."

"So I hear, over and over again. I wonder why."

"It's not your place to," she said severely.

"All right, Harriet, you don't have to remind me that I'm merely an employee in this house."

Her eyes softened.

"I'm not wanting to be harsh, child, but you can't go around accusing someone of being a murderer and expect to be believed. Especially a respectable lawyer like Mr. Deacon."

I gave up. I dropped onto the bed, defeated, and she covered me with a rug. I thrust it aside, complaining of the heat, and lightning zigzagged across the room, followed by the crackle of thunder. If only it would rain! I wanted to feel large, cool raindrops splashing against my brow. My head had begun to ache again, but that had nothing to do with my accident; it was the result of tension and shock and frustration.

"There now, rest, my dear," Harriet said, and left me to do so. There was forgiveness in her voice, but when she reached the door I said, "I meant it, Harriet. Remember that, please, later on."

"Why later on?" she asked patiently.

"When David comes."

If she was surprised at my being on Christian-name terms with the doctor, she made no comment. "I dare say he'll be along shortly," she said. "Mr. Deacon was sending for him right away."

"He won't get him . . ." I began, but the door was already closing, leaving me alone. I sat up abruptly, reached for my dress, and waited until Harriet should have reached the foot of the stairs and disappeared across the hall, then I tiptoed down. No one was about. I hurried to the telephone and picked up the receiver. I had to ring London right away and nothing and no one must stop me.

"Don't waste your time," said Matthew Deacon's voice. "The line is dead."

I dropped the receiver with a crash. He was standing a few feet away, watching me with a derisive little smile. "So unfortunate!" he sympathized. "I was most anxious to get the doctor for you, but will have to wait until I drive back to the village. The lightning must have struck the wires."

I turned and ran back upstairs. I thought I heard him laughing, but couldn't be sure because at that moment all sound was deadened beneath another roll of thunder. Then came the rain, pelting against the windows. Relief had come. But not to me.

I sat down on my bed and thought hard. What could I do? Go on waiting and, while I waited, let this girl and this man get even further ahead of me? Wait for David to return, hoping he would bring good news? I couldn't be certain that he would, and with the telephone out of order, I couldn't even hope for a call from him.

I flung myself against the pillow in despair. I had bungled things badly, but what else could I have done? No human being could have stood back and not accused that girl of stealing the Bible; no normal person could have remained

343

silent in the face of such effrontery. And, of course, no average person could be expected to believe such fantastic accusations as mine, so I could hardly blame my mother and Harriet for not doing so.

★ ★ ★

Later, Harriet returned with a tray. I lay where she had left me. But now I was passive. There was no fight left in me. There was nothing I could do until I made contact with David again.

I made a pretense of eating, beneath Harriet's watchful eye.

"Nasty storm that was. Fortunately it didn't last long. Still, it was long enough to do a bit of damage. Mr. Deacon tells me the telephone wires have been damaged. He couldn't get through to the doctor. Miss Belinda has persuaded him to stay to lunch, and he'll call at the surgery on his way back."

"He'll be wasting his time."

"Well, we don't think so, dear. If you won't go to bed proper, someone has to make you, and maybe you'll obey the doctor. Is that all you're eating?" She clucked her disapproval. "No wonder you young things are skinny nowadays — don't eat enough to keep skin and bone together!"

I smiled and said, "Is Lady Katherine all right?"

"Of course, she's all right. I admit she was a bit upset about you, but we all were."

"Not her daughter, believe me."

Harriet looked at me keenly.

"You don't like her, do you? Well, no more do I, sad as I am to admit it. She's not a bit like her mother, despite all our hopes."

"It's a mistake to have preformed ideas about people — what they are like, or should be like, or what we expect them to be."

I spoke with feeling, having had preconceived ideas about my mother.

Harriet picked up the tray. "Did you sleep, love?"

"I dozed."

"Do so again, dear."

"I'll try. And, Harriet — "

"Yes?"

"Make sure Lady Katherine has her afternoon rest, won't you?"

"Miss Belinda is seeing to that."

The door closed behind her again. I must have slept, after all, for the next thing I knew I was opening my eyes and seeing clear skies instead of gray. The sun shone, but it was fairly low in the sky. I washed and dressed and went along to my mother's room.

She was asleep. Nursing the doll again.

22

I CROSSED the room quietly, and was about to ease the doll from her arms when she stirred and looked up at me. And at the precise moment the door opened.

"What are you doing here, Miss Conrad? I thought you were in bed," my impostor stated.

"I decided to get up."

"I hope you are feeling better?"

"Yes, thank you."

My mother was lying there, looking from one to the other of us. For once, I could not read the expression in her eyes. The girl came over, saying in a tone of indulgent amusement, "Really, *Maman*, don't you really think you are too old to play with dolls?"

Katherine looked surprised. Her glance focused on the doll in bewilderment,

"I — I don't understand. How did it get here?"

"You asked for it. You wouldn't rest

without it. 'I always take my baby to bed with me' you said, and refused to be denied. What could I do, but give in to you?"

Katherine made no answer. She just lay there, looking puzzled and a little frightened. Then she said slowly, "I don't remember . . . "

The girl said soothingly, "Do not try to, *Maman*. It is not important."

"But it is! Surely, if I had asked for the doll, I would remember?"

"Did you remember before?" the girl asked, significantly.

"Before what, Belinda?"

"Before I came. Oh, come, do *try* to take things in! You were lucid enough this morning."

I said sharply, "Don't talk to her like that. You are frightening her."

"Frightening her!" The girl gave a short laugh. "I like that! Do you think she doesn't frighten me?"

Katherine said tremulously, "Belinda, what are you saying? What do you mean?"

"That when you start being eccentric, dear, I don't like it very much. Who

348

would? A woman who plays with dolls can hardly be accepted as normal."

"Get out," I said quietly. "Leave this room at once."

"And who are you to give orders? You have no authority here. I heard Mr. Deacon say you were to pack your bags and go."

"I refuse to."

"I will tell him."

"Do so, if you wish. Meanwhile, leave Lady Katherine alone."

She gave me a level glance.

"You have gone too far," she said. "Don't say I failed to warn you."

Before I could answer, the door closed sharply behind her.

"Gillian! *Gillian* . . . "

The frail hands were trembling, clinging to me with all the uncertainty which they had revealed long ago. Long ago? Only a short while ago. Scarcely three weeks. Yet it *did* seem that I had been at Lyonhurst for a long time.

I put my arms about my mother and gathered her close.

"Don't be afraid," I said.

"But *why* am I frightened?" she

whispered. "What is the matter with me?"

"Nothing. Nothing at all."

"But there must be. She — my own daughter — says so."

"She is wrong."

"I'm not so sure that she is," Katherine answered slowly. "There are things which make me wonder."

"Like what?"

"This, for one . . . " She indicated the discarded doll. It lay on its back, eyes closed, the eternal smile on its waxen lips. "It's only a doll, but sometimes I think it is my baby."

"Only because that is what it was to you as a child," I said, but she refused to be reassured.

"I'll bring you some tea." I moved to the door, hiding my concern. This slip back alarmed me, and even more alarming was her own fear of it.

My feet were soundless on the faded stair carpet, so that the voices which drifted from the open drawing room were not silenced by my approach. They were sharp and raised in argument. I recognized them at once and listened unashamed, pausing with my hand on the banister.

"Don't be a fool. If she had any proof she would have used it long ago!" It was Mathew's voice.

"But why should she come here incognito?"

"I've answered that one already. Obviously she did so because she has no proof. God only knows why, but I am content to accept the fact. If she could have proved her identity, she would have done so in the first place; it wouldn't have been necessary for her to come here the way she did. So pull yourself together, girl. You've done well, so far — "

"I doubt if I can keep it up. For goodness sake, get matters settled quickly."

"I intend to, with your help. I haven't finished with your services, yet."

"My services! Is that how you regard me, as someone employed for the job?"

He laughed. There was the sound of movement, muffled words, as if her voice was subdued by his shoulder — or his mouth. Then she gave a long, tremulous sigh. "God," she said, "how I hate you!"

"You don't. You love me."

"Love? What is love? I've dabbled in it too much to know."

"Call it sex then. It's what you want, isn't it?"

"With you, yes."

Silence again. Something told me she was in his arms and I waited, holding my breath, ready to run back upstairs at the first indication that either one of them was coming to the door. But then his voice came briskly. "Now don't be frightened anymore. The woman trusts me implicitly — "

"I don't trust that girl."

"Then you're a fool. What can she do now? The only tangible evidence she had is lost to her now, so what can she try to do? If she had a single card, she would play it."

"But how did she come here in the first place?"

"As to that, I've never found out. It is the only thing at which I've failed."

"Oh, no, it isn't, my dear Matthew. What about that brush fence?"

"*Be quiet!*"

His voice was like a whip cracking.

The girl said, "You needn't try to frighten *me*, you know. That would be most unwise. I know too much about you. Just remember that."

His footsteps echoed abruptly on the polished floor. A chair crashed over and she laughed.

"You look ridiculous when you're angry, Matthew. All red in the face like a balloon about to burst." Then her voice sank to a purr. "There, darling, forget it. Let me kiss you . . . "

"Get away from me!"

"All right," she said sharply, "if that's the way you feel! But remember this; I can explode your whole plan, if I wish to."

"You wouldn't. You'd lose too much."

"Then we understand each other, don't we?"

"We must try to."

"We must even try to trust each other — difficult, I agree, but perhaps not impossible, if you do what I ask."

"And that is?"

"You know damn well what it is! *Get rid of her!*"

23

I SPED back upstairs, but the second tread from the top creaked loudly beneath my weight and I turned abruptly, walking down again with a nonchalance which I hoped would be convincing. Apparently it was, for Matthew appeared at the drawing room door, looking up at me and saying, "Ah — it's you. Feeling better, I hope?"

"Quite, thank you. I'm just going to get Lady Katherine's tea."

"I hear she's unwell again."

"Unwell? In what way?"

"You know the way I mean. Not herself. As you were not yourself this morning."

"I was perfectly all right, and so is Lady Katherine." I walked straight past him, heading toward the kitchen, sparing him not another glance or word.

The kitchen was deserted. Through the window I saw Harriet talking to Buxton in the kitchen garden. I filled the kettle and placed it on the large, old-fashioned hob, and while it slowly came to boil, I set the tray, made the cress sandwiches my mother was particularly fond of, placed some of Harriet's queencakes on a plate, and as I did so Harriet entered.

She smiled at me, surprised but pleased.

"You look yourself again," she said.

"I am, thank you, Harriet. But I meant every word I said to you. I want you to remember that."

She frowned.

"Well, I won't. No one can make such terrible accusations against Mr. Deacon to me."

"So I gather. That won't stop me, however, when I know them to be true."

She sighed and shook her head. "And I thought you were all right again, dear!"

I laughed.

"Believe it or not, I have been perfectly all right since I wakened this morning."

"You were mightily upset before lunch."

"Yes, I admit that." I poured boiling water into the teapot, set it upon the tray, smiled at her, and said, "I still like you,

Harriet — bless you!" and sailed out of the kitchen.

I felt extraordinarily lighthearted and unafraid, ready to face whatever had to come, ready for action if need be.

But my spirits evaporated when I reached my mother's room. She was seated on a chair beside the window, and Matthew was with her. He had papers outspread on a small table, and after taking one glance at them, I said brightly, "Excuse me, Mr. Deacon, I want that table . . ." and placed the tray on it deliberately.

His quick temper flared. "Couldn't you see Lady Katherine was about to sign those documents?"

"She can sign nothing until she has had her tea," I insisted, "and after that I'm taking her for a little fresh air and exercise, so you can gather up these tiresome papers and bring them back another day. They are in the way. As you can see, the tray is unbalanced."

I picked it up and, using it as a shovel, swept the papers onto the floor. His fury pleased me and I enjoyed watching him on his knees, gathering them up. "So sorry I didn't bring another cup," I said to him, "but I'm sure Harriet will give you tea in the kitchen if you want some."

It was insulting and meant to be. I had reached the stage where I just didn't care anymore. I wanted to draw this man's fire, and the sooner the better. If he aimed at me, he might leave my mother alone.

To my surprise and delight, Katherine laughed. It was hastily suppressed, but Matthew heard it, and frowned. He had gathered up the documents and I was satisfied to see that they were in hopeless disorder.

"I shouldn't sign anything, Lady Katherine, until you've read it thoroughly, or had someone do it for you," I advised. "Legal documents can be tedious, I know, but I'm sure Doctor Harvey would examine them and save you the trouble."

"My dear, I have no need to read them! Matthew has told me what they are about. Just the assignment of various properties to my daughter."

"Including Lyonhurst?" I asked un-abashed.

"What business is it of yours?" Matthew's voice was sharp.

Katherine hastened to assure me that he would never ask her to dispose of her home.

"Forgive me. I thought I saw the words 'Lyonhurst and all estates pertaining thereto,' on one of those papers . . . "

"I — I don't think so, dear . . . " my mother said uncertainly.

"What about witnesses?" I added, turning to the solicitor, but that he ignored.

He was placing the papers in a briefcase, calmly and precisely. He was every inch the family lawyer — trustworthy and impeccable. He said pedantically, "My dear Kathy, your companion is right, you should always be absolutely sure of what you are signing. But I explained everything, did I not? You were quite sure a moment ago. Surely you cannot be certain one moment and uncertain the next? Otherwise it must be assumed that you are not in full possession of your faculties, and that would be unfortunate, because I would then be obliged to overlook your authority. An unreliable

358

mentality cannot be held responsible for its actions. Someone else must take control."

With that he was gone, leaving my mother trembling and afraid. Her panic-stricken eyes turned to me in helpless pleading. "Take no notice!" I cried. "He cannot hurt you. No one will hurt you, I promise."

"Matthew would never lie to me. Whatever he says is right."

What could one do or say in the face of such implicit trust? Yet, Katherine's feelings toward this man contained more than trust. I sensed something else which I could neither define nor understand.

I persuaded her to drink some tea and chatted idly about the garden, the weather, anything to take her mind off personal things. It was quiet and pleasant in the old-fashioned bedroom. When the two of us were alone together, we were both content. Only since the arrival of the girl had discord and uncertainty crept in. Nevertheless, Katherine had been loyal to me this morning, refusing to send me away despite her solicitor's advice, and the memory of this pleased me. It proved not only her affection for me, but her trust as well. Even more than that, it proved that she still had a will of her own — so long as she was allowed to retain it.

I knew that if this man and girl had their way, they would undermine every shred of her confidence. Already they had started, insidiously planting little germs of doubt and confusion in her mind. The doll — had she really asked for it before she lay down? I didn't believe so. The whole thing had been a fabrication of the girl's, intended to frighten Katherine.

As for Matthew Deacon, he had deliberately hinted at her mental derangement, determined to frighten her, and in that he had succeeded despite my intervention.

And what of myself? I had no illusions about his plans for me. I only prayed that David would return in time.

★ ★ ★

The rest of the day passed peacefully enough, lulling my apprehension. When I went to bed I even wondered if I had been overanxious and imaginative.

In the morning a telephone engineer came to repair the wires, but he could find no fault outside the house. The damage was traced to a joint box in the hall, which had somehow become dislodged from the skirting, interfering with the wires so that contact could not be made with the exchange. "Funny," said the man, "the storm couldn't have done that. Perhaps it was knocked with a vacuum cleaner."

But Harriet had not used the vacuum that day.

* * *

I let the incident pass, making no comment, but uneasiness returned.

Shortly before lunch I said to my mother, "May I ring friends in London, Lady Katherine? The friends I wanted to visit last Sunday."

"Of course, my dear. You have no need to ask."

For once the girl wasn't around. She had driven to Canterbury, and the feeling of no longer being watched was like a reprieve. Until this moment I had hardly been free of her presence and never free from an awareness of being spied on. Now I knew why. Both she and Matthew Deacon knew my identity and were puzzled by my silence. It was a cat-and-mouse game between us, with the odds stacked in their favor. That they were determined to bring things to a head, and soon, I was convinced. My mother was to be persuaded, cajoled, or intimidated into doing whatever they wished, and she had no one but myself to protect her.

My feeling of inadequacy was enormous.

But at last I was able to telephone Hilda McClellan.

"Hilda, it's me!"

"Belinda! Where are you? Why haven't we heard from you?"

"We? Who do you mean?"

I hoped she would say, "Françoise and I," but she didn't. "Everyone at the shop," she said, "and especially me. Françoise actually sent you a picture postcard from Paris, but I didn't know where to forward it, so I gave it to that nice man who called here yesterday . . . "

"David! So you've seen him! Where is he? And where is Fran — ?"

The line cut off with a jerk. I called, "Hello! Hello! Hilda, are you there?" holding the receiver in my hand and suddenly realizing that there was something wrong with it. The cord trailed loosely, unattached.

I followed its trail and saw that it was severed from the wall, the end lying — cut clean across — beside a pair of immaculately shod feet. They wore French Court shoes with elegant heels.

"So you didn't hear me come in?" the girl said. "I'm not surprised. You seemed very excited. I'm sorry you didn't get news of David, but I shouldn't try anymore, if I were you. You can't now anyway, I've cut the wire. It also prevents anyone you were talking to from ringing back. Lucky that Harriet asked me to get her dressmaking scissors sharpened in Canterbury, wasn't it? My cuticle scissors would have been unequal to the job."

There was nothing I could say. She walked away down the hall, carrying some parcels with her and calling as she went, "Harriet, where are you? Send

Buxton out to the car to bring in the rest of my shopping, will you? And where's my mother? I have a present for her."

She disappeared into the drawing room, and I followed slowly, trying to gather my senses. So the gloves were off between us, pretense discarded. Well, in that there was a measure of relief, but also of fear. It meant that she was now so confident that she could call my bluff, when in fact I was trying desperately to call hers.

Katherine was sitting in her wing chair, some knitting on her lap. The girl crossed to her, walking with her usual grace. She kissed my mother affectionately and I looked away as she did so, for these little demonstrations always seemed like mockery to me.

The morning paper had fallen to the floor and I stooped and picked it up. As I did so my glance fell on a small paragraph tucked away at the bottom of the page. I read it a second time, memorizing it, feeling a tingling of excitement run through me, and then I laid the paper aside and looked at the girl.

She had carried a dress box in with her, and now she was opening it, scattering tissue paper about the floor and shaking out folds of transparent black chiffon which my mother, in her innocence, mistook for a nightdress, but which I recognized as a see-through gown which was not only intended to reveal bare breasts but plunged deeply to the waist to reveal a great deal more. She held it against her, executing a little waltz in front of my mother and saying. "Do you like it? You must! It's the loveliest thing I've ever seen and absolutely made for me! I certainly didn't expect to pick up anything like this in a stuffy cathedral city . . . What's the matter *Maman*?"

"My dear, isn't it a little brazen, even for a nightdress?"

The girl's laughter pealed.

"Nightdress? You dear thing, this isn't a nightdress!"

"Then something is missing, surely? There seems to be no lining . . . "

"The only thing missing, *Maman*, is my beautiful body inside it!"

"You are joking, Belinda."

"Why should I? I have a beautiful

body. Many men have told me so and many will do so again when you give that promised party for me. It must be soon, very soon! Matthew tells me he is going to arrange for decorators to do up the ballroom. Imagine, Miss Conrad, a ball at Lyonhurst, to welcome home the unacknowledged daughter and introduce her to local society! And very respectably accounted for, of course. My mother contracted a secret marriage in France, long ago, and then the war came, separating her from husband and child, both of whom were eventually presumed killed, but after years of searching, the family solicitor traced the daughter and brought her back to Mother. How's that for a tearjerker? All very touching, if you dig that sort of thing; revoltingly sentimental if you don't. I don't. But so long as it serves its purpose, what the hell do I care? It will be convincing enough, providing no one tries to probe further, and the clever family solicitor will prevent that!" She pirouetted happily, quite unaware of Katherine's pained reaction to her words. "Well, thank God for a party at last! I'll

make everyone sit up, especially in this."
She whirled from the room, crying, "I'll
put it on at once! I can't wait!"

"Belinda, come back!"

My mother's voice was calm and
authoritative, arresting the girl's flight,
but only momentarily. "I'll come back
to give you a dress rehearsal, *Maman*!
Oh, I nearly forgot! I have a present for
you." She picked up a package, ripped
the paper off, opened a box, and took
out a doll. A larger, bigger, brighter doll
than Katherine's. A doll with a cheap
face and enormous eyes. It had the false
animation of an overdressed puppet, and
she flung it into my mother's lap saying,
"Here, play with that, you dear, batty old
thing! It's far better than the rubbishy doll
I threw into the dustbin this morning. If
you *must* play with dolls, at least have
something worth looking at!"

Her laughter came back to us, echoing
with hideous mockery. For a moment
which seemed like an eternity my
mother stared at the creature in her
lap, a vulgar, sexy doll clad in sequins,
with a plunging neckline revealing an
overdeveloped bosom. And then she

367

began to sob. Her sobs rose to cries, harsh with distress — the cries of someone deeply wounded.

At that precise moment Matthew Deacon walked in.

24

HE said sharply. "What's going on? Why is she screaming? What have you done to her?"

I took the doll from my mother's lap and flung it away. "It isn't what *I* have done! It was that girl's doing, the girl you brought here!" I cradled my mother's head against my shoulder, stroking her hair and murmuring, "Hush, darling, hush, you're all right. I am here . . . " She clung to me, sobbing wildly.

"She threw Belinda away. Belinda, my baby!"

"What the devil is she rambling about?"

I replied sharply, "She is not rambling. She is speaking the truth. The girl threw the doll into the dustbin this morning and replaced it with that!"

I took a kick at the tawdry thing. It lay spread-eagled on the floor, painted mouth smiling with hideous coquetry, false eyelashes curling from ogling eyes, exaggerated bosom rising from sequined dress. It was the sort of doll which would adorn the bar of some low nightclub.

"Take it away and burn it," I said to the lawyer, "or give it back to the girl to keep for herself, if that's the sort of thing she likes."

He paid no heed. Instead, he picked up the doll, viewed it appreciatively, then threw back his head and laughed aloud. "It's delicious!" he declared. "It's the sexiest thing I've seen in years."

I went to the door and called loudly for Harriet, who came hurrying from the kitchen. At the sight of her mistress, her face creased in concern and she hurried toward her saying, "Why, your ladyship, my dear, whatever is the matter? Don't you feel well, my love?" Her maternal arms went out to her, only to be thrust aside by Matthew.

"Don't indulge her, Harriet. Pampering is the worst possible treatment for anyone in her mental state."

The housekeeper drew back as if struck. She looked at Matthew Deacon for one shocked moment, then stammered,

"Why, sir, what do you mean? She's upset, that's all."

"My dear Harriet, don't be a fool. What is wrong with your mistress has been obvious for a long time. Don't delude yourself that she's sane. It's about time the truth were faced in this household."

His voice had the cold, sharp edge of a razor and it was plain that Harriet had never heard that note before. She stared at him as if he were a stranger, and despite my own anger I felt gratified because he had been foolish enough to reveal himself to her now. If he had been wise he would have done nothing to antagonize or shock the old woman; he would have retained her as a loyal ally. She had been ardent in her defense of him ever since I came to this house, as admiring and devoted as Katherine herself. This sudden transition from affability and courtesy to coldness and cruelty was a mistake. Was he now so overconfident because he believed he was in sight of his goal?

I said quickly, "Pay no heed to Mr. Deacon, Harriet. Only the doctor can testify to Lady Katherine's condition and I know that Doctor Harvey is well satisfied with her."

"I doubt if he would be, if he could see her now."

Matthew's voice was both smug and contemptuous. My glance reverted quickly to my mother. The charming, gentle face was twitching and distorted, the mouth slack, the eyes staring into space with a mixture of vacancy and fear. The Dresden figure seemed to have shrunk, crouching within the depths of the wing chair as if for refuge, fragile hands clawing the arms in a frenzy of anxiety.

I was with her in an instant, covering the trembling hands with my own, kneeling beside her, and saying, "Listen to me, listen to me! *You are all right!* Understand? There is nothing wrong with you, nothing at all! He is making it all up, he and the girl between them. They want to frighten you, to convince you — "

Harriet interrupted anxiously. "Oh, miss, call the doctor! Call Doctor Harvey at once!"

"You'll be wasting your time," Matthew

Deacon said calmly. "The industrious doctor isn't at home. He has gone to London on a wild-goose chase."

"How do you know?" I demanded.

"There is precious little I don't know, but for Harriet's peace of mind I'll consent to another doctor being called."

"*You* will consent? And what makes you think you have the right?"

His only answer was an enigmatic little smile, and Harriet said anxiously, "I don't think her ladyship would let any other doctor examine her, sir."

"*I* won't let any other doctor examine her," I stated forcefully, "and, what is more, it would be unethical for any other doctor to attend a patient who was not his own, without the consent of her regular practitioner." I snatched the vulgar doll from Matthew Deacon's hands and held it out to Harriet. "Put that in the dustbin, Harriet, and rescue the one which the girl threw there."

She accepted the new doll distastefully. "Wherever did this come from?"

"It was a present to Lady Katherine from her daughter, and apparently has Mr. Deacon's full approval."

"Oh, surely not, sir? You wouldn't let Miss Belinda give a thing like this to her ladyship!"

"Don't be a fool, Harriet, I didn't even know about it."

I wasn't so sure of that, but merely said, "Quickly, please, Harriet!"

When she had gone, I ignored Matthew Deacon altogether and he, to my surprise, was silent, although I could feel his calculating eyes on me as I gave Katherine my full attention again. When Harriet returned I would send her upstairs for the tranquilizing pills which, since her pseudo-daughter's arrival, my mother had no longer needed. In the meantime, I refused to leave her alone with this man.

It wasn't long before Harriet came back, her face even more shocked and puzzled. She held out Katherine's doll. "It's filthy now," she said. "I'll have to clean it up. Whatever made Miss Belinda do such a thing?"

At the sight of the doll, my mother gave a cry and held out eager hands toward it.

I said gently, "Harriet will wash the

clothes and clean the doll thoroughly, and it will be just as good as before — ”

"No one but me must bathe my baby!"

Matthew Deacon uttered a contemptuous sound.

"For heaven's sake, let's end this farce! Throw that doll out, once and for all. Belinda was right; the thing is only fit for refuse. Where is the sense in keeping it? Why don't you listen to me, Katherine, or can't you? Have your senses gone completely?"

"Get out!" I cried. "Leave this house at once! Harriet, get rid of him."

"Mr. Deacon, sir, what's come over you?"

I declared, "If anyone is insane, it is *he*!"

I was totally unprepared for his reaction. He took a blind step toward me, his hand uplifted. I saw it poised above me — thick, strong fingers covered with dark hairs, blunt fingernails with unpleasant, dry ridges. He clenched them into a brutal fist and I stood rigid, my brain wondering for one paralyzing moment just how I was to dodge the oncoming blow. Then, to my amazement, Harriet went to his side, placed her hand on his uplifted arm, and said, "Quiet now, Mr. Deacon. Quiet now."

Her words had a surprising effect. Matthew was calm immediately. The thick fist unclenched and the hand fell. He passed it across his eyes, then turned and walked toward the door. He had almost reached it when the girl appeared, standing within the aperture. She was wearing the black chiffon. It clung in all the right places and revealed all it was intended to.

"Like it?" she sang. "*Maman* — look at me! And you, m'sieur! Look at me, everyone!"

I saw swift admiration in Matthew's face and shock in my mother's. She was suddenly still, her trembling and uncertainty gone, then in a tone of surprising authority she commanded, "Go upstairs and take that thing off, Belinda."

"Don't be stuffy, *Maman*! I know this is provincial England, but please remember that I am French. In France a woman's body is not regarded as something to be covered."

"There are ways of revealing it, Belinda, which can make it appear charming and lovely, and others which make it seem crude and indecent. That is the way you look now."

"How *dare* you speak to me like that!"

"Because I have the authority to do so." My mother leaned wearily against the tall back of her chair, exhausted by her recent outburst but very clearly in possession of her faculties. "I am your mother and, as such, can decide your future at any moment I wish."

The girl's eyes flashed her anger, but it was a look tinged with sudden alarm. Her glance flew to the lawyer and there was accusation in it.

He avoided her glance, and the girl's anger changed to pleading.

"You wouldn't turn against me, would you, *Maman*?"

"I have never opposed you, Belinda."

"No? Then why did you not acknowledge me until recently? Why ignore my existence? You owe me something for that. You promised to make it up to me, to be generous. Surely you intend to keep that promise?"

"I have another kind of promise to fulfill, my child. My father placed a responsibility on me — the responsibility of deciding whether you were a right and fit person to inherit what is, to a Tredgold, a sacred trust, a family legacy which should be cherished with pride and served with respect."

The girl moved impatiently.

"Do you really expect me to appreciate family obligations when, all my life, I have been considered unworthy of them, outside them?"

"You are not outside them now, Belinda. You are part of Lyonhurst. It is your heritage."

"*And* I shall have it!"

"If I decide so."

The girl looked at the older woman for a long moment, eyes narrowed, mouth tense.

"I do believe you are not such a fool as you seem," she said slowly, "but *I* am not a fool, either. I didn't come all this way just to be questioned and looked over and chucked out again. Two can play at that game, believe me! If you say I am not good enough to inherit, I will say *you* are not fit to decide, and your trusted solicitor will back me up. Isn't that so, Mr. Deacon?"

"If necessary," he agreed, "and, of course, if it is true." He seemed evasive now. Unsure of himself. Anxious to tread carefully again.

"What do you mean? *If* it is true? The woman goes round the bend at times. We have all seen that! She plays with dolls! She calls one by my name! She bathes it as if it were her baby! How can she be in her right mind if she behaves like that? And how can anyone not in their right mind be fit enough to sign documents and make decisions, and delegate property and money and bequests? Look at her now! She's trembling again. She's crying like a child, blubbering like an idiot!"

Anger charged my voice as I rapped out, "For the second time, Matthew Deacon, get out of here and take this girl with you. She is deliberately upsetting Lady Katherine. Both of you are. You are trying to break her down, to terrorize her, but I won't let you.

Understand?" I gathered my mother close again, protecting her as if she were my child.

The girl came and stood before us — tall, slim, and brazenly arrogant.

"The only person who is going to leave this house, my dear Miss Conrad, is yourself. I will see to that. You have no control here, but *I* am going to have plenty. And when I have it, do you know what I intend to do? Do you, my dear *Maman?* Well, listen while I tell you! I'm going to make this crumbling old ruin pay. I'll turn it into a first-class, money-spinning hotel, lavish and luxurious and lousy with the rich and the famous. It will be the first of a whole chain of luxury hotels, all financed with the Tredgold money. *My* money!"

"As you once told me, ma'am'selle," I put in sarcastically, "you speak faultless English. As if it were your native tongue."

She flushed, faltered, then rallied, but before she could answer, I continued relentlessly, "As for the plushy hotel you visualize, it all sounds terribly familiar.

380

There was one in Park Lane, built to outplush all others, and another at Brighton, more garish than any — flash-in-the-pan places which enjoyed brief and spectacular popularity and ended as disastrous flops, and all thought up by a speculator-*cum*-financier named Hubert Clayton. You've heard of him, I'm sure. He came from these parts originally, didn't he, Mr. Deacon? Wasn't he a client of yours before he went into bankruptcy from which he never recovered? Funnily enough, I was reading about him just now — a paragraph in that newspaper over there. He died some time ago but his name is back in the news because some company with which he was once associated, another of his South Sea bubbles, went into liquidation recently. It is reported on the City page, with a brief biography of Hubert Clayton himself. He had a daughter who went on the stage. A promising actress, the newspaper called her."

Harriet was looking from one to the other of us, frankly puzzled. My mother was leaning against me, her eyes closed, tears forcing themselves from beneath tired eyelids, too distressed even to hear what I said. She looked beaten and exhausted. Only the girl and the man were comprehending and attentive. The girl shrugged her shoulders and drawled, "My dear Miss Conrad, I don't know what you are talking about."

"I think you do, ma'am'selle. Harriet, will you fetch Lady Katherine's tablets? They are in the drawer of her bedside table. And then make a cup of tea for her, please. Come," I said to my mother, "we will sit out on the terrace until Harriet comes back. You can put your feet up and rest."

She obeyed, allowing me to lead her to a reclining chair just a little out of the sun. I sat beside her, longing for David's return, wondering when he would come and what news he would have when he did, praying for the sound of his step and the sound of his voice; for suddenly I felt more alone than I had ever felt. Despite my show of assurance, despite my anger and determination, I was afraid of Matthew Deacon and this girl, who would stop at nothing to gain their ends. I knew there would be no more cat-and-mouse game between us, for I had flung down the gauntlet with a vengeance and had only myself to blame if they picked it up.

25

I THOUGHT my mother was dozing, for her eyes were closed, but after a while she said, "Was I hard on my daughter, Gillian? Did I show intolerance and a lack of understanding?"

"I don't think so," I answered carefully.

"And her dress, did you react toward it as I did?"

"It surprised me."

"You are being tactful, I think. Which means that you, also, did not quite approve."

I couldn't approve of anything that girl did, for I hated her, I thought ironically. Aloud, I said, "It was a beautiful dress."

"She is a beautiful girl, too stunning to cheapen herself like that." She opened her eyes and looked at me. "Shall I tell you something? I was wrong about her. Yes, wrong about my own daughter. When I first saw her I believed her to be lovely in every way. But she isn't." Katherine's voice was suddenly old and sad.

"She is extremely pretty, Lady Katherine."

"I am not talking about her looks, my dear. I am talking now about her nature. Belinda is cruel. Vicious and spiteful and cruel. And it breaks my heart."

Seeing my mother in such distress tore my own heart to shreds. But what could I do? Tell her the truth and beg for her secrecy until David returned? How could I expect her to believe me now, when she didn't before? And if by some miracle she did believe me, how would she react to Matthew Deacon and the girl? She would be even more frightened of them than she was now, and since this morning's scene I knew that the terror they had implanted in her was very real. They had gone more than halfway to convincing her of her own insanity. No, I decided. She had faced enough stress and bewilderment for today. A few more hours could make no difference and David was bound to return before long. He couldn't stay away from his practice indefinitely, and so long as I stayed at my mother's side, forestalling any move which Matthew and the girl might make, what could happen?

Despite these thoughts I shivered involuntarily. Katherine said, "You should have a cardigan about your shoulders, my dear. There is a coolness in the wind today."

"I'm all right," I told her, wishing she would discuss her so-called daughter again, for I wasn't saintly enough not to enjoy hearing the girl summed up so well, especially by the very person she wished to deceive.

At that precise moment the girl reappeared. She had changed from the scandalous gown into a simple skirt and blouse and nothing could have been a more effective contrast. She wore no jewelry and no makeup. She had brushed her hair until it hung in a smooth curtain about her shoulders, imparting an air of cleanliness and goodness and simplicity. She had adopted the very role which would most please my mother and it had an immediate and gratifying effect.

Katherine looked at her, pleasure lighting her eyes, relief curving her mouth.

"My dear, you look yourself again — as you were when you first arrived."

The girl dropped to her knees and buried her head in my mother's lap.

"Forgive me, *Maman*. Forgive me and understand. I've had so little all my life! That gown went to my head and oh, I am so ashamed now!"

I wanted to scream, and yet I sat quite still, almost mesmerized by the scene. "A promising actress . . . " the newspaper paragraph had said. But this girl was more than promising.

Was she really the daughter of 'Rogue' Clayton, as the press used to call him? The man had made big news at one time. He had been behind big city frauds as well as spectacular business ventures — a man without conscience and without mercy, just as this girl was. Had I really hit upon her identity?

I thrust down a sense of alarm, regretting my impetuosity, a characteristic which had landed me into this whole sorry plight. If I had introduced myself legally and properly in the first place, this terrible situation would never have arisen and Matthew Deacon could never have denied my existence or thought of producing someone in my place, for he himself was the Tredgold lawyer and it would have been to him that I would have presented the indisputable proof of my birth.

Which brought me right back to the still unresolved question as to why, having guessed who I was, he didn't immediately challenge me with it. Could David possibly be right in declaring that the solicitor's original intention was not to look for Belinda Lemaître at all, and that only when faced with my arrival had he done something about it? Or pretended to.

But the conversation I overheard yesterday as I descended the stairs — even before the girl stole my Bible they knew who I was. That was why she searched my room at the first opportunity and removed the one possession which linked me with this house. How and when I had betrayed my identity still eluded me.

Katherine was stroking the girl's hair and I experienced a swift jealousy, which made me look away. It was then that I saw my sketchbook at the girl's feet and realized with a cold sense of shock that my Bible was not the only thing she had stolen from my room.

But my portfolio was still in my wardrobe. I had seen it only today! It was at the bottom, standing propped against the back, just as I had left it, but it hadn't occurred to me to open it and look inside. It must have been lying there, empty, ever since she extracted these sketches, retied the portfolio, and replaced it as if untouched.

Slowly, I stooped and picked up the sketchbook, and as I did so the girl lifted her head and watched me. There was a faint smile on her lips and I knew she was secretly laughing at me. She leaned against the long reclining seat, her head still resting on my mother's knee. She was like a cat, quietly purring . . .

"Your companion is examining my amateur drawings, *Maman*. I hope you are not too severe a critic, mademoiselle. I have a very meager talent, I'm afraid, but Lyonhurst offers so many opportunities for sketching that I have been unable to resist them — especially the beautiful wrought-iron gates. I have drawn them in detail, as you see."

389

I was looking at the sketch in my hand
— my sketch, my handiwork, bearing my
signature. I sat very still, shocked into
silence. Now I knew how I had betrayed
my identity to Matthew Deacon, and
when. Right at that first moment of our
meeting, out there in the lane, before
I ever presented myself at the manor
or even thought of doing so. When
he looked at my fallen sketchbook and
then at me, there had been a subtle
change in his manner — a watchfulness,
a wariness, hidden curiosity which made
him unwilling to let me go. That was
why he had ridden after me, trying to
make me admit who I was and where I
was staying. Into what devious channels
had his astute mind then plunged when
he later saw me in this house as Gillian
Conrad? What game had he decided to
play, and why?

That was the last remaining question,
the one piece of the jigsaw puzzle which
I had still to fit into place. It seemed
obvious that, knowing the full extent
of the Tredgold fortune, he wished to
acquire it, or at least a share of it, but
how would he have done this without

producing the girl if, in the first place, it had not been his intention to do so? It was my arrival on the scene which had precipitated that step. He had produced her, complete with apparently watertight evidence, legally testifying to its authenticity and thus forestalling any action I might take — providing he and the girl acted quickly and effectively.

I felt terrifyingly alone. Why didn't David come? Had he drawn a blank in London, abandoned the quest, returned to Oakwell, gone back to his house and his work and given up the whole thing? Not David! He was too tenacious, too determined, a man who climbed mountains and explored jungles and did things which the average person would never dare. He disliked Matthew Deacon; mistrusted him, too. He had gone away, determined to outwit him by bringing back evidence which would counter the girl's completely.

But, oh, God, make him hurry! Bring him back soon, because it is vital, urgent!

The girl's hand reached out, took the sketchbook from me, and handed it to my mother. "Doesn't this prove how

391

much Lyonhurst means to me, dear *Maman*? I have been here so short a time, and already I have made several sketches of the place . . . "

Katherine was touched. She studied my drawing of the gates with pride. I knew she was regretting her earlier criticism and was eager to make amends.

"I had no idea you were so talented, Belinda. I am proud, very proud." She hesitated, and looked at her with a pleading little smile. "You must forgive me, my dear, I fear I misjudged you."

"In what way?"

"I was afraid you were avaricious, seeing Lyonhurst only as a source of gain, not as a home of which to be proud."

"But I am proud of it, *Mamam*. So proud that I want to share it with the world."

"That could easily be done," I pointed out, "by presenting it to the National Trust. Or it would make a wonderful convalescent home as a subsidiary to one of the hospitals in Canterbury."

"That is an excellent idea, Gillian! I must suggest it to David. We could still retain this wing for ourselves . . . "

The girl cut across my mother's words.

"I'm all for opening it to the public," she said. "*There's* a money-making scheme for you! It could become another Woburn."

"We don't need money, my dear. The Tredgolds are still fortunate in that respect."

"Death duties will swallow it, *Maman*. Be practical."

Katherine laughed.

"My dear, I am not dead yet, nor likely to be so long as I have Doctor Harvey to look after me! And long before that I shall avert ultimate financial depletion by giving a great deal of it away to worthwhile causes. Cancer research, needy children — there are many organizations which could benefit from a fortune such as ours, and still leave enough for us."

The girl said lightly, "Charity begins at home, *Maman* — remember that. If you give me my rightful share now, you will reduce ultimate death duties considerably."

"I am aware of that, my dear. Matthew

393

will see to everything. You have no need to worry your pretty head about that. Please, no more talk about turning our home into a hotel."

"Very well, *Maman*. I won't speak about it."

It was an ambiguous remark, but it made Katherine happy.

"And there is something else I won't talk about," the girl promised. "You."

"Me, my dear? In what way?"

"You know what way. Your moods, shall we call them? That seems the kindest word."

I said sharply, "Enough of that! Don't start again, ma'am'selle."

"You see, *Maman*, even your devoted companion admits that we mustn't discuss your condition, so I promise to be good. I will never refer to it again. I will even pretend not to notice it!"

"I meant nothing of the kind," I said angrily. "I was warning you not to distress Lady Katherine, or to make false accusations . . . "

Wide-eyed and innocent, the girl answered in hurt tones, "False accusations? What can you mean?"

"Precisely that. Your insistence that Lady Katherine is unbalanced is cruel and totally unfounded. Everyone can be emotionally upset at times." I found that I was standing beside my mother, my hand on her shoulder. She reached up and patted it gratefully.

"Belinda doesn't mean all she says, Gillian, but you are kind to defend me."

The girl took Katherine's hand and kissed it gently, saying, "You are beginning to understand me better, *Maman*. You realize that I am a tease. I cannot help being so!"

"Were you teasing when you gave her that tawdry doll?" I asked.

"But, of course! I thought it fun! I expected it to make her laugh!" The girl pouted prettily. "Am I so very naughty, *Maman*? Your companion seems to think so."

I couldn't stand much more of this. I wanted to turn away and leave them, but refused to allow this girl one moment alone with Katherine, so went back to my seat, and at that moment Matthew Deacon came walking across the terrace — smiling and affable, compelling in that strange way of his. One was always aware of this man: of his sheer brute strength, his animal magnetism, his unreadable personality.

I was afraid of him, but I smiled to cover it up. The girl smiled, too, saying, "Here comes Mr. Deacon. Let us ask him how he thinks the future of this lovely old house should be planned."

"That sounds as if you are thinking of changing it," he said, "but why can't it continue as before?"

"Because we are all agreed that good use should be made of it, that the public should have a chance to enjoy it."

To my surprise, he answered sharply, "That is unthinkable. It has belonged to the Tredgolds for generations and must continue to. The very thought of the public enjoying it in any way at all is utterly distasteful!"

The girl threw him a hateful glance, but since she was still sitting on the terrace with her head close to my mother's knee, Katherine did not see, and if Matthew himself did, he gave no sign. He continued imperturbably: "But

I agree that others should be given the opportunity to appreciate it. Lyonhurst has remained closed for too long. It should open its doors. Life should return. I remember the balls which used to be held here, the gaiety, the dinner parties, the entertaining which made it one of the most famous houses in Kent. You will reinstate all that now, I hope. Your daughter's arrival should open a new era."

The girl clasped her hands ecstatically.

"Oh, *Maman*! Was life really like that here, once upon a time? Will it really come back?"

The longing in her voice was irresistible, so I was not surprised when Katherine responded.

"Of course, my dear. It is wrong that anyone so young and so alive as yourself should live as I have all these years — cut off from the world."

"Then you won't abandon the idea of the dance to launch me into society, to introduce me to people?"

"Naturally, I won't abandon it. Did you really think I would?"

"Well, darling, after your reaction

to my dress I wouldn't have been surprised!"

"If it could be made a little more modest . . . " my mother began tentatively.

"It most certainly will be," Matthew put in, and it was significant of my mother's complete acceptance of him that she didn't seem to find his authority over the girl surprising. That her solicitor should dictate in such a way must surely have struck anyone else as odd, but Katherine saw him only as the man who was responsible for finding her daughter and for this reason accepted his attitude toward her without question.

"When will the dance be held?" the girl demanded impatiently.

"As soon as everything is settled, my dear."

"Meaning legal tie-ups, proper acknowledgment of me as your daughter, strict adherence to the terms of that tiresome will? No time limit was imposed, surely? Is there any reason why you cannot sign all the necessary papers or what-have-you right away?"

"Absolutely none," Matthew stated. "I have everything with me. It can be settled immediately. In fact, if Miss Conrad had not intervened, the papers would have been signed yesterday."

"Miss Conrad?" the girl said sharply. "What has it to do with her?"

"Nothing at all," said Matthew. "Except that I wouldn't allow Lady Katherine to be bothered with business matters at that particular moment. I had brought her tea, that was all, and saw no reason why an hour which she enjoys should be spoiled by dreary legal matters for which there was no urgency."

"Who says there is none?" the girl rapped. "And what has it to do with you, may I ask?"

"Hush, Belinda! Gillian's actions are all prompted by concern for myself. She is right. There is no urgency. A few hours, a few days, even a few weeks can make no difference. I will sign the documents and everything will be settled satisfactorily, so why be impatient?" The gentle voice broke off, then continued in surprise, "Why, who is this?"

Each one of us followed my mother's glance and each one of us was equally surprised. Visitors to Lyonhurst were virtually unknown these days, but a woman had appeared around the side of the house and now she came toward the terrace, approaching diffidently.

I saw to my astonishment that it was Mrs. Tracey.

She came toward us shyly, mounting the steps of the terrace with a touch of embarrassment which, I could see, vied with curiosity, but her discomfort was nothing compared with my own. I wanted to hide, to run away, but could do neither. In another minute we would be face to face.

Then I felt an extraordinary relief, although to see David approaching with Françoise, complete with infallible evidence, would have been preferable to an embarrassing meeting with a village woman with whom I had lodged under another name.

Her eyes were on Lady Katherine, but they flickered momentarily to the girl and then to the man. The girl caught her attention and I wasn't surprised, for she was certainly eye-catching.

Mrs. Tracey said diffidently, "Excuse me for coming round this way, Lady

Katherine, but I could get no reply from the front — "

"If you mean the front doors, that isn't surprising, Mrs. Tracey, since they are never used."

It was Matthew who answered, assuming authority with typical assurance, and the woman said, "I didn't know that, Mr. Deacon."

"How could you? In any case, you should have gone to the tradesman's entrance. It is at the side."

"I did go there, sir, but the housekeeper didn't seem to be around."

"Harriet is probably busy in another part of the house," my mother said pleasantly. "Can I be of help, Mrs. Tracey?"

"I just brought this telegram, madam. Millie, that's the girl who helps me with the postal, couldn't be spared."

"So you trudged all the way from the village? That was good of you."

My mother took the wire. I could see Matthew Deacon's eyes focused on it with curiosity, and knew that he longed to get his hands on it.

Mrs. Tracey's mouth fell open in

surprise when she saw me. "Why, Miss Masters! I thought you had gone on to Margate . . . "

Katherine said, "This is my companion, Mrs. Tracey, who looks after me, very kindly, too. This telegram is for you, my dear."

She held it out to me. I took it mechanically and saw that the envelope was addressed to Gillian Conrad, care of Lyonhurst, Oakwell, Kent. Had Mrs. Tracey recognized the name of Mrs. Butler's niece? The question was replaced by an urgent hope that the telegram was from David. I willed it to be, and knew that I was right even before I opened it. Nevertheless, I was almost afraid to do so. Wasn't it possible that the telegram might be for the real Gillian Conrad, from someone unaware that she had never arrived?

My eye fell on the sketchbook again, the pad which Mrs. Tracey had examined so eagerly. She would vouch that these drawings were mine! That would be one lie proved, at least, so I said quickly, "Mrs. Tracey, do you remember . . . " but the woman had already turned and walked away, murmuring something about making a mistake and being "sorry for troubling you, madam." She was now making her getaway as fast as possible, too shy to remain. A moment later her hurrying figure disappeared.

"You must have a double, my dear," my mother said. "Poor Mrs. Tracey, she was quite embarrassed by her mistake. I wish I had offered her tea before she left. I wonder, Belinda, if you could catch her — "

"Let the woman go," Matthew said in a peremptory tone. "She was only doing her job. She is paid by the GPO for the service." His eyes were upon me as he spoke. He was waiting for me to open my telegram — alert, watchful.

I slit the envelope. I read the message several times. It needed every ounce of my self-control to hide my reaction and to still the wild elation within me.

"Not bad news, I hope?" said the girl.

"Far from it, mademoiselle. Good news. Very good news, indeed."

I couldn't keep a note of challenge from my voice. She sat very still, watching me, no longer laughing, no longer purring. To tantalize her more I tore up the telegram very slowly. Then I went to the balustrade of the terrace and threw the tiny fragments into the air. The wind carried them away like snowflakes.

I turned and saw Matthew Deacon watching me and I looked back at him in open challenge. *Run after them, try to catch them!* my eyes mocked.

His face flushed an angry red, but it was a fleeting betrayal, soon overcome. He rose, pushing back his chair so that it scraped loudly on the flagged terrace. "I must be off," he said, "but before I go, Katherine, let's get the formalities over, shall we? Your signature to the documents will only take a moment."

"It will take her much longer to read the documents through," I said. "What's the hurry, Mr. Deacon?"

He opened his mouth to snub me, but my mother forestalled him by saying, "Could they not wait until this evening, Matthew? Come to dinner, and then I will sign them. Gillian is a wise little soul, much wiser than her years, and she is right to insist that I read them, although I confess I shall probably not understand a word!"

"Then you must take my assurance that they are in order," the man answered curtly.

"Of course I do, Matthew. Please don't imagine that I doubt you."

"Then why stall?" the girl demanded.

"Stall?" my mother echoed. "I don't understand, my dear."

I said, "You don't have to understand, Lady Katherine. You don't have to worry about a thing. Just relax and let everything slide. In any case, documents have to be witnessed, and your signature must be appended in the presence of witnesses."

"We could get Harriet and Buxton," Deacon said impatiently.

"But they are beneficiaries, Matthew. As you know, I am settling pensions on them before I die because I see no reason why they should wait, and what with life becoming so expensive these days, I think it a good idea. Besides, I want David to witness my signature, also Gillian herself. I could not have two more reliable friends."

The girl protested, "But Doctor Harvey

405

is away, *Maman*."

"He will return, ma'am'selle," I said pleasantly. "He will return very soon."

I saw Matthew's eyes narrow speculatively.

I was annoyed with myself for the slip, but on the whole didn't regret it. It was well for him to know that, very soon, I would no longer be alone.

He changed the subject by saying, "As far as I am concerned, Katherine, you can have anyone you like as witnesses. Meanwhile, let us discuss more pleasant things. The coming ball, for instance. You told me you wished to have the house redecorated for the occasion, the closed wings opened up, and the ballroom made ready, so the sooner this work is put in hand the better. I will attend to everything for you immediately, but as regards redecoration, this is something a feminine mind should decide on. I am a better authority on horseflesh than curtains, and stables than drawing rooms."

Katherine smiled. "All the same, you appreciate beautiful things. You have admired many pieces in this house, many

406

treasured antiques, and your judgment has always been good, but if you wish to have my daughter's cooperation, do so, by all means."

"But I don't. The whole thing must be a surprise for her. Cinderella mustn't set the stage for her own ball! Spare your companion for an hour or so. Her advice would be helpful."

All too soon I was standing in the empty ballroom wing, alone with Matthew Deacon.

26

AS soon as we were out of ear-shot I said, "I can't think why you should want my advice."

"I don't. I want your company. Does that surprise you? I have made many attempts to get to know you since the day we met in the lane."

"Time is short, Mr. Deacon."

He frowned.

"You never call me Matthew now. Why?"

"Because I never think of you as Matthew."

"Nor do I, as a matter of fact, ever think of you as Gillian. Why did you say time was short? Are you afraid?"

"Of what?"

"Of it slipping by."

"I am young. My whole life is before me."

"Isn't it strange," he said as he opened the door leading into the unused part of the house, "how we always assume that

408

life is to be long? But why should it be? 'Only the good die young,' or so the old saying goes, which means that your days could already be numbered, for I am sure you are a very good girl, Miss Conrad. A girl who would never do anything wicked, or underhanded, or deceitful."

"Such as pretending to be someone else? Assuming another person's identity? And yet you know I have done precisely that and am still, in fact, an impostor."

The door closed behind us. We stood beneath the minstrel's gallery, the vast, marble-floored hall ahead of us, the vaulted ceiling spanning it like an enormous dome and the sweeping marble staircases rising from either side like those flanking the entrance to the palace of Fontainebleau. He walked ahead, saying appreciatively, "Magnificent, isn't it? And yet there's no reason why it should remain a relic of the past. It could come into its own again. So you admit to being an impostor at last? I must confess that I admire you for keeping it up so long. You have guts, Miss Conrad. Or is it merely audacity? Tell me, do you think it will be sufficient to have

409

this old marble work washed down, or should it be whitened? There's some new and ingenious process, I believe, which restores the surface of stone without any suggestion of artificiality. It is a pity you will not be here to see it when restored, since it is obvious that you love this old house. But you don't belong, you know. You can never belong. Not as I do."

"I belong by right of birth, a birth which is now acknowledged. That doesn't apply to you."

His reaction was startling. *"Don't you dare to say that!"*

I quelled a little spark of fear and retorted, "Why not, since it's true? You know who I am. You have known all along. I didn't realize that I had betrayed my identity out there in the lane, but it has been obvious for some days that you were aware of it."

His flash of anger had gone. He looked pleased instead.

"When did it first become obvious, Miss Conrad?"

"The day you tried to kill me."

"Are you calling me a murderer?"

"You would have been, had you

410

succeeded. Instead, you killed Rufus."

"*You* killed Rufus with your incompetence as a rider, your inability to handle him, your stupid bungling of a perfectly straightforward brush fence! You killed a magnificent horse who was more to me than any human being, and for that I shall never forgive you."

We began to climb the sweeping marble stairs on the right of the hall. We took them slowly, looking at each other, sizing each other up.

"Was Rufus more to you than that girl you brought here in my name?"

"But your name is Conrad. Gillian Conrad. You said so yourself. Prove that it is anything else!"

"It will be, soon. Meanwhile, you heard what Mrs. Tracey called me — Masters. You know what a near French translation of Masters is, surely?"

"Lemaître, of course. As for Rufus meaning more to me than the girl, naturally he did."

"But you love her. Are having an affair with her."

"So you know about that? Well, that is the right word. It's no more than that. To tell the truth, she's a tiresome creature, but at the moment she has her uses, not the least of which is her histrionic talent. She could succeed as an actress if she were not so infected by her father's grandiose get-rich-quick ideas . . . "

"Such as turning Lyonhurst into a plushy hotel?"

He shuddered distastefully.

"Dreadful thought, isn't it? I wouldn't allow it, of course. I have other plans for this house."

We were halfway up the stairs. He paused, looking up at an ancestral portrait — dark, forbidding, depressing. He touched it with his thick fingers; they were surprisingly gentle. "These portraits must be cleaned," he murmured. "I doubt if that swine of a man ever bothered to have them done."

"Meaning my grandfather?" I asked pleasantly.

"Meaning Sir Humphrey." He turned and laughed at me. "My dear, how can you claim him as your grandfather in the face of the indisputable evidence that girl produced?"

"And which you, as my mother's

lawyer, confirmed as genuine? It will be easy enough, when David and Françoise arrive."

"Françoise?" he said sharply. I had startled him. "And who is Françoise?"

"You know perfectly well. My father's sister. The woman who brought me up. The woman whom this girl — prompted by you? — claims to have been killed in an air raid. That was a ridiculous story and a foolish mistake. Hasn't it occurred to you that Françoise Lemaitre could still be alive and traceable, and that I, Katherine's real daughter, could be too?"

He shrugged. We had reached the long landing and now began to walk toward the deserted ballroom. Tredgold ancestors watched us as we passed, staring silently and accusingly from their tarnished frames. Rows of eyes, as cold as this man's . . .

I stood still, staring at him. He turned in his tracks and said sharply, "What's the matter?" His voice echoed in the high reaches of the ceiling, coming back to us mockingly. I couldn't answer, because I was suddenly bereft of speech, full of fearful dawning comprehension.

He was standing directly beneath a massive portrait; the features were identical with his own. The thick neck. The sensual mouth with its hint of cruelty. The handsome, rather brutal features which, nonetheless, held a certain charm and certainly great physical appeal. My glance went from the portrait to Matthew Deacon, and remained there. A slow smile spread across his face.

"So — you see it at last. There's no escaping certain Tredgold features, once their blood is in you."

"It is in me, too."

"No one would believe it. You must resemble your father — that impecunious young Frenchman who seduced poor Kathy."

"He loved her! They loved each other!"

"Love!" he scoffed. "The thing singers croon about and romantic writers weave dreams about? That isn't love. Love is an appetite, insatiably greedy."

"You are wrong."

"Don't dare tell me I am wrong! I am never wrong! No Tredgold can be."

"You're not one of them. You don't

belong to them, not to Lyonhurst."

I was taunting him deliberately because it was the only way to get the truth out of him. Strangely, beneath my dislike, pity was beginning to stir. Was it this which had made my mother treat him as a brother and earned Harriet's loyalty?

He took a step toward me — swift and angry, with a threat of violence in it. I stepped aside, but he caught my wrist and pulled me close to him. I could feel his hot breath fanning my cheek as he gasped. *"That isn't true! Take it back!"*

"I can't."

He struck me. The back of his hand fell heavily across my cheek, the knuckles hard as iron. Pain was a blinding flash, a thunderclap in my ears.

"Who are you?" I gasped.

"The son who should inherit. The one who should belong. The man no Tredgold will acknowledge."

His voice was thin and venomous. Then, with one of his surprising changes of mood, he put out a hand and touched my cheek gently. "I'm sorry I hit you, Belinda. But you shouldn't have come here, you know. You should have stayed away forever, and now you leave me no choice. I shall have to get rid of you. A pity, because in your rather quaint way you're attractive. Not pretty like your mother was once, but very endearing. I've wanted to kiss you many times. Did you guess? But I knew I repelled you. Most women find me attractive — physically, at least. That is the only use I have for love, just as my mother had. Her appetite for sex was insatiable. I'm not referring to poor Henrietta, of course. She wasn't my mother, although she did her best for me. I can never make up my mind whether I admired her or despised her for that. Henrietta Deacon couldn't have children. Everyone thought that a tragedy, especially your grandmother — another Belinda."

"Prudence? Was she your mother?"

"Of course. Prudence the imprudent. What a tart she must have been!"

"Don't talk like that, Matthew. Have pity for her."

"Pity — for *her?* Why should I have? She had no pity for poor Henrietta."

"Did you care for Henrietta?"

He pondered the question. "I've never really thought about it, but I suppose, in a way, I did. At the same time, I grew to despise both her and my father. Oh, yes, Sir Basil Deacon was my father and I suppose it must be said that he did the right thing by me. At least he accepted me as his son and gave me his name and his home, but that couldn't compare with Lyonhurst."

"All the same, it must have been a good place to be, Matthew." It was easy to call him Matthew now. Pity had removed my dislike of him, but not my fear. That still stalked along the icy corridor, ready to clutch me.

"A good place?" he echoed. "Would you regard a place as good if you were there on sufferance, patronized, tolerated, endured in the name of respectability? The things which respectable people do, the situations they will face, the shams and pretenses they will perpetrate to preserve their precious facade! Sir Basil Deacon wanted a son and heir. His wife wanted a son and heir. Between them, they couldn't produce one. But Prudence Tredgold did, and it was his.

Scandal! Imagine the wagging tongues and the shaking heads — even worse, the newspaper reports! A man who aspired to become a leading judge and the daughter of one of the most respectable British families! Imagine Sir Humphrey's sister being the guilty party in one of the tastiest divorces of the century! There was the little bastard — me — to prove it. So Henrietta and Basil did the noble thing; they adopted the child as their own, scandal averted, and Prudence conveniently took sleeping tablets to speed her way out of their lives."

His voice was as bitter as his words, but I wiped my cheek with the back of my hand. Matthew said wonderingly, "Why — you're crying, Belinda!"

I made no answer. He put his hands on my shoulders and shook me gently. He even smiled — compassionately, gratefully. "You have a soft heart, Belinda. Such a thing is a burden in life. Get rid of it."

"I should hate to go through life without it, Matthew."

His hands fell away impatiently.

418

"Then you're a fool, but I am not. I feel nothing for anyone. Not even Katherine, who has been kind to me. I have used her without compunction, and shall continue to. And that foolish old woman, Harriet — I've kept on the right side of her, too. Both of them know the truth about me, and actually feel sorry for me. I despise them for it, but don't discourage it — pity can have its uses, especially from a woman."

"And the girl — the girl you brought here? Why did you do that?"

"My dear, I had to, thanks to you. When Sir Humphrey died and his will was read, I naturally hadn't the slightest intention of tracing you, because I knew that if I did Katherine would pass everything on to you and that would be the end of my own chances forever. So I merely pretended I was looking for you. I have never given Katherine any cause to mistrust me. I think, even as a small boy, I sensed that it would be wise to bide my time, to keep on the right side of the Tredgolds."

"How did you find out the truth?"

"About myself? Guessed it, partially,

but not until I was actually grown up. My father's law firm always handled the Tredgolds' affairs and when I graduated and joined it I was sent there one day with some papers. I stood down there in the hall, looking at the family portraits, disliking them and yet coveting them, feeling resentful and envious and wondering why. And then I saw my own reflection in a mirror and it was like looking at one of them. I'm only surprised you didn't notice it yourself."

"It isn't all that apparent, Matthew, but I admit it is there."

"You see?" he said triumphantly. "That proves I am a Tredgold, doesn't it?"

"Not really. Only through your mother."

"And so are you — only through your mother! So why should you inherit so much? Why not I? Especially since they owe me some compensation for not acknowledging me."

"They didn't acknowledge me, either."

"Belatedly, they did. But, even so, their obligation to you was not so great as their obligation to me. I was something to be fobbed off onto another woman, taken on by her. You, at least, were wanted and loved by your father and his sister. Katherine told me the whole story years ago, fondly believing I would be sympathetic. Of course I pretended to be. I've always pretended to be. I knew, one day, it would pay. As for my own birth, eventually I made Henrietta admit the truth."

"Stop feeling sorry for yourself, Matthew. Your lot could have been much worse. Henrietta is the one to pity and to admire. Spare some for your mother, too. She must have been a desperately unhappy woman."

"Don't preach to me!"

I became aware that we had moved toward the ballroom, and now he flung open the double doors with a flourish, saying with a grandiose gesture, "Walk into my parlour!" and again I felt, as once before, that I was no more than a fly, to be devoured by this man, but I entered the ballroom and walked beside him, our footsteps echoing on the bare floor.

Matthew stood still and waved his hand aloft.

"Look at them! They are everywhere.

In the hall, on the stairs, along the landing, even in here! Sanctimonious, self-satisfied, and — oh, so damnably respectable! No illegitimate births marred the family archives, no one born on the wrong side of the blanket was acknowledged by them! But *I* will be acknowledged. I will be master here. I will take their name legally and I will own all that was once theirs!"

"How do you propose to achieve this? By forcing my mother to sign documents handing everything over to the girl?"

"Of course not! She will think she is handing everything over to her daughter. Instead, she will be signing everything over to me. You don't imagine I would be fool enough to put *your* name on those deeds, do you? I'm much too clever for that."

"But if she reads them?"

He shrugged.

"She can, if she wishes. So can you. So can the girl, the doctor, anyone at all! 'Read them, all of you!' I will say, and you will think, my poor Belinda, that that fool of a girl is getting what should be yours, and she will think she has been cleverer than her father ever was, and Katherine will think that her dear long-lost daughter is the genuine article, and as for David Harvey — even he, damn him, will be outwitted, because whatever you say and whatever you hope, he will arrive too late."

I didn't pursue that. There was something I wanted clarified.

"Tell me, Matthew, have you prepared two sets of papers?"

"Of course. The ones I have shown to the girl, with her name on them, and the others which I shall substitute when your mother signs on the dotted line. I can do it, have no fear. Hubert Clayton taught me lots of tricks. We were good friends, he and I. He always said I was an apt pupil, but he was too conceited to realize that I was really far cleverer than he."

"Why did you say that Gillian Conrad had looked after his wife?"

"I had to say something, and quickly. Your unexpected appearance caught me off guard. I didn't show it, did I? I can never be outsmarted. That first meeting of ours in the lane startled me; at least it did when I saw your name on the sketch. I didn't even know you were in the vicinity, and besides, I had visited Katherine only that morning so I knew you couldn't be staying at the manor. Later, when I went to my office, I had a call from the Conrad girl turning down the job. I knew her, of course. I met her when she cared for Henrietta."

"So you knew from the beginning that I wasn't Gillian Conrad and you just let me continue with my masquerade."

"You were not cautious enough. Everyone must always be very, very careful of me."

I suppressed a shiver.

"Let's go back to the terrace, Matthew. Katherine will be wondering why we haven't returned."

"Oh, no, she won't. She believes we are making wonderful plans for redecorating the ballroom." He gave a high-pitched giggle. "As if I would do this place up to please anyone but myself! It is *I* who will live here. I'll be a king in my own domain. Anyone who wishes to see me will have to request an audience. Katherine and Harriet will have to wait on me. I will rule!"

"Don't be ridiculous," I said too abruptly. It provoked his anger again, only this time something else was added to it, something which made his hands tremble and his mouth quiver and his eyes stare with a hard, bright, glazed look from which I turned away.

"I've had enough of this," I said. "Stop play acting and realize you can't get away with any of these far-fetched plans. We don't even have to discuss them further. Our cards are on the table and we have acknowledged the truth to each other. David is bringing Françoise. He caught the night plane to Paris, contacted her at Balmain's and she came straight back with him. She even skipped two other shows to come, and if you knew Françoise, you would know that only life or death would make her do that! It was all in David's telegram, which he sent from the bank — "

"The bank? What bank?"

"Where Françoise keeps her deed box and all personal documents, including everything relating to my birth, which will prove that the girl you produced is nothing but a fake."

425

Matthew said with pride, "*I* produced her identification. I have very good contacts — mainly through Clayton originally. She's his daughter, but you guessed that, didn't you? You're a bright girl, Belinda. We'd make a good partnership, you and I. We could get married and share Lyonhurst between us. There would be a touch of ironical humor about that, don't you think? The two unwanteds sharing everything in the end."

"No!"

"Why? Am I so distasteful? You have always been slightly repelled by me, haven't you? I sensed that very early in our acquaintance, just as I sensed how potentially promising you were as a woman. And suddenly we were aware of each other. You felt my physical attraction — "

"I felt that you could attract other women and wondered why such an attraction would seem unnatural to me. Now I know. We are related."

"Second cousins have married before now."

"You can't possibly be serious!"

426

"Why not? You should be grateful. I'm giving you a second chance, Belinda."

"A second chance for what?"

"A second chance to live."

★ ★ ★

I have no idea how long I stood there, staring at him, before I took to my heels and ran. It might have been an age or a fleeting second, but in that time I saw the fanatical glare of his eyes and the way in which his lips drew back in some hideous mockery of a smile, revealing pale gums and teeth which reminded me of a tiger's. A cold and creeping terror ran up my spine. It was the first time I had ever consciously stood face to face with a killer — my killer.

Fear seemed to drag at my legs, making them move as in some ghastly nightmare when the body races panic-stricken, only to tread air on the same immovable spot. Somehow my paralyzed limbs actually did speed across the ballroom to the nearest door and on down a long corridor which was vaguely familiar but which, in my bewilderment, I could not place. Nor could I think of where it led to. All it represented was a means of escape from the man whose heavy body came lumbering after me. I could hear his footsteps hard on my heels and his breath, sharp and excited, charged with a frenzied laughter as if he were enjoying the chase as a preying beast enjoys the hunt.

I was sobbing and screaming David's name at the top of my lungs, and Matthew shouted behind me, "You little fool, he can't hear you! He's nowhere near! He'll arrive too late!" His hand clutched my hair and pulled me back, viciously jerking me to a standstill. "You bitch!" he gasped. "You lovely little bitch!"

His huge body pressed against mine, and even in my dazed condition I was aware that the chase, short as it was, had winded him. "You're out of condition!" I mocked. "You're growing old!" The taunt was a mistake, boomeranging back on me in the shape of a blow from his fist. Some reflex instinct made me dodge sideways, so that although he still held me imprisoned by my hair, the blow fell upon my shoulder, knocking me to the ground. The fall released me from his grasp.

He made a wild grab as I scrambled to my feet. I saw his hands, huge and merciless, reaching for my throat. I felt a scream rising in me, heard it ringing in my ears and echoing down the long corridor in hopeless, helpless terror. I was on my feet, leaping for a glass door through which the sky was framed like a tranquil picture. Yet contrary to that exterior calm, a girl was running from a killer, running for her life . . .

I reached the door. My hand was on the latch. To move it required a superhuman effort, for every nerve in wrist and palm and finger seemed paralyzed. I had no idea where the door led, nor time to think. I was only aware that outside was sky and air and on this side was a maniac with hot and savage breath. I could feel that breath again, close to my ear, and his voice — incoherent, babbling, meaningless — pouring out a frenzied jumble of sound. His hands, those terrifying, brutal hands, incensed with the strength of madness, were reaching for my throat.

The door swung open. The latch fell from my hand. I stumbled through blindly, then pulled up with a jerk for I could go no farther. I was standing on a small stone balcony outside a window, faced by a balustrade in which a hole gaped like a missing tooth in a giant's mouth.

Memory pierced me. I was out on the balcony where the girl and I had stood, where I had leaned against the parapet and sent the copingstone hurtling to the ground below. I was standing, stupefied, before that yawning gap, with the killer close behind me.

He was ominously quiet. I spun around, my back to the danger spot, and saw that he was crouching, his hands outthrust, ready to spring. As he did so I leaped aside, seeking refuge in a corner of the balcony with the stone balustrade supporting me, watching his heavy body plunge to its death.

27

I SANK to my knees, whimpering like a child, leaning my head against stone, clutching a pillar for support. I was crying helplessly, my whole body shaking — weak, spent, exhausted, scarcely aware of noises from below, of voices and shouts and a car engine suddenly braking. Aware of nothing but a sensation of having escaped from a nightmare which still refused to release me.

Someone shouted my name from below, but it took a long time to penetrate, and then I recognized it and the sound lifted me up from the bog of terror. I pulled myself to my knees, clutching the short stone pillars with shaking hands, peering between them to the dizzy ground below. It swayed appallingly and I shut my eyes, only to open them again because I had seen someone for whom I had been waiting and praying.

David cupped his mouth in his hands

and called, "*Don't move. Stay where you are! I'm coming!*" I obeyed like a child, sinking back on my heels in the corner of the balcony, refusing to look down there again — down to where a man's body lay spread-eagled like a broken puppet and which Harriet's black-clad figure was gently covering with a rug.

I did look again. I had to. The scene mesmerized me, like a play upon a distant stage viewed from an unusual angle. David's car was there and a woman was standing beside it, as if she had just stepped out and didn't know what to do or where to go. She was staring aghast at the covered figure, then she moved to Harriet who knelt beside it, put her hand on the housekeeper's shoulder and comforted her, just as, throughout my childhood, she had comforted me when in need.

I called weakly, "Françoise! Françoise!" but she didn't hear me. My voice was carried over the balcony and away on the breeze, and then David was stepping through the open window, picking me up, and carrying me indoors.

It was over. Everything was over, and I was safe.

"I can never turn my back on you, Belinda, but you land in trouble. Françoise was telling me what a penchant you have for it — always getting into some escapade or other, she said, and agreed that you need looking after. You'll be quite a responsibility for a man. There's a hell of a lot to be explained and I suppose I'll have to do it."

"Certainly not," I managed to reply. "I got myself into this mess. I'll get myself out of it."

"Then I'll stand by and watch — with pleasure."

He did, too. So did Françoise, looking on with her kindly tolerance and saying to Katherine every now and then, "She is Pierre all over again, is she not?" But I knew, when I looked at David, that although I had inherited my father's looks and much of his spirit, I had inherited something from my mother, too — the ability to love a man with passion and not count the cost.

433

Much later, the four of us sat alone in the dusk and there were no more questions, no more explanations. Even Françoise's spate of reproach was over and now she looked on benignly.

"Ever since Belinda was born I have hoped for this," she said. "To see the pair of you together, as my brother wished it to be." In the twilit room my mother's hand reached out to the older woman in mute and eloquent thanks.

And David's hand reached out to me, and I took it, allowing him to lead me outside. The garden was deserted, the drive empty, the ambulance gone. So, too, had the girl, leaving the house with a defiant toss of her head, blaming Matthew for everything and declaring she couldn't get away from this ancient ruin fast enough, anyway. My mother had watched her go with a sigh of relief.

Beside me, David said, "Perhaps there'll be time now, Belinda."

"For what?" I asked.

"To get to know you. I want to do that."

I wanted it, too. To know one another intimately and well was suddenly tremendously important to us both.

When we returned to the house, Harriet met us. She stood just within the French windows, holding something. I saw that it was Kathy's doll — clean and spick-and-span again, tended with Harriet's ever-loving hands. I reached up and kissed the old lady's cheek, and saw that she had been crying. I wanted to comfort her, but could think of nothing to say. It would have been hypocritical to sentimentalize about Matthew Deacon now that he was dead, but I understood Harriet's grief. She had pitied the man and, in her pity, had seen no fault in him. With my mother it was different. She, to my surprise, had revealed an amazing understanding of him, condoning none of his faults, but forgiving them — all but that last desperate attempt to get rid of me. Even that, she pleaded in excuse, he had not been responsible for — and although the memory of it would forever fill me with horror, I knew that she was right.

"This doll should be put back on the window seat in my mother's old room," I said to Harriet.

The woman nodded, and smiled.

"What is more," I added, "I will put it there myself, Harriet, and it will stay there always."

THE END

TO FIGHT THE WILD
Rod Ansell and Rachel Percy

Lost in uncharted Australian bush, Rod Ansell survived by hunting and trapping wild animals, improvising shelter and using all the bushman's skills he knew.

COROMANDEL
Pat Barr

India in the 1830s is a hot, uncomfortable place, where the East India Company still rules. Amelia and her new husband find themselves caught up in the animosities which seethe between the old order and the new.

THE SMALL PARTY
Lillian Beckwith

A frightening journey to safety begins for Ruth and her small party as their island is caught up in the dangers of armed insurrection.

THE WILDERNESS WALK
Sheila Bishop

Stifling unpleasant memories of a misbegotten romance in Cleave with Lord Francis Aubrey, Lavinia goes on holiday there with her sister. The two women are thrust into a romantic intrigue involving none other than Lord Francis.

THE RELUCTANT GUEST
Rosalind Brett

Ann Calvert went to spend a month on a South African farm with Theo Borland and his sister. They both proved to be different from her first idea of them, and there was Storr Peterson — the most disturbing man she had ever met.

ONE ENCHANTED SUMMER
Anne Tedlock Brooks

A tale of mystery and romance and a girl who found both during one enchanted summer.

CLOUD OVER MALVERTON
Nancy Buckingham

Dulcie soon realises that something is seriously wrong at Malverton, and when violence strikes she is horrified to find herself under suspicion of murder.

AFTER THOUGHTS
Max Bygraves

The Cockney entertainer tells stories of his East End childhood, of his RAF days, and his post-war showbusiness successes and friendships with fellow comedians.

MOONLIGHT
AND MARCH ROSES
D. Y. Cameron

Lynn's search to trace a missing girl takes her to Spain, where she meets Clive Hendon. While untangling the situation, she untangles her emotions and decides on her own future.

NURSE ALICE IN LOVE
Theresa Charles

Accepting the post of nurse to little Fernie Sherrod, Alice Everton could not guess at the romance, suspense and danger which lay ahead at the Sherrod's isolated estate.

POIROT INVESTIGATES
Agatha Christie

Two things bind these eleven stories together — the brilliance and uncanny skill of the diminutive Belgian detective, and the stupidity of his Watson-like partner, Captain Hastings.

LET LOOSE THE TIGERS
Josephine Cox

Queenie promised to find the long-lost son of the frail, elderly murderess, Hannah Jason. But her enquiries threatened to unlock the cage where crucial secrets had long been held captive.